THE TIDINGS TREE

THE TIDINGS TREE

Sheila Spencer-Smith

CHIVERS

British Library Cataloguing in Publication Data available

This Large Print edition published by AudioGo Ltd, Bath, 2011.
Published by arrangement with the Author.

U.K. Hardcover ISBN 978 1 445 83768 0
U.K. Softcover ISBN 978 1 445 83769 7

Printed and bound in Great Britain by
MPG Books Group Limited

To Geoff

CHAPTER ONE

Jenny stared, aghast, at the young oak sapling as she adjusted her scarf round her throat even though the soft spring air warmed her face with a gentleness that was soothing. 'The Tidings Tree can't really be this small after all these years,' she said in dismay.

Her daughter's blue eyes sparkled back at her. 'Two metres would you say? Don't they call it bonsai or something when you deliberately stunt the growth?'

'Stop teasing, Saskia. This is serious. How can this spindly thing be the replacement of that lovely tree? They felled it thirty years ago.'

Saskia wrinkled her nose, considering. 'A bit of a mystery here then.'

Jenny nodded. Even the triangle of grass on which it grew seemed smaller. She had expected change, but not as much as this. 'Maybe the replacement tree suffered a severe fate, too,' she said. Unbidden, a memory stirred of a group of village women beneath the spreading branches, their heads close together as they meted out blame for the demise of the ancient elm.

When she left home early this morning to take Saskia back to Exeter University, she had no idea that a few hours later she would be in

1

Mellstone gazing nostalgically at what should have been the real Tidings Tree. She had no idea either that the sudden glimpse of Marigold Cottage's photo in the estate agent's window in Hilbury would have such an effect. But the long-forgotten familiarity of the white fence, the thatched cottage roof and the dark trees behind had made the blood rush to her throat and her limbs tremble.

She had taken a deep breath of Dorset air and let it out slowly so that the fuzzy outlines in the photograph cleared. Then she had pushed open the door and made an appointment to view.

Only afterwards, as they sat sipping coffee had she wondered at the impulse. Though willing to go along with it, Saskia, of course, considered her crazy. But now, any lingering guilt that she had no real intention of buying vanished in Jenny's shock at the new-look Tidings Tree. She needed to know what someone had done to the interior of Marigold Cottage too in the intervening years.

Saskia moved impatiently. 'Eleven o'clock the estate agent said. We'd better go.'

Jingling her car keys, Jenny nodded.

*   *   *

'A desirable residence in a much sought-after village,' the young man said as they met outside the gate.

2

Jenny wondered if he believed it himself. The clipboard he carried looked like one of those boards school children used on out-of-door projects on which to amass useful information. Maybe he had escaped from the school next door on a sudden whim as she had once done in the distant past? But the building was shut down years ago by the run-down look of it.

She blinked, and smiled at him. 'Sought after by whom?'

He looked smug as he pushed open the gate and paused on the brick path. She was glad the bricks were still there. Slippery in wet weather, but old and attractive. She had always liked them.

'Retired people mostly, from towns and cities.'

Oh heavens, did she look that old? Her hand flew to her auburn hair.

A flicker of assumed patience slid across his face. 'Mellstone is an attractive village you see, Miss Finlay, not far from Hilbury. All that thatch. And not too big.'

Encouraged by her nod, he brightened and smiled at Saskia as he unlocked the door and stood aside for them to enter the small hall. No potpourri smell now, Jenny noticed, and the paintwork was brilliant white. A radiator too that hadn't been there in the old days.

'I'd like us to see the studio first, if we may,' she said.

3

'Studio?'

'On the back lawn. It's still there, isn't it?'

A startled glance at his clipboard and then he shot her a worried look. He indicated the door at the end of the hall. 'The garden? Shall we take a look?'

She went ahead of him into the kitchen. Gone were the old fashioned sink and the free-standing kitchen unit. Completely unrecognisable, of course, but she would look and appreciate later. He unlocked the back door and they went up the steps to the lawn.

'A patio?' she cried.

'Tastefully done with the riven stone. Weathered York, no, Cotswold I think. Good for sunbathing.' Again he smiled at Saskia, who grinned back at him.

Her daughter was enjoying herself. Egging him on? It seemed like it. Jenny stood on the tasteful riven paving stones, York or Cotswold she didn't care which, and looked round her, frowning.

'But the studio's gone,' she said.

His patient expression remained in place longer this time. 'There's been a patio here for a few years, Miss Finlay. That's all I know.'

The studio had been one of the reasons all those years ago for their coming to live here and she and her mother had been happy at first until that dreadful day of the gale when she was nine years old. Jenny rubbed her fingers through her hair, remembering.

4

She had stared out of the school window at the black clouds scudding past. The exciting wind outside made her want to rush out to dance and shout for the joy of it. Slipping out to the windy playground and into the lane was easy. She ran past Marigold Cottage to the Tidings Tree with its branches swinging and creaking above her.

The wind caught at her clothes as she scuttled down into the safety of the churchyard. She danced from grave to grave through the long, unkempt grass. She paused, breathless, as Mrs Pengold came out of the church and stumped along the path with her broom and mop. The wind pulled at the old lady's coat, showing her flowered blue pinafore beneath, and snatched her duster from her pocket. It went dancing off, a wild thing bright yellow among the tombstones.

Jenny darted after it, grabbed it and bore it back to Mrs Pengold. 'You're the lady with the cabbages in the front garden.' she said.

'Better than cluttering the place with them old flowers.' Mrs Pengold's face was grim. 'What are you doing here, Miss? You ought to be in school by rights. You'd best come along with me.'

The old lady marched to the gate looking so formidable that Jenny obeyed.

The Tidings Tree moaned and wailed. Jenny felt Mrs Pengold grab her as a tractor swung round the bend. The man on it leaned

5

towards them, shouting.

'What?' Mrs Pengold screeched back at him.

His words had vanished in the tremendous crack as a branch tore from the trunk and hurtled downwards.

Jenny blinked. Today the soft spring air in the sheltered garden was still and the studio that had played such a part in their lives was gone. She saw the young man with his clipboard and her grown daughter in her skimpy skirt gazing at him as if taking in his every word. But that expression on Saskia's face meant that she was miles away mentally. Already back in Exeter perhaps, planning the first celebratory evening back with those disreputable university friends of hers.

Suddenly Jenny felt ashamed. What did it matter whether the building was there or not? Highly unsuitable for her kiln anyway, even if she had been a genuine prospective purchaser. They were wasting his time.

'Have you seen enough out here? Shall we see upstairs in the cottage now?'

He looked relieved when she nodded. 'It's been modernised well,' he said as they moved across the grass. 'We've had one offer already, and there are others as well as yourselves interested. Mellstone's a sought-after place, like I said. People moving in find plenty to interest them and help them settle down to country life . . . the dramatic society, badminton and indoor bowls. And the Rambling Club, of course. The Village Society is active too, arranging away-days. I'm told they go as far afield as the Eden Project or St Ives.'

Jenny looked at him, appalled. She had lived here as a child for goodness' sake, when the village was a real place for living and working in and not some suburban overspill for fantasy-seekers. She had attended the school next door. She was different . . . she belonged. No retired stranger was going to move into Marigold Cottage, wanting bowls and badminton and far-flung away-days if she could help it.

'I'll take Marigold Cottage,' she said. I'll pay the asking price.'

Saskia's gasp of astonishment rivalled Clipboard Man's. Mum really was the limit jumping in like that without a moment's thought. True, her mother needed a place of her own at this to start up her business but why here? Not St Ives where Gran lived or Chester where they had been based for the last three years. Or even Exeter. Oh no, Mellstone it had to be, and if she herself didn't like it she could take a running jump. Her hurt was all the more severe for being brought on so unexpectedly. Maybe she would have to start making plans of her own from now on and not consider other peoples' feelings either.

'I'm off to have a look round,' she called

7

back as she left them.

A young boy was hanging over the stone bridge that spanned the brook. 'What's going on?' she asked.

He heaved himself back and grinned at her. She knew better than to show, even by a flicker, that she had registered his reddened eyes and flushed cheeks. His hair stood up in peaks and his light sweatshirt had grass stains down the front.

'Your mum'll never get those marks off,' she said.

'So?' He looked down at himself and shrugged. 'Did you know that otters are coming back now the water's much cleaner?'

'Is that what you were looking for down there, otters?'

She leaned over, watching the strands of green weed in the water spreading elegantly in the strong current.

'Look on the bank. Can you see that tiny brown patch down there? It could be otter spraint. They leave that behind to mark their territory. Does it look like an otter's spraint to you? Anyway I haven't got a mum.'

'You haven't?' Saskia felt cold inside. How could she have been so tactless? How did she know who had mothers? Or fathers for that matter. She hadn't herself. Or not one that counted since he'd gone off and left them when they were still living in New Zealand. Here was she, a trainee teacher supposedly

8

tuned to the young, and out she came with a remark like that.

'I said so, didn't I?'

'So who looks after you?' There was something so vulnerable about him she simply couldn't help the words tripping off her tongue.

The smile he gave her was beautiful, lighting up his face with warmth and sensitivity. 'Dad's got someone in. She's all right.'

'I see.' She leaned on the rough stonework of the bridge again. Down below, the waterweed still strained in the current, tugging ineffectually against its roots. Suddenly she remembered the time. 'I've got to go.'

To her surprise he walked along with her, his auburn hair bobbing and his hands deep in his pockets.

'What's it like living in Mellstone?' she asked.

'I dunno. All right I suppose. I'm just staying here with Gran and Grandad.'

They walked up the short hill to the Tidings Tree, a high brick wall on their left overhung with dark yew trees. Saskia saw that the wall leaned outwards and all the spaces between the bricks were filled with moss to hold them together. Or so it seemed. It couldn't be really, of course, or it would collapse. She put out a finger to touch it, and a piece of coarse moss came away, falling to the ground in a flurry of

9

green dust.

'That's the vicarage,' he said. 'My Grandad used to live there.'

'He did? Where do he and your gran live now?'

'Down the lane past the Tidings Tree. That's where I'm going. Is that your car outside Marigold Cottage?'

'My mother's.'

'Marigold Cottage is always being sold.'

Saskia was silent, considering. They had reached the car now. She stopped and put her hand on the bonnet. 'Bye then,' she called to his retreating back.

She looked at the cottage. It seemed to stare back at her unblinkingly. Was it lonely, unloved? But Mum had loved it as a little girl and was excited at seeing it again. Was she to be one of the long line of people who came to live here in Marigold Cottage and then went away again?

'Whatever it is you do to people,' she muttered. 'Just make sure you don't do it to my mother, that's all.'

*   *   *

The school building hadn't changed much from the outside. Jenny, investigating, saw that someone had filled two stone troughs by the door with bright yellow pansies. A wooden notice board encased in cracked glass

10

informed her that the building was now the village hall, bought by the Village Society when the school closed.

The door opened. The grey-haired woman who emerged looked startled. A dull flapping garment smothered her stout figure. 'Oh, you've come to view the exhibition. I was just going to close for the day.'

'Idle curiosity on my part, that's all,' said Jenny, backing away. 'I used to come to school here.'

'You did?' The interested look invited further information.

'A long time ago. We lived next door in Marigold Cottage for a time, my mother and me.'

'You're never Jenny!'

Jenny, flushing a little, smiled. She might have known that Mellstone memories were long. No surprise, then, that this woman appeared to know her. But who was she?

'This is wonderful!' the woman said. 'I can't believe it after all these years.' She opened her mouth and then shut it again.

Jenny's lips twitched. She wasn't going to say she had grown, surely?

'We get news of your mother on her Christmas cards. And you too, of course, Jenny. You're on your way to stay with her in Cornwall?'

'Not this time. I've got to get back for the last term of my own floristry studies after dropping my daughter off in Exeter. My mother doesn't know yet, but I've just bought Marigold Cottage.'

Approval shone in the woman's grey eyes. 'Are you planning to live here then?'

Jenny shrugged but made no reply. There was a lot of thinking ahead of her and she still felt shaky at what she had done. She looked across what used to be the playground to the three terraced cottages across the lane. The middle one was Mrs Pengold's . . . she who grew cabbages in her front garden.

Catching her glance, the woman smiled wryly. 'Holiday cottages now except for the end one. Some new people, from Kent. Or Hertfordshire. I forget which.'

'New people?'

'We have a lot of those now. People have died or moved away.'

'Alice Pengold?'

'Not Alice. She went off to live with her son and daughter-in-law ages ago.'

'She can't still be alive?' Jenny was amazed. 'She brought me back to school when the branch came down all those years ago.'

Her companion moved her weight from one foot to the other. 'I remember. But what am I thinking of? Come inside and see what we've been doing.' She gestured for Jenny to go ahead of her. 'Remember the two classrooms with the wooden partition between? You'd never think it but this space was my room.'

12

Jenny looked at her in astonishment. 'Then you must be Miss Mellor?'

'Varley now. You remember Varley's Farm down the lane? I married Ralph, the eldest son. We've a grown up son and daughter.' Her eyes lit up and her voice softened. 'Oliver's due home on leave from Africa soon. But please, call me Cathy.'

'Of course.' Looking at this ungainly woman Jenny would never have recognised the slim nervous creature who had once taught the Infant Class all those years ago. Except that there was something . . . a tremor of the mouth, a listening look about her and a hint of kindness in her eyes. She had always liked Miss Mellor who had been kind to her when she needed kindness.

To give herself time to adjust Jenny looked around her at the craftwork laid out on long white-clothed tables. She moved to the nearest and saw that the embroidery was exquisite, the lace so ethereal it took her breath away. There were oil paintings and watercolours, beadwork and dough craft. No pots, though.

'Wonderful,' she said.

'We've put this show on to raise money for our own meeting hall. This place has been condemned. Only fit to be pulled down apparently and the land sold. There's heaps of talent in the village.'

'I can see that,' said Jenny, humbled.

'Have you time to come back with me for a

13

cup of tea, Jenny? There's a lot of catching up to do. Do say you'll come and your daughter too of course. I wish Oliver was home already.

'We've got a long journey ahead of us, I'm afraid. Here she is now by the car. We'll have to make a start.'

'Of course.' At once Cathy Varley was all concern, an anxious frown creasing her forehead just as it used to do in the old days.

Jenny unlocked her car and slid behind the wheel. She smiled at her daughter as she fastened her seat belt. 'Sorry about all this, Saskie. I wasn't expecting to meet anyone I knew. The person I was talking to was a teacher when I was at school here. I always liked her.'

'But she's old. You need friends your own age.'

Jenny laughed. 'You sound just like your grandmother. Cathy can only be about twelve years older than me. She's got a son, Oliver. Too young for me, of course. What a shame.'

Turning the car, Jenny drove slowly past the Tidings Tree and down Church Lane. She pulled up outside the church. 'I won't be a minute, Saskia. I just want to check the notice board.

Saskia sighed. 'I can't get used to it. Are you really going to come and live here, Mum?'

'Sometimes you have to grab at what life offers when the chance comes.'

Smiling, Jenny got out of the car and

14

climbed the steep pavement and read the notice board on the church wall. The service times had changed. And the vicar's name of course, now *The Reverend Lesley J Bond* in shiny gilt lettering. She could hardly expect the Reverend Robert Moore's name to be there still, faded now and perhaps chipped a bit, but its absence sent a frisson of surprise through her. It was like that poem she'd had to study in college about a tree in the park not existing if you weren't there to see it. With few thoughts from herself, year in, year out, Mellstone had been going on without her.

Now, when she decided to come back, she found its existence amazing.

CHAPTER TWO

'Guess who I saw today?' said Cathy in the farmhouse kitchen. 'Whom, I mean.'

Ralph grunted from behind the evening paper.

'Remember Jenny Finlay who used to live in Marigold Cottage? She's coming back to Mellstone to live. She was a nice little thing, Jenny. I'd never have thought she would grow so tall. And a short skirt, as short as her daughter's.'

'Good legs?'

'Mmn.'

Ralph lowered his paper. 'Takes you back, does it, meeting someone from the past?'

Cathy nodded. Of course it did. She was pleased to see Jenny so unexpectedly of course but some of the memories she brought with her were painful.

Deep in thought, she strained carrots and spooned them out on the plates she had forgotten to warm. Where had all the years gone since she had been the young naive assistant teacher at the school? Ah well, it didn't do to dwell on what used to be when the young Ralph Varley, fresh from agricultural college, had been there for her when she needed him.

'Don't stand dreaming, woman. I'm hungry.'

Cathy put the pan down and reached for the shepherd's pie. As she dished it out she couldn't help thinking of the passing years. And now Jenny Finlay, once the child who started all the trouble years ago, had returned to Mellstone. No one ever quite knew what had got into her young head to make her escape into the wind-blown afternoon. She had recovered from the injuries and gone back to school for a while but her head teacher, who was held responsible, always had it in for her after that and for Jenny's mother Elisabeth too.

*   *   *

16

'Jenny! I thought something had happened. You're all right? You got back safely?'

Jenny smiled at the relief in her mother's voice on the other end of the phone. She could imagine her perched on the low windowsill of her studio-apartment in St Ives with her back to the twinkling harbour lights. Her own flat here in Chester was so different, poky with no view but that didn't matter now she was nearing the end of her three-years of hard work for her diploma in floristry and ceramics.

'Very much so,' she said. 'And Saskia's happy to be back with her friends.' She glanced at the photograph in one of the silver frames that stood on the low table near the window. Fine silky hair, was tucked back behind her daughter's ears. Her smiling mouth looked sensitive and her eyes were as blue as her shirt.

'That's good, dear.'

'I'm on a real high,' Jenny said. 'On the way down we detoured to Mellstone to have a look at the place, and I've bought Marigold Cottage.'

'Marigold Cottage? Oh Jenny, why? Aren't there hundreds of other more suitable country places?'

'Not for me.'

'But what will you live on?'

'I'll manage,' Jenny said lightly. 'With my settlement from Nick it's enough for the asking price and a bit left over for a kiln and

17

removals.'

'I can't help thinking . . .'

Jenny smoothed her forehead, in her mind seeing her young mother with her sketch book in hand moving from window to window in the studio attempting to capture the stance of trees blown sideways and the feel of blustering wind in grass and bush. And then the wailing of the ambulance siren and the rush to the front gate and the horrified realisation that it was her child lying injured beneath the mass of fallen branch and leaves.

'It was a terrible time,' Elisabeth said with a catch in her voice.

Jenny suddenly felt shaky with what she had done. 'I'll make it work. I'll be all right, Mum, I promise.'

'I know it will, love,' Elisabeth said, her voice stronger now. 'You're a grown woman, Jenny, with your own decisions to make and I mustn't interfere. You must do what you feel is right for you. Perhaps it's a good thing to bring old memories out and air them knowing they no longer matter.'

Long after their conversation ended Jenny sat still, thinking about the decision she had made and how it would affect her mother. Elisabeth's dream of having the freedom to paint had become reality, thanks to a great-aunt's will, with the purchase Marigold Cottage when she herself was seven. Elisabeth had been living as part of her cousin's family in their North London flat and already devoted to her three-year old self when her own parents died when they were on their way to the West Country on a second honeymoon. As soon as the news came she had clung to Elisabeth, refusing to let her out of her sight. It had been natural for the family to assume that Elisabeth would continue to look after her and perhaps adopt her legally as her own.

Other members of the family had chipped in with financial help and they had lived fairly comfortably until the legacy came and they had moved to Mellstone. She knew that Elisabeth had male friendships but only one meant anything to her and he had failed her in the end. Heartsick, Elisabeth had left Mellstone with Jenny and finally settled elsewhere. But she had said that perhaps the time had come now to lay old ghosts of memories that were best forgotten. All so long ago, Jenny thought now. Present-day Mellstone was still a beautiful place. She hoped that already Elisabeth would be imagining the new Tidings Tree growing tall and strong with summer sunlight filtering through its leafy branches to the grass beneath just as it had with its predecessor in the old days.

*   *   *

Emerging from the Olde Worlde Tea Shoppe

in Hilbury a few weeks later, Jenny paused to admire the sunlight illuminating the tubs of tulips outside the art shop across the road. Everything was going ahead as planned. All her demonstrations for her course were behind her. She could relax and think about Marigold Cottage that hopefully would soon be hers. Now she was on her way for a window-measuring visit and a general look round.

Perhaps that should include a brief visit to her mother's old friend, John Ellis. He had played such a large part in their lives years ago and she herself had been in contact with him sometimes during her growing up years. She had started writing to him about a school project because he knew about forestry. It was a new thing round here when they were living in Mellstone, and John had always had an open mind about new things.

She gazed thoughtfully at her mobile, and then made up her mind. No harm in dialling Nether End Farm. John Ellis' deep voice was so reassuring and welcoming that she knew she had done the right thing in contacting him.

A brief shaft of silvery sunlight brightened the front of the old house for a few moments as she drove through the gates. The front door opened as she got out of the car, and there John was with a black and white collie at his side.

He was older, of course. She had expected that but she hadn't expected the energy emanating from him or the twinkle in his blue eyes as he came towards her. How old would he be, sixty five? He certainly didn't look it.

His handshake was firm. 'Good to see you, Jenny. You look well.'

But aged too? Well, of course. It was a wonder he'd recognised her.

'You too, John. I'm so glad to see you at long last. And who's this?' Smiling, she bent to stroke the dog's silky body.

'Meet Lassie. Come in, my dear. Let me take your jacket. Do go in.'

She looked round the long, low room with pleasure. Lassie lay comfortably on the rug in front of the wide fireplace where a wood fire crackled. John seemed as calm and unruffled as she remembered him.

'Sit down, my dear Jenny. Are you hungry after that long drive? Lunch is prepared but first we'll have a drink. I hope there's nothing wrong?'

'Wrong? Oh no.' Was he thinking of Elisabeth, worried perhaps that she was ill or worse? She hastened to reassure him. 'Everything's fine. I had some things to attend to in this area. Then I thought of calling on you.'

He smiled. 'I'm glad you did, my dear.'

'I'd love something non-alcoholic.' She now saw that a table behind the sofa on which she sat held bottles and glasses. He poured a whisky for himself and a ginger ale for her.

'Perfect,' she said, sipping it.

He sat down in the deep armchair that she could see was his usual one. Lassie raised her head, seemed to smile and then collapsed again in slumber.

Jenny glanced round the warm, chintzy room. 'It hasn't changed a bit,' she said with pleasure.

'A little perhaps, through the years, but nothing drastic. I like these dull colours.'

'Not dull, subdued and old-looking and beautiful. Who needs bright colours with those lovely wide French windows and the lawn outside and the hills?'

'It's a thought. But it's dull out there today, I'm afraid. I wish you could see them on a perfect summer's day.'

'Maybe I will.'

'You'll come again?'

She nodded and looked down at the glass in her hand. For some reason she was reluctant to tell him about Marigold Cottage.

He smiled, nursing his glass. 'You'll have seen changes in the village.'

'Well yes a few, but not many. The tree, of course. I expected it to be much bigger.'

'Vandals, I'm afraid. The parish council had to replace the young oak planted after the old elm was lost. This one will grow.'

She smiled. 'Oh John, it's good to be back. And to see Nether End as I remembered it. How have you managed to stay so young?'

'No pipe-rack any more, you'll notice. I gave that up a few years back. For my health, if nothing else.'

'You look so well, John. Better than a man half your age.' The skin round John's eyes crinkled in his tanned face.

'You're flirting with me, my girl.'

'I know. Fun, isn't it?' She took another sip and finished her drink, suddenly saddened by memories of Elisabeth and John together and the part she had played in trying to separate them.

John finished his whisky. 'I expect Mrs Horlock will be ready for us now.'

They went into the dining room. There were no memories here. She could remember only the sitting room on their few visits, not this dark room that looked out at the front of the house. An invisible Mrs Horlock had placed bowls of steaming celery and cheese soup in the two places set at the table. Silver cutlery gleamed on the white cloth. The scarlet table napkins made her think instantly of blood. Now why should that have come into her mind? Of course . . . an aftermath of that day when the branch from the Tidings Tree had come down. Later she knew of Elisabeth's anguish at seeing her lying unconscious on the stretcher with her red hair on the white sheet and then the swift transfer by ambulance to Hilbury hospital and all the trauma that caused.

'So how is Saskia?' John asked as he passed her the basket of granary rolls. 'Still enjoying university life?'

Jenny took a roll and crumbled it on her plate. 'Oh yes.'

'No ideas for her future yet?'

'Apart from travelling the world. She enjoys new places and new experiences.'

'She wouldn't be your daughter if she didn't.'

Jenny smiled. Nick's daughter too. She didn't think often of her ex-husband these days. It was at his instigation that they had gone out to New Zealand to live and work when Saskia was only tiny. They had settled, after a fashion, but it was she who had a growing awareness that she didn't really belong there. When the marriage began to fall apart she had already half-decided to return to this country when the divorce came through. Now here she was and her daughter too. But when Saskia got her degree she might well decide to move on.

John smiled. 'And you've nearly finished your college course now? Any plans?'

'Oh plenty. A new location, of course. I never intended to stay up there. Actually I've just found a good place. I need to be fairly accessible to hotels and guesthouses. I don't think many people have set up in business combining the two crafts, pottery and flower arranging. Not, hopefully, in this area anyway.'

24

He raised his eyebrows. 'This area?'

'Bounded by Salisbury, Poole, Bath and Exeter.'

'A lot of travelling.'

'Well yes. There are plenty of smaller places in between though. I'm hoping for regular contracts with the pottery containers as a one-off and regular arrangements in them in situ from then on. I'll take samples and photographs to show. In fact I can get started on the research for that at once and the setting up of meetings. With luck the hotel guests will give me commissions for the pots. That's the big idea.'

'And a good one too.' John bent to stroke Lassie. The dog raised her head, loving it. 'You say you've found somewhere. Am I to know where?'

He would have heard that Marigold Cottage was on the market, perhaps even that it was sold subject to contract. She raised her head defiantly. 'Marigold Cottage.'

He nodded, gazing into the fire, one hand idly stroking Lassie's head.

To her surprise he said no more but asked instead about the technical part of the course in floristry that had occupied her for the last three years. Then they discussed farming in general and Nether End in particular. They didn't mention the village that lay a mere two miles away and which she had decided to make her home as well as her place of business.

John returned to the sitting room when Jenny left. Lassie raised her head in greeting, and then lowered it again. He piled on more logs and then sat in his chair watching them as they began to burn.

He had become fond of Jenny through the years even though they hadn't met again until now. How like Elisabeth she was in some ways. Blood relations of course, though distant. Elisabeth had done a good job with Jenny and they had always been close. Too close, he had once thought.

Some inherited gene in both of them ensured a similar approach to life, a misplaced optimism that could lead to disillusionment. He didn't want to see Jenny's bright enthusiasm dulled as Elisabeth's had been for a time. Yet he had said nothing.

He thought of the day all those years ago, when his grandparent's cottage was on the market. Elisabeth was the only person who wanted to see it and he had shown her around. At first he had felt only amusement at this attractive creature's enthusiasm for the property. It was obvious that she found it hard to remove her gaze from the view of the wooden building on the back lawn even when they had returned to the cottage. At the upstairs window at the front she had watched

26

with interest as Alice Pengold came hurrying along the lane, her arms full of leafy branches. When he told her that Alice did peculiar things with roots and berries her laugh had contained an element of panic.

She had looked as if she thought he was judging her when he had tried to put her off the place by pointing out that there would be heavy fire insurance premiums on Marigold Cottage because of the thatch.

That was the effect Elisabeth had had on him, a desire to look after and protect and the very qualities Elisabeth hadn't wanted from him, ever.

But Jenny was a different matter. She, too, knew what she wanted, even if things hadn't worked out well for her as yet. He had no right to put obstacles in Jenny's way and indeed had no wish to. But could Jenny try to re-write history and be happy and fulfilled in Mellstone as her mother palpably couldn't after the loss of the Tidings Tree? Only time would tell.

CHAPTER THREE

Jenny sprang up from the kitchen floor of her new home and brushed down the knees of her jeans. The move had gone well. She was able to proceed with the purchase of Marigold Cottage and complete at the beginning of July.

The store in Hilbury that specialised in antique pine delivered two hours after she had taken possession and she now had the minimum furniture needed to make Marigold Cottage habitable.

Stacking the units could wait. She made coffee in her favourite mug and carried it into the back garden to drink seated on the top stone step in the sunshine. She hadn't thought much about the garden. Now as she looked about her she could see that someone had cared for it in the past although she would have to start weeding and cutting back very soon. The cerulean blue of the delphiniums rose above a mass of milk thistle and groundsel that would soon be in the compost heap before they knew what hit them.

As Jenny sipped her coffee she half-closed her eyes so that the colours of the flowers blurred into each other. She found this helpful in choosing subtle shades for the pots to complement her arrangements. A bumblebee droned heavily and perfume wafted across to her.

The day after tomorrow she would check that the order for the electric kiln was going ahead. Old cottage walls were thick and didn't take kindly to having holes made in them to insert extractor fans. A brick-built construction in the garden seemed the best idea to house the kiln in safety. Sited near the back door, it wouldn't be intrusive. At least she hoped not.

The local chap, Jason Gedge, seemed to think it would be easy enough to construct.

The priority at the moment was to get everything properly sorted out indoors so it didn't look too much of a mess when Saskia arrived. Then she would allow herself the pleasure of unpacking her precious pottery and arranging it on the shelves she'd had installed in the downstairs bedroom. Although small this would make a fine studio and workroom when she had leisure to equip it with all she needed. Elisabeth's offer to supply the money for all this as a housewarming present meant there were no problems about the extra finance. She must then install her computer and other office equipment in the room on the other side of the passage. Saskia would be able to help with that.

The shrilling of the front door bell cut short Jenny's thoughts. She put down her mug and sprang to her feet.

On the doorstep stood a short woman whose pencil-thin skirt emphasised her thinness. Her perfume cloyed the air about her with musky sweetness as she stepped forward. Hugged to her white polo-necked jersey was a basket of fruit covered in cellophane paper.

'Oh,' the visitor gasped as if the opening door was totally unexpected. 'I couldn't help noticing the furniture van from Hilbury. This came for you. I saw it on the doorstep earlier and I took it in. I'm not one to pry but . . . I hope you don't mind?'

Jenny took the crackling bundle from her. She could see a book tucked in beside the grapes and avocados. Intriguing! 'Thanks. Good of you to take the trouble.'

'I'm Tess, Tess Hartland. My husband's Nigel.' She waved her hand at the terraced cottage opposite. 'We live in Ivy Cottage. We retired here a few months ago. Five actually, five and two weeks. And three days. We used to holiday here for years and got to love the place. I do hope people will be friendly.' She looked anxious. 'It's so beautiful round here with such pretty villages.' She paused again, her head held to one side waiting for Jenny's agreement. 'Nigel loves the countryside, you know. He reads about it all the time and he belongs to all sorts of organisations, the RSPB and Plantlife and Save the Whale.'

'Save the Whale?' said Jenny, bemused. She knew there were fish in Mellstone brook, but whales? Things had changed more than she thought.

'I hear you came to school here in Mellstone when you were a little girl?'

Oh heavens, had she heard that already? 'Well, yes . . . '

'Wasn't Mrs Moore a teacher there once? Or was that since your time?' Tess Hartland's enquiring expression deepened.

'Mrs Moore?' Could she be her disapproving head teacher, Jenny wondered, married to the then vicar, the Reverend Robert Moore? Her eyes opened wide in speculation.

'They moved in to Lynch Cottage last year, she and her husband. Well, I won't keep you as you're busy. The fish and chip van calls every Thursday down by the post office and the mobile library comes every Friday. Do say if there's anything else you want to know . . .'

Jenny smiled. This sparkly little person wouldn't be able to tell her how her business was going to take off. Or whether her clay supplies would arrive on time and what contracts would prove most successful in this area.

'Thanks,' she said. 'I'll be in touch.' But she would take care not to. Tess and her energetic Nigel could be a distraction she could ill afford. Single-mindedness from her from now on or she would never cope with everything she had taken on.

When her visitor had gone tapping down the brick path in her high heels Jenny carried the basket into the kitchen. She ripped off the shining cellophane and extracted the book entitled *Mellstone Magic* by Therese de Possièrre. A folded piece of notepaper fell out.

She picked it up. *'Welcome to Mellstone,'* she read in John Ellis' firm handwriting. *'I didn't dare send flowers to an expert like you. Hope you like the book. The author knows her stuff. Enjoy it, and the fruit, John.'*

31

Jenny flicked through the pages of the book and saw the line drawings and colour illustrations among the pages of clear print. How thoughtful of John. She put the book down beside the basket, picked off a grape and popped it into her mouth and then went at once to the telephone to thank him.

*   *   *

Jenny threw open the fridge door and glared at the contents. 'Not much here, Saskia. We'll get fish and chips later.'

'Fish and chips?'

'A van comes every Thursday down by the pub. So I'm informed.' Her eyes narrowed as she thought of Tess Hartland so eager to please and obviously lonely. There might well be a problem here. 'First, bread,' she said. 'There's a baguette somewhere and some rather runny Brie. Will that do as a stop gap? Oh, and fruit. Some came just now. That's lucky. I wasn't going to bother much myself.'

Saskia smiled. 'Perfect. Fish and chips next week.' She had already downed a mug of steaming chocolate and half a packet of biscuits and looked much better. 'You didn't mind me coming a day early, Mum, only . . . '

'Ash?'

Saskia nodded. 'We've finished.'

'Oh, Saskie, I'm sorry. But why . . . '

'No heart-to-heart Mum, please. Let's just

say it's over. Someone else, for him I mean. Or that's what it looked like and I didn't give him chance to talk himself out of it. I just got on the first train this morning and here I am. I nearly passed out at the bus stop in Hilbury. Why are you looking at me like that, Mum?'

'There's nothing wrong is there? You'd tell me at once . . .'

'Grow up, Mum. There's nothing wrong with me that food won't put right.'

'So was the chap who brought you?'

'He offered. The bus had just gone. I was going to phone but my mobile's dead and I'd no spare cash. I was starving. I didn't eat breakfast or anything. And then Oliver stopped his car.'

Jenny raised her eyebrows as she rummaged in the drawer for the bread knife. 'Oliver?'

'Oliver Varley. He lives in the village. He knew I was coming here.'

'So that's Cathy's son?' Jenny paused, the knife in her hand. She had caught a glimpse of him as he shut the front gate behind him after carrying Saskia's luggage to the front door. She had seen that he was broad shouldered and not very tall. His hair was receding a bit. His face was so tanned that all the little lines round his eyes seemed etched in white as he smiled at her daughter. She had felt a strange desire to have him smile at her like that.

Saskia leaned back in her chair. 'He was kind.'

'He takes after his mother then.'

'He offered to stop at a café but I said I'd rather get here. We talked. He's really nice. He told me about going abroad to work straight after agricultural college. He's been in Africa for years but his sister lives near here with someone with a young son called Jem. Oliver thinks I'm clairvoyant because I asked if the boy's got red hair.' Saskia giggled. 'I met Jem you see when we came to look at the village. He was down on the bridge looking for otters.' She gave a huge yawn. 'Maybe I'll stay for the whole summer after all. I'll need a job though. Any ideas?'

Jenny frowned. 'Have a heart. I've only just got here myself. Have a holiday for a bit, why don't you? You've been working hard and you look simply terrible.' And that was definitely the wrong thing to say. 'Let's get your stuff upstairs.'

Saskia swayed a little as she stood up.

Jenny was alarmed. 'Sit down. I'll do it.'

Her daughter gave an ear-splitting yawn. 'I didn't sleep last night, that's all. Don't fuss, Mum.'

'Bed for you as soon as you've eaten.'

'OK, you're the boss.' Her smile was so sweet that Jenny relaxed.

Later, with Saskia settled, she seated herself on the sitting room windowsill and looked out over the front garden to the yellow roses against the fence. She was glad Saskia had

34

come straight here to Marigold Cottage at the end of term. For the last four years there had been only temporary homes. Saskia's schooling hadn't appeared to suffer though it was a wonder after the upheaval of her parents' divorce in New Zealand.

But Saskia was young. Hopefully it would be different for her.

Jenny sighed again, took a last look at the slant of summer sun that turned the roses to shining gold. A coffee in the back garden and a determined look to the future instead of the past.

* * *

Cathy Varley straightened the duvet in the double guest bedroom and stood back to admire the new, flowered wallpaper. Ralph, grumbling as usual, had arranged to have the local chap in. She had always gone for the country cottage look and this room was their best. Bed and Breakfast bookings were up on last year anyway so they must be doing something right.

Another had come by post that morning with a deposit for the first weekend in September, the Wayside Arts Open Weekend. Frowning, Cathy pulled the letter out of her apron pocket. Mrs Betty Bronson. Not a common name. Could it be? Arnold Bronson would be in his fifties now, probably married.

To Betty?

Her mind travelled instantly back to herself as new young school teacher at her first social occasion in the village. Arnold had come in with Ralph Varley. How good looking Arnold had been and so self-assured! Ralph introduced him as a forestry student here in the area to study something. Trees, of course. Arnold had come straight to the sofa where she sat. Surprised and flattered, she had listened avidly to all he had to say in that deep husky voice that had sent shivers through her. Love at first sight . . .

Among much laughter the drink flowed. After a while Arnold wiped his hand across his moustache and suggested the pub. Ralph's thick fair hair had shone in the lamplight as he sprang up but she had got up slowly as if doing so would make her invisible because she felt guilty at leaving the party early.

While Ralph got the drinks in Arnold inspected the horse brasses and warming pans hanging on the walls between lighted carriage lanterns. 'Amazing how they flicker so realistically,' he said. 'Would you have believed anything so sophisticated in a dump like Mellstone?'

His poor opinion of the village surprised her. She hadn't liked to ask what forestry there was round Mellstone in case she sounded stupid. All she knew about Arnold was that he was staying on a local farm. She felt the

36

pressure of Arnold's leg against her own and warmth flowed through her. The talk turned to bell ringing because the experienced Arnold had agreed to join the Mellstone band of bellringers.

When it was time to go Arnold caught hold of her arm. 'You'll come up to the Tower on Tuesday evening and learn to ring?'

The beam from his torch made patterns on the uneven surface of the lane. He turned it off when they reached Lynch Cottage where she lodged. In the sudden darkness she felt his nearness and wondered, her heart lurching, if he would kiss her.

'See you on Practice Night then,' he said as he moved away from her.

Now Cathy blinked and glanced at her watch with an exclamation of dismay. She hurried downstairs, untied her apron and removed the letter to place safely on the mantelpiece to answer later. If she wasn't careful she would be late for the emergency meeting of the WI Committee and that wouldn't do.

Puffing slightly, she arrived outside the old school building at the same time as the President, Hilda Lunt, who stumped ahead of her with her broad back registering disapproval of the laughter and chatter going on in the committee room.

A hush fell as they went in.

'Good afternoon, ladies.' Hilda dumped her

37

briefcase on the floor and sat down at the head of the table, flanked by secretary and treasurer. 'We won't beat about the bush as this is an extra meeting. Wake up, Cathy. You look as if a goose has walked over your grave. The minutes, please.'

Cathy jumped and scrabbled in her bag for notebook and biro to look efficient as the secretary began to read aloud.

'We'll get down to brass tacks straight away,' Hilda announced in a sonorous tone. 'The speaker for Tuesday has done a runner,'

'Done a runner, is it?' said the press secretary in her soft Welsh voice.

Was this all? Hastily Cathy coughed, bent her head and began to write. *Done a runner/ Speaker?* Best to keep her eyes down. Fatal to catch the treasurer's eye or they both might dissolve into giggles.

'A bolt from the blue. Since our meeting is an Open Meeting and advertised as such we've got to find someone at once to step into the breach. Any ideas, ladies?'

They all looked at each other.

'Quick' said the competition organiser waving one arm dramatically. 'Think of someone or we'll have the *Mellstone Emasculated* woman offering her services again.'

'*Mellstone Magic* you mean,' said the secretary, busily writing. 'She's clever and good on research.'

38

'Clever, maybe. Interesting, no.'

'She's just brought out another book,' said the programme secretary, wrinkling her nose. 'Now let me think what it's called?'

'I never open a book,' the press secretary said with pride.

The treasurer grinned. *'Hilbury Hookers.'*

'Hilbury Hiking you mean.'

'Of course, that's it. All about the new long distance footpath starting from Hilbury and the history of all the places you pass through. How about it as a suggestion for our Autumn Outing?'

The outings organiser shuddered. 'She knows nowt for all her talk. I can't stand the woman. She's only been in Mellstone five minutes. I'll not give her the satisfaction.'

'Stourford Strippers, that's another,' said the treasurer.

'Stourford Serendipity you mean.'

The President's thick neck was a mottled pink. She rapped on the table. 'Ladies, ladies, keep to the matter in hand if you please. Cathy, are you still with us?'

Cathy, flushing, looked up. 'Sorry.' She glanced at the blank faces of her fellow committee members. A talk about some of her more eccentric Bed and Breakfast Guests, perhaps? No, too trivial. Jenny now, freshly qualified and . . .'

'I know!' she said. 'I've thought of someone if she would do it.'

39

'Anyone, good or not, if it will get us out of a hole.'

'Some sort of flower arranging, possibly. Jenny would be good. She's in the floristry and the pottery business.'

The competition organiser looked interested. 'Hasn't she recently moved to Marigold Cottage?'

Cathy nodded.

'Someone said she used to live there as a child. Interesting.'

'I knew her aunt years ago,' said the secretary.

'Or was it her mother?' said the treasurer. 'My father bought one of her paintings. Elisabeth Turner, that's the name. There was some story about them, something fairly tragic, I think. I'll give him a buzz this evening and find out.'

'Interesting, I'll not deny,' said the outings organiser, her eyes gleaming. 'I can't wait to hear.'

'Me neither,' said the secretary.

Cathy frowned. Human nature was odd. These were caring women but sad events in the past engendered only lively interest and curiosity. It was like historical battle scenes laid on for public entertainment to which present day crowds poured for a family day out. Past tragedies were today's entertainments. For an instant she saw the committee members disguised as a pack of

40

wolves. The Treasurer's grin seemed to widen, Hilda's hat change to rugged fur . . .

'Cathy!' The President's sharp tone made Cathy blink. 'Better get on to your person at once. We don't want her to slip through our fingers.'

'Time and tide wait for no man,' murmured the treasurer in Cathy's ear.

But Cathy didn't feel like giggling now. What was she throwing Jenny into? She should have kept her mouth shut.

CHAPTER FOUR

Jenny was at her front door, about to go inside, when Cathy arrived at Marigold Cottage. She smiled and waited.

There was something different about the younger woman today, Cathy noticed, a bubbling confidence that hadn't been there before. Encouraged, she rushed up the path. 'I've got something to ask you, Jenny. I hope you don't mind.'

Jenny dumped her bucket of lilies by the hall table. 'Sounds intriguing. Time for a coffee?'

Cathy, following her into the kitchen, paused in surprise. 'The white roses in the shiny blue vase, so pretty. One of yours?'

Jenny nodded, smiling. 'Sit down, Cathy.

Instant? I won't be a moment.'

Cathy seated herself comfortably and then remembered why she was here. 'I've just come from the WI committee meeting. We're short of a speaker for the Open Meeting on Thursday evening and I thought of you.'

Jenny reached two mugs down from a shelf. 'Me? You're crazy. I've never done such a thing in my life.'

'I wondered if it might be good for business.' Cathy feared she didn't sound convincing. She slumped in her chair, and stared down at the table. Was it fair to involve Jenny in something that might have unwelcome repercussions? The Hartlands had come across a fair bit of unpleasantness when they threw themselves into Mellstone affairs. This was different, of course, but still . . .

Jenny made coffee, deep in thought. Then she flashed a smile. 'I'll do it! Any subject? Can I bring some of my own pots? I like a challenge.'

'Of course. I'd love to see some of your pottery some time, Jenny.'

'Now?'

'Oh lovely, if . . . '

'Come on then, this way. Bring your coffee with you.'

The workroom on the ground floor was already stocked with a wheel and a sturdy workbench. Several large plastic containers stood about on the bare wooden floor. One of the shelves lining the walls was stacked with clay pots.

Jenny waved her hand at them. 'Those are ready for firing. The kiln's not in place yet in the back garden. Soon will be, I hope.'

Cathy moved carefully towards one of the other wide slatted shelves holding a variety of pottery containers. 'You've done all these? Such lovely colours like jewels.'

'I made these over a period of about three years.' Jenny picked one up a tall narrow ultramarine one and handed it to her. 'What do you think of that?'

Cathy stared down at it, struggling for the right comment. 'Well, it's different.'

Jenny laughed and took it from her. 'I designed that to complement trails of ivy for a very high landing windowsill in an old house where the light slanted in at midday. It got high marks in one of my exhibitions at college.'

'Yes, I see,' said Cathy doubtfully. 'It must be good then.'

'Or this?'

Cathy brightened on seeing the shallow rose-pink bowl shining with rainbow lights. 'That's lovely! Felicity would approve of that. She's into rainbow-coloured things.'

'Felicity?'

'My daughter. And your daughter is now home I hear. Have you other children too, Jenny?'

'Sadly, no. A hysterectomy took care of that

43

in my mid-thirties.'

'So young? I'm sorry.'

'Saskia's in Hilbury now, job hunting.' Jenny laughed suddenly, her eyes alight with enthusiasm. 'Oh, Cathy, I must tell you or I'll burst. I had an extraordinary piece of luck this morning. I've landed a superb contract for six months, possibly longer. You know the Roselyn Guesthouse at Wernely? I'm to look after their floral arrangements in all the main rooms and landing and hallways and some bedrooms, using my own pots. Most of these and some special designs.'

Her excitement was infectious. Cathy smiled her delight. No wonder she had seemed different with this news bubbling up inside her 'That's marvellous, Jenny. But the demo?'

'Don't worry. I'll think up a suitable theme and let you know. I'll need the right foliage, of course, not garden shrubs. I'll look for some in the lanes. There's plenty about at this time of year and I need some exercise.'

'If you're sure?'

Jenny smiled. 'Of course I'm sure.'

'Then that's fine,' said Cathy, preparing to go.

*   *   *

Later, Jenny fetched her bucket of yellow and white lilies and placed it outside the back door where their heady perfume mingled with the

44

honeysuckle on the nearby trellis. Then she went inside and stretched luxuriously. She had made a good start. As well as this contract she had three more meetings set up with prospective clients. It seemed that this sort of thing was welcome at the moment. She was lucky to have got in first in this area, and one contract might well lead to others by recommendation.

But the demonstration talk she had agreed to give was another matter. What on earth had she let herself in for? Maybe now would be the moment to reconnoitre a bit, and revisit some of the places she had loved as a child to see what they offered in the way of greenery. Brooklands, for one. Hopefully, the rough area at the bottom of the field near the brook would still be there and the wooded area nearby where she had once seen an otter.

She fetched her walking shoes from the hall and grabbed a jersey. In the lane she saw someone in a grey jacket and skirt whose white dog collar gleamed against her pale grey blouse.

Jenny did a quick retake. The Reverend Lesley J. Bond, whose name shone in gilt lettering on the church notice board. The young estate agent hadn't mentioned that in his prattle about the sought-afterness of Mellstone. She smiled.

The vicar approached with hand outstretched and gripped Jenny's hand. 'Nice

45

to meet you. I've been meaning to call on you. Jenny Finlay, isn't it? I'm Lesley Bond. I've heard a lot about you from the Varleys. So, how did you come to choose to settle in Mellstone? You've been doing a college course in the north I hear.'

'Mere chance. I was struck by the co-incidence of the advert in the estate agent's window in Hilbury just when I happened to be there. You see I lived in this cottage as a little girl.'

One of Lesley's bushy eyebrows shot up. 'Co-incidence? I wonder.'

'A chance too good to miss.'

'And you're glad you took it?'

Jenny smiled. 'Everything seems to be working out so far, touch wood!' Oh dear, she shouldn't have said that! She glanced at Lesley, wondering if an apology for being superstitious in front of a member of the cloth was called for.

But Lesley Bond seemed unperturbed. 'I've been meaning to ask someone. Was Mr Moore the vicar here once?'

The new vicar smiled. Jenny could see that with a bit of attention she could look quite attractive. Her eyes were good. 'Ages ago, about three back. Was that when you lived here? He moved away to a Living in Somerset. Then when he retired he and his wife came back to Mellstone to live in Lynch Cottage.'

'And who did he marry?'

46

'His wife's called Karen. Maybe you knew her? Well, I must be on my way.'

Jenny stared after her brisk retreating back. The lane past Lynch Cottage was definitely out of bounds now. Her old head teacher, now Mrs Moore, still had the power to send shivers down her spine. She would lay that particular ghost in her own time and in her own way.

*   *   *

To Jenny's pleasure Hodman's Hollow, the track that led up the downs, hadn't changed much since her very first walk with Elisabeth. Suddenly the vision of the old woman, Alice Pengold, shot into her mind. To her childish eyes Mrs Pengold had looked like a witch in her black coat especially as she was carrying an armful of dead grass and twigs with a single scarlet-berried head of lords and ladies that shone like a torch from the middle of the bunch. Petrified, she had tugged at Elisabeth's arm. 'Why is she picking all those things? She made the branch fall off the Tidings Tree.'

What was it about Alice Pengold that filled her young self with such abject terror? They had walked further than they intended that day and were glad to accept a lift from a neighbour when they got down to the lane again. She had asked if Mrs Pengold could make the Tidings Tree grow again and had remembered the reply as if it was yesterday.

'No human being can make it grow. It'll grow on its own.'

Or not, as the case might be, Jenny reflected.

Today, as then, the vale stretched into the far-distance, dark with trees. Across on Mellstone Hill a pearl necklace of sheep clung to the olive hillside and above her a kestrel hung in the clear sky. Invisible lark song hung in the air. The mossy earth smell of the bank was the same now as then.

Jenny moved her armful of branches to her other arm. Then she picked some late pink campion to add colour.

The sound of voices reverberated in the quiet air as a group of walkers, heavily kitted out, climbed over the stile. Their bulky gear looked suitable for an arctic expedition. As they came towards her she recognised Tess Hartland's animated face beneath her bright blue woolly hat.

'Hello,' Tess shrilled. 'Lovely up here, isn't it? Meet Nigel, my husband. Nigel, this is Jenny from Marigold Cottage. Clever with flowers.'

Jenny smiled at Nigel Hartland. He too was well wrapped up against the pleasant summer air.

'Glad to meet you, my dear,' he said, pulling off a thick glove to grasp Jenny's hand. To her surprise his felt cold. There couldn't really be snow and ice up there, could there? The sunlit sheep looked happy enough.

'This is our little walking group,' Tess said. 'We meet every week to explore the countryside and do a bit of a recce. Lovely up here, isn't it?'

Nigel looked smug. 'It all needs looking after and we're the people to do it. Mostly retired, of course. We're planning to start Mellstone Countryside Association to do the job properly. I always say the people who have always been here don't appreciate it as it ought to be appreciated.'

'Nigel's the man to get things going,' said Tess. 'Aren't you, dear? We can't have all those managerial skills going to waste.'

Jenny, leaving them, was thoughtful as she turned back towards Hodman's Hollow. Outwardly there hadn't been as many changes as she had feared. But the spirit of the old place was fast disappearing. Where were the eccentrics she remembered from her childhood? All these affluent incomers made differences, good and bad. Something was definitely lacking in present day Mellstone.

But would she really rather have that awful Mrs Barden screeching at her cronies round the Tidings Tree than people like Tess Hartland and her manageering, pleasant Nigel? Well no. So what was she complaining about?

* * *

A few days later Jenny drove her car through the wide gates and into the drive of the Linton Guesthouse on the outskirts of Poole. From the car park at the side of the red brick building she caught a glimpse through the willow trees of the harbour backwaters and the faint mauve line of the Purbeck Hills beyond. This could be miles from anywhere if she didn't know that in the other direction she would see a huge industrial estate.

She got out and stretched. The front door was shut. Jenny rang the bell. After a few minutes' wait she rang it again and was rewarded by a clatter of chains from inside. The door opened.

'Yes?'

'Mr Cant?'

He looked at her in silence. A short man, devoid of any humour as far as she could tell by the sour expression on his face.

'I have an appointment at twelve. May I bring my containers in to show you?' She indicated her car. 'I won't be a moment.'

He followed her across the gravel, and stood waiting while she unearthed a shallow yellow bowl designed for a table in a hall or foyer.

'What's that?'

She looked at him in surprise. 'I've brought six, all different. Perhaps we could discuss the colour of flowers you would like. Or would you

50

prefer me to make my own choice?'

'I said nothing about wanting anything.'

'We spoke on the phone. We made an appointment for today.'

'I don't think so.' He rubbed the tip of his nose, not looking at her. 'You've made a mistake. We do our own flowers.'

'But you said . . . '

A ginger cat came sauntering towards them round the side of the building but returned faster than it came with the help of one of his suede shoes. 'I've changed my mind. I'll say good day.'

There was nothing for it but to replace the dish in the box with the others, get in her car and drive away. Jenny made a civilised farewell although she was seething. To get her all this way for a put down like this? This was a complete waste of time.

Once out on the main road Jenny pulled into a handy lay-by and stopped the car. She took several deep breaths. No way was she going to let this sort of setback get to her. You win some, you lose some. She had to accept it. Calmer now, she put the car into gear and set off again.

She could do without the Mr Cants of this world. All the same no one liked having their work rejected.

Nick hadn't approved when his mother, a well-known potter, had interested his wife in the craft. Would things have been different if

51

she had listened to his urging to give up her pottery classes? It was something she would never know for sure. The uncertainty of this struck her sometimes in the small hours when she couldn't sleep. Examining her latest work laid out on the shelves of her workroom, she would remind herself that the past was behind her and this was her life now. But sometimes, when the moon shone fitfully through the racing clouds, she wondered if her new life would continue to satisfy her as year followed year.

A Red Admiral butterfly came flickering nearby, landed on a plumbago bush and was instantly off again. Jenny smiled as she watched it flutter away.

*   *   *

Saskia's supermarket application came to nothing. The work was for two days only and temporary full-time work was what she was after. She needed money fast since her mother's resources after the move were not at their best. Mum worried about her contracts and all the rest of it. With luck she would get some more soon.

Her plans to move on elsewhere were quite out of the question now because of Oliver. Just as well she'd been taken on at the pub for evening work. Luckily she'd done bar work before, though she wasn't quite as experienced as she had given the landlord to understand. Never mind, it would be quiet at first and she would soon pick up on what he wanted.

Melvin Gedge was a big man, florid of face and much given to hearty laughter. He looked at Saskia approvingly as she pushed open the door early on Friday evening and went into the public bar.

'Early, my dear. Well done. And looking as pretty as a picture.'

Saskia blinked at the sudden dimness after the brightness outside. Then she smiled, liking what she saw. The large collection of brass horseshoes on the beams shone and the bar counter was polished to a deep attractive brown. The whole place looked welcoming.

The others'll be here soon and the wife's out the back. She wants to show you all the ropes. Go on through while we're quiet.'

They were busy because it was Friday. After a while her legs ached and she had a dull pain at the base of her spine. She pushed her hair away from her face and leaned on the bar. The sound of church bells came drifting pleasantly in each time the outside door opened. She liked hearing them. Melvin's wife Janis was here too now, deftly serving pints and taking money. To Saskia she seemed tireless. 'Used to it, that's all,' she said when Saskia asked her how she did it.

Well, she would get used to it, too.

The bells had stopped now and she was

53

sorry. At this distance they were mellow and musical. More people came in amid much talk and laughter. Among them she saw, with a quickening of her heart, Oliver Varley. Oliver, oh great! Aching limbs, backache, what were they? All gone. She moved as deftly as Janis Gedge could wish, her skirt loose about her waist and with the feeling she was least an inch taller.

Oliver looked somehow bigger than when she had last seen him. The sides of her mouth curved. People raised their glasses to him and greeted him in slow, burry voices. Dorset voices, she thought, liking the sound of the deep vowels and rolling rrrs.

He looked at her and smiled, looking younger in his jeans and light jersey. Of course he wasn't exactly young. Quite old really. Gazing at his animated face, she wondered how old. Getting on for thirty probably. His mother had been a young teacher at the school when Mum was small.

'The bellringers always come in after Practice Night,' said Janis Gedge.

'Yes, yes, of course,' Saskia murmured, moving forward to take their order.

They crowded round, remarking on their new barmaid with friendly banter. She liked it and joined in easily. Oliver ordered the first round of best bitter and lager. They stood at the bar drinking as if they hadn't tasted liquid for months. Once or twice she was aware of

Melvin Gedge glancing at her with approval. She was loving it and all because of Oliver.

'Thirsty work, bellringing,' said the eldest man, wiping the back of his hand across his mouth. His blue eyes twinkled at her from his deeply tanned face.

This is Tom Barnet,' said Oliver. 'Tower Captain this many a long year. Took over from Melvin's old dad. Saskia from Marigold Cottage, Tom.'

'Oh aye?'

More people needed serving and Saskia found herself busy for a while. The bellringers carried their glasses across to a table they had obviously made their own. She hadn't expected Oliver to be one of them. Maybe he always came in here after the ringing on Fridays? Great! Her job here was doubly worthwhile. She would gladly work for nothing for the chance of seeing Oliver. She gave a little giggle and glanced across at him but he was deep in conversation with the man called Tom Barnet.

Then, in a quiet period, Oliver came to the bar.

Her face glowed.

'Great to see you again,' he said, and she could see he meant it. 'So they've got you working already?'

She smiled. 'I was lucky. Two evenings a week, Friday and Saturday.' No harm in getting that in straight away. 'But I need more work really to stay here all summer.'

'You're at university?

She hesitated. 'I've just done the first year of a B.Ed. But I don't know. I think I've made a big mistake. I thought I wanted to teach but I don't know now.'

His eyebrows rose up then down again in the way she remembered from when he gave her a lift home. 'So what else will you do?'

'That's the problem. I don't know any more.' Not since Ash did the dirty on her and she began to think more deeply about her future. 'People can change their minds, can't they?'

He hooked forward a stool with his foot and sat down. 'I know, I know. Tell me.'

Great to pour it all out and she felt better now. All it amounted to really was that she felt a definite leaning towards something she had never considered before.

'I felt so sorry for that boy Jem,' she said. 'The one I met on the bridge. He seemed so lost somehow. That's what set me thinking.'

'OK, so what are you going to do about it?'

Saskia noticed some spilt liquid on the shiny surface and ran her finger through it. Then she got the cloth to wipe it away. Not looking at him she said, 'I don't know.'

'Can you switch degree courses?'

'I don't think I want even that.'

'You mean you'd give up university?'

For a moment she didn't answer. Mum would go mad. She had done so much for her,

56

supported her when she needed it, encouraged her to follow her to this country from New Zealand. How could she explain to her mother when she didn't really understand herself?

'I see. Phew, rather you than me. It was bad enough when I didn't want to go into the same branch of agriculture as my father. Can you imagine . . . the farm involved and my father coming up to retirement age and the only son swans off to a remote country in Western Africa?'

'What for? Charity work?'

'In a broad sense, I suppose. Fairly broad anyway. Have you ever heard of the parkia tree? We're doing a project on it to help the local economy. It's a long story. I'll tell you one day if you're interested.'

'Oh, I'm interested.'

'Once I get on to the subject I can't stop. I've come back for a while to raise money, write articles and lecture. That sort of thing. Good to have someone to talk to about it. Dad doesn't want to know of course.'

Saskia smiled. Oliver was a very understanding sort of person. He deserved to be understood in his turn by someone who really cared. Suddenly she longed to feel his head on her shoulder while she listened with her whole being, understanding him as no one else could. 'And your sister,' she said. 'Is she interested in your parents' farm?'

He laughed. 'Not a bit of it.'

57

'It makes my problem sound trivial.'

'Not if it means a great deal to you.' He leaned forward. 'Go for what your heart says, OK? Now is the time to do something about it, not in a few years time when you've resented not taking action earlier.' He smiled suddenly so that the tiny lines round his eyes disappeared. 'And now for more drinks. Same again I think, though Tom's paying. What time do you finish?'

'Not till eleven.' Would he hang around waiting for her? It was only twenty past nine now.

'Past my bedtime.'

'Mine too but needs must.' She was proud of the lightness in her voice as if she didn't care one way or the other.

Tom Barnet came up to the bar, fishing in his pocket for cash. 'We got to talk about Saturday week, Oliver.'

'OK, Tom, I'm coming.'

Saskia watched them carry the drinks to the table in the corner. What was happening Saturday week? In any case she would see Oliver again next Friday if not before. She hoped very much that it was before.

*   *   *

In the small Office off the kitchen at Varley's Farm Cathy placed a pile of paper in the printer and switched on the computer. Betty

58

Bronson's letter enquiring about the booking of a double room for the first weekend in September needed a reply. She would write that she had pencilled in the date in the Diary. The deposit would make this a firm booking and she looked forward to hearing from her in due course.

But instead of getting on with it Cathy stood with the Bronson letter in her hand, thinking. Pink young things? What had made that shoot into her mind? It came from a poem by Thomas Hardy. Arnold had given her the book, one of his rare presents to her . . . his only present to her. For some reason that particular poem had remained in her memory. She had thought it sad . . . pink young things turning into market women and the poet looking at them and marvelling that such a thing could happen.

But she had never worn pink in her life. Except underwear, of course, and that didn't count. She had never been conscious of feeling young either. Probably because she was the eldest child in her family. With two younger sisters pushing her from behind she had always felt old. Gawky, yes, young no. So what had Arnold seen in her? Or Ralph for that matter.

Cathy looked in the glass above the radiator reflectively. All she saw was an overweight middle-aged woman. A market woman, except that she never accompanied Ralph to market. He had never suggested it, of course. In any case she would rather be at home preparing for their Bed and Breakfast guests. And with Oliver home now for a few months she wanted to be here for him.

She wished Ralph could accept that his son had his own life to live. Felicity was doing what she wanted so why not Oliver? If his mother could accept it why couldn't Ralph even though where their son was working was too remote for her to have much peace of mind about him while he was there. Ralph had never approved of his only son giving up the prospect of lucrative work to do research on parkia trees or whatever they were called in such a place. He hadn't approved of his botany degree either. A good agricultural degree would have been far more useful according to Ralph. At least their daughter had the good sense to qualify as an agricultural secretary. The sun shone out of Felicity's eyes as far as Ralph was concerned.

Cathy sighed. Arnold wouldn't recognise her now. She had nothing to fear. Now what had made her think like that? And why would Arnold Bronson suddenly wish to visit Mellstone when he had loathed the village in the first place? She was being ridiculous. She shouldn't assume that someone called Betty Bronson should automatically be married to someone called Arnold.

Smiling at herself, Cathy got out of the program and switched off the computer. The letter would have to wait until tomorrow. Back in the kitchen, she propped it on the table where Ralph would be sure to see it when he came in later this evening.

CHAPTER FIVE

Jenny, suddenly nervous about her talk and demonstration in the old school building next door, was glad that Saskia was with her for moral support and to help carry in the scented selection of flowers whose colours brightened the dim room.

'Hilda Lunt,' said a woman with sleek grey hair and broad shoulders greeted them in a deep authoritative voice. 'President. And you are?'

Jenny told her, feeling slightly uncomfortable. 'I've brought my daughter to give me a hand. I hope you don't mind?'

The President shot a fierce look at Saskia and then smiled. 'Not at all. I can only apologise for the decrepit state of this place. We need to do something before it collapses about our ears.'

Saskia, trim in a skimpy green skirt and top, grinned at her. 'It'll last out the evening, I hope.'

Jenny frowned. The President's grim look showed this was no laughing matter.

Someone had placed rows of chairs in readiness. Probably done by this large woman whose ultra-short hair appeared stuck to her head. She looked strong enough to deal with any number of chairs and anything else too, if it came to that. At a snap of her capable fingers a new building might well spring up from the ruins of the old.

Jenny planned to demonstrate some of the arrangements that had been successful for her in the past. As well as flowers she had brought some of the tools that she used in making her containers.

The business part of the evening started and all went smoothly for a while. Then, seeing the President's forbidding expression. Jenny knew that something important was coming.

Hilda Lunt cleared her throat. 'And now ladies we come to the matter of this hall.'

A ripple of conversation rose and died.

'The news is bad.'

'Well it would be,' Saskia murmured at her side. 'Just look at her. I'm beginning to feel it's all my fault.'

'The surveyor has found more faults, among them subsidence.'

'Subsidence?' squealed someone from the front row. 'But doesn't that mean it could fall down round our heads?'

'It might well come to that. But not yet.'

Not until after her talk and demo anyway. Jenny bit her lip to stop it twitching.

Apparently the problem was even more desperate than foreseen and the speeding up of money raising activities for a new hall was crucial.

Then it was time for the talk and demonstration. Jenny had a heart stopping moment as she walked to the front but to her surprise she enjoyed herself once she began. The four containers she used for the arrangements brought forth cries of admiration and so did the arrangements themselves. The questions poured in after she had finished and the flowers auctioned for funds.

'Tell me,' boomed the President. 'How do you get those wonderful colours?'

I use various oxides to stain the clay slips. I paint it on the fired pots either with brushes, or this.' Jenny picked up the engobing horn.

'So what's the most exciting part about it all?'

'The most exciting?' Jenny smiled. 'It's different for everyone. For me it's when I open the kiln door after the final firing. You can never be sure how the glazes, colour and textures will look.'

'Why don't you start pottery classes and teach us?' someone asked breathlessly.

'One day perhaps.' Jenny felt her face flush with pleasure. It was good to feel appreciated. Thoughtfully she began to pack away the tools into the large bag she had brought with her.

63

Cathy and Saskia joined her. Together they carried the containers to the kitchen to empty the water.

'D'you think they liked it, Cathy?' Jenny said.

'They wouldn't have crowded round like that at the end. They were so interested. Well the majority . . .' Cathy's voice trailed off and a doubtful expression flicked across her face. Then she smiled. 'They loved it, Jenny.'

Saskia said nothing but Jenny knew that she could rely on her daughter for an honest opinion once they were home. Meanwhile Saskia went on ahead with the door key and some of the containers.

'She's a good girl,' said Cathy, watching her go.

Jenny, busily packing her pots, nodded. 'And to think if it hadn't been for my interference in my mother's affairs long ago she might have known Mellstone from the beginning.'

'Interference . . . what do you mean?'

'I rather put the boot in between Elisabeth and John Ellis. Deliberately, I'm afraid.'

Cathy looked bewildered. 'A child of nine, how could you?'

'Easily enough as it proved.'

'But Jenny that's wrong. Oh Jenny, it wasn't you. There's no way you could have known the implications of everything, and it's so long ago. Karen always was . . . I mean. .'

Jenny looked at her in astonishment. Cathy,

64

obviously unhappy at what she had said, seemed to be struggling with herself.

'You'll have to tell me now,' Jenny said.

Giving in, Cathy looked entreatingly at her. 'It can't make any difference now, can it? Everyone thought that Karen, the head teacher, would marry John Ellis. Their mothers were friends. They'd known each other from childhood. Karen thought so too you see, and made life difficult for your mother when Elisabeth moved into Marigold Cottage. It was Karen who . . . well, I was never really sure, but everyone thought that because she couldn't have John herself she saw to it that Elisabeth didn't either.'

Jenny, silenced, stared at the older woman.

'I would never have brought this up, only I couldn't let you think

'But she married the vicar.'

'There was that as well. Robert was interested in Elisabeth too, which of course made it even worse. So when Karen saw her chance to spoil things for John she took it. Then it was too late.' Cathy's voice tailed away.

Jenny, saying nothing, packed the last container in newspaper and placed it carefully in her box. This needed thinking about. What had she done in returning to Mellstone with the idea of providing a home here for Elisabeth in due course? After what she had just learned a hornet's nest sprang

65

immediately to mind.

Saskia was back now, anxious to help with the rest of the things. And someone wanted to lock up. No time to ask Cathy any more now even if she wanted to.

*   *   *

Saskia had only decided at the last minute to attend her mother's demo feeling she needed moral support. She had helped with the flowers a bit too. But later, seated at the back beside Oliver's mother she was able to sit back and observe the reaction Mum was getting from this crowd of women. Some, the older ones, sat huddled together looking as if they were glued to the same chairs they sat in at every meeting. Others, a little less decrepit, crowded round the table at the end, their excited voices rising higher and higher. Another group looked disdainfully on.

She was the youngest person here by many years, and she didn't like the feeling. The saving grace was Oliver's mother who was kind to her, making sure she had biscuits with her coffee and trying to explain who everyone was. Not that Saskia cared, wanting only to talk about Oliver. She felt her eyes begin to glaze over and longed for the evening to end. Oliver reminded her a little of Dad. Much younger of course and better looking but there was that some grave look about Oliver as he looked at you with his head bent a little to one side as if he was considering carefully everything you said. She liked that. In Dad's case, though, it was all just an act. She knew afterwards that his wandering mind was on anything but her. Somehow she knew Oliver was different.

'Oliver is your son, isn't he?' she said at last.

The older woman's face lit up. 'You know him, Saskia? Yes, of course you do. Oliver gave you a lift home didn't he?'

'He's very kind.' Kind? Is that all she could think of to describe Oliver? She wanted to say how wonderful he was, how she couldn't stop thinking of the way his hair waved slightly at the back. She thought all the time of his steady hands as they held his pint, his lovely enthusiasm as he talked about his special tree . . . the parkia tree that no one was interested in except herself. She had spent part of this morning, after she got back from town, on the computer gleaning sparse knowledge about this tree he loved. And all she could say to his mother was that he was kind.

Cathy nodded, looking proud. 'He's a good boy.'

'He lectures, doesn't he?'

'They have to raise money for the autumn when they go out to Burkina Faso for the next stage.'

Autumn was a million light years away. It was only July now. 'How long will it be for this time?'

His mother looked troubled. 'Who knows? Indefinitely, I think.'

'Indefinitely? You mean for ever?'

'A year or two anyway. A few new people will be going out with them.'

'Wow!' What a great idea. If only she could go with him too. She would have to find out more. From the little she'd heard of it so far Oliver's work out there sounded fantastic.

Saskia smiled, imagining it.

*   *   *

Cathy saw that the Bronson letter was still on the kitchen table. She hoped Ralph would see it when he came in from overseeing the improvements in the milking parlour. If he did then he might recognise the name as being the same as the man to whom she had once been engaged. Unofficially, of course. Arnold had insisted they keep the wonderful news secret for a while although she longed to shout it from the top of the church tower. At the time the decision had seemed perfectly reasonable. Now, it didn't. There hadn't been any reason for secrecy as far as she knew. Except, with hindsight, one very obvious one.

She took the letter into the office, switched on the computer and set to work answering it. She needed to do something positive to bury her regrets about her impulsive words to Jenny. It was all in the past now and forgotten

68

surely and shouldn't matter now? But Jenny
had obviously remembered and felt guilt at her
imagined part in separating her mother and
John Ellis so she had hastened to set her mind
at rest. Had she stirred something up in
Jenny's mind now that would have been better
left in ignorance? So difficult to know. She
sighed in an effort to concentrate on the job in
hand.

Ralph, entering the kitchen a little while
later, made no comment as he glanced at the
envelope on top of the pile left ready for
mailing.

'Another booking, Ralph. Did you see?'

'Good show. I've been thinking, Cathy. It's
about time we had John Ellis over for a meal
before we get too busy.'

'Funny you should say that. I was thinking
too. We haven't seen anything of John for
ages.'

'How about inviting your pal from Marigold
Cottage at the same time?'

'Jenny? Good idea. I've been meaning to
ask her.'

Ralph sat down on the nearest chair and
pulled off his boots. He grinned up at her as if
he'd done something really clever. 'They know
each other, don't they? Make a bit of a party
of it.'

Cathy frowned, deep in thought. 'What shall
we have to eat?' Something different to make
a good impression. And what about that new

dessert recipe she had been reading about somewhere or other, Banofee Cheesecake with toffee pecan sauce?

'You'll think of something,' said Ralph with confidence. 'I've done my bit, suggesting it. It's down to you, now.'

'Or up,' said Cathy. 'We always used to say up. When did it change to down?'

Ralph, slipping his stockinged feet into his slippers, shrugged. 'Crept in unnoticed, I suspect. Most people have other things to think about. What's it matter anyway?'

'It sounds odd, that's all. Irritating. We could invite the Hartlands too. Nigel and Tess are good company. You like them.'

'Good idea.' Ralph hooked the *Dorset Gazette* out from behind the microwave and went to the door into the hall.

'And Lesley Bond,' said Cathy before he could escape.

'If you like.'

'But we need another man.'

'Oliver? Or don't you think he's fit to show in company after where he's been for the last six months?'

Cathy smiled. 'Oh yes, Oliver, of course.'

'He'd qualify as a man wouldn't he?'

'Don't be silly, Ralph.'

Ralph, poised for flight, hesitated for a moment. 'Have you thought of the Moores?'

Cathy looked at him in horror. 'Karen and Robert?'

70

'We owe them, don't we?'

'Definitely not the Moores.' Cathy shuddered. 'Not with Jenny coming too. Remember the Tidings Tree, for goodness sake.'

'The Tidings Tree? You're not seriously suggesting that something that happened years ago is going to cause trouble now? A load of rubbish.'

'Some people have long memories.' Cathy thought suddenly of Thomas Hardy. On the bookshelf in each of the guest bedrooms she had placed a book of Hardy's poems as well as local guidebooks of the area. She hadn't read anything of Hardy's for ages, not his novels anyway. His poems were easy to dip into when she needed a break from dusting.

She had read somewhere about Thomas Hardy's knack of burying an emotion in his heart for many years until some trigger made it spring up as fresh as ever.

Suddenly a vision shot into her mind of Karen Moore seated at her desk in her empty classroom that fateful day when the branch came off the Tidings Tree. The howling wind slammed shut the door Tom Barnet had left open as he blundered into school to tell them what had happened. From the Infants room beyond the partition she heard Karen's sharp voice haranguing her children in a desperate attempt to establish exactly when Jenny had slipped out of the classroom.

71

When both classes had departed into the windy afternoon she joined her head teacher who stared wild-eyed at Jenny's desk at the back of the room.

'Go home,' said Karen, her voice tight. 'I've got to think. Mr Moore will be here soon on the attack. I must plan what to say. Go on, Cathy, you're doing no good here.'

Cathy had been only too well aware of that. She hadn't been much help either in the events that followed. The pain and bitterness was like a living river, increasing in volume until something had to give. Robert had asked Karen to marry him in the end and they moved away. The school didn't recover either with the drop in numbers and so that when it closed no one had been surprised.

The surprise had been that the Moores had decided to retire to Mellstone.

But the Moores and Jenny? No, it wouldn't do at all.

CHAPTER SIX

'So how was the meeting?' Robert Moore asked as his wife joined him in their dining room at the back of the house. Rain had started to fall and with the branches of the yew almost tapping the window the room was already dim. He pulled the heavy velvet

72

curtains across early as it was. 'That's better. Another lamp, d'you think?'

Karen Moore picked up the teapot and shook her head. 'One's enough.'

Her voice sounded strained and he looked at her in concern as he lowered himself into the chair at the head of the table. She looked pale and the dark shadows were back beneath her eyes. He had hoped getting out to the WI meeting this afternoon would be good for her. She had been confined to the house too much of late and they had had few visitors. He sighed. 'Did they manage to find another speaker?'

She began to serve the chicken casserole and passed his plate to him without speaking. He removed the lids from the two vegetable dishes and helped himself to carrots and one small potato. He knew better than to ask her again. She would tell him in her own good time.

They began to eat.

'You'll never guess who the speaker was,' she said at last. 'I was rather taken aback when she was introduced. Jenny Finlay, the Turner woman's child. Red-haired still, I may say. Oh yes, and the same direct look about her she had then.'

'Do I know her?' Robert thought hard. 'D'you mean the little girl who once lived at Marigold Cottage? But that was years ago.'

'Of course I'd never have recognised her if

Hilda Lunt hadn't announced who the speaker was.' Karen looked at him, tight-lipped. 'I might have known she would return one day to haunt me.'

'Haunt you? What can you mean, my dear? She didn't.. ?'

'Of course not. She had no idea who I was.'

Robert ate his food thoughtfully. Jenny Finlay, a child who once lived here had now come back. People were doing similar things all the time for whatever reason. But this particular child they had known at a traumatic time in their lives and he feared for the effect on his wife now. He thought of his visit to Jenny's mother in Marigold Cottage on the day of the gale that resulted in the tree being felled, perhaps unnecessarily. Mellstone people had never forgiven Elisabeth Turner for something that wasn't in any way her fault. She had always remained in his memory because of it. A pleasant young woman who didn't deserve the way things turned out.

'So how did Jenny Finlay come to be here in Mellstone at your meeting? But she won't be Jenny Finlay now I suppose. Married, is she?'

'Didn't I tell you? She's moved in to Marigold Cottage. I don't know about marriage. Hilda Lunt introduced her as Jenny Finlay.'

'So we shall be seeing something of her.' In spite of everything his interest was aroused. 'What was her subject?' He tried to imagine an

74

adult Jenny and failed.

'She'd brought some strange-looking containers with her. I wouldn't have given them house-room.' Karen glanced at the mahogany sideboard that had belonged to her mother and took up far too much space in the room. On it were some large glazed vases in magenta and cream. 'Then she did some flower arrangements in them. The arrangements were auctioned afterwards for funds but not the pottery. She took that back. People were interested in those, the new people mostly. They were still crowding round when I left.'

'So you didn't chat with her?'

His wife looked horrified. '1 took good care not to be recognised. I think she's making a mistake listening to all the ideas they seemed to be throwing at her. Pottery classes if you please. And then she'll need someone bigger to display it all, no doubt. Ridiculous. Can you just imagine what people are going to think, especially the older ones? It won't be Mellstone anymore . . . new car parks, crowds at Bank Holidays, delivery vans. They won't like it. There'll be trouble. Bound to be.'

'Demonstrations?' he couldn't resist suggesting.

She threw him a scornful look and he ate the rest of the food in silence. He couldn't help thinking of the young woman, Elisabeth Turner, who had interested him so much at the time. Where was she now? Older, of course, as they all were. He hoped the intervening years had dealt kindly with her.

Karen got up to remove their plates which she placed on the sideboard. The bowl of fruit was already on the table and he leaned forward to take an apple. He still regretted the old-fashioned puddings, apple pie, rice pudding, roly-poly. Fruit was all very well in its place, on apple trees preferably. But heavy puddings brought on his indigestion so fruit it had to be.

He peeled his apple slowly, remembering the gale that had brought down the fruit early as well as the branch from the tree. Vividly he remembered walking along the lane the day after the gale. From the group of people gathered there with heads close together he recognised Mrs. Barden, blowsy and loud-mouthed, shouting that the child had no business here. When he pointed out that something would have had to be done in time because it was an old tree she'd had her answer ready.

'It's always been old, Vicar,' she had screeched. 'It was the child's fault. If she weren't hurt no one would have done nothing and we'd still have our tree.'

The day before they had been shocked and sympathetic about Jenny, but when she was known to be out of danger emotions ran high. He hadn't liked the sound of it and with justification as things turned out.

Robert stroked his forehead thoughtfully. He liked the thought of Jenny Finlay's return. Indeed he wished her well. It seemed that she was anxious to take part in village life, and, in spite of what Karen said, this could only be good.

*   *   *

The kiln was now in position in the back garden, surrounded by a brick wall roofed with grey tiles. Several times already this morning Jenny had come out to inspect it merely for the pleasure of knowing it was there.

'Cooee!'

Startled, Jenny saw a small head appear round the end wall of the cottage. This was the third time Tess had called on her since yesterday.

'Come and look at my kiln, Tess,' she said as pleasantly as she could. 'I'm going to be packing it later so I'm really busy. I've lots ready for firing.'

Tess was enthusiastic. 'You're doing so well, aren't you dear?'

Jenny closed the kiln door. 'My six months contract at Roselyn Guesthouse is better than I dared hope. They want twice as many floral displays as they said at first. And there's a strong hint that the contract will be extended.'

'Wonderful, but don't get too immersed in

77

all it, dear. It's so important to get involved in village things and be accepted here. Why not join us in our Countryside Group? There's land on the other side of Larksbury Rings that needs looking at. It makes a fine walk, Jenny, and you get to know people. What d'you say?'

'Tess, I wish I could.'

'You'd be helping to do something for the good of Mellstone. And to be seen doing it. It's important, dear, to be seen or how will anyone know? Can't you really take the morning off?'

Jenny glanced at her kiln, and then thought of the promised clay delivery. This morning was her only chance for several days to get ahead. She had to make her choice, and stick with it. She shook her head. 'It's no good Tess. I'll leave the involvement with the village to you and good luck.'

'So many people are interested in what you're doing. Pottery classes are the thing. Have you thought any more about that, dear? Why don't you set up something here?'

'Space,' said Jenny. 'There's no room here to set up classes and it's only viable with a biggish group. I'm a working woman with my living to make.'

'Then let's find somewhere for you.'

Jenny laughed. 'You're going way too fast, Tess. 'I couldn't consider expanding the business yet. I've only been here a few weeks. I'd have to get established first.'

'But it would get you accepted here. People admired your things so much.'

Jenny smiled. Admiration was as heady as the sweet honeysuckle perfume wafting across from the fence. She thought of her plans to start slowly and build up over several months of hard work. She must be strong, able to resist the blandishments Tess insisted on pouring on her.

'I'll leave you to it then, dear. But it makes me sad that you won't make the effort.'

As she watched Tess trip across the grass on her way out Jenny wished she could think about setting up the pottery classes. She loved her craft and wanted others to share her pleasure in it. Saskia approved of the plans she had made so far and was anxious to help in between her job hunting expeditions to Hilbury. 'When's Gran coming to stay?' she had wanted to know only this morning. 'I hope she'll like it here too and approve of us.'

Did Elisabeth approve? Well yes, of course, and she was looking forward to coming to see for herself very soon. Jenny stared at the roses, quite still for a moment. She hadn't thought things through properly since Cathy had come out with all that about her mother and John Ellis and the part her old head teacher had played in keeping them apart. But that was years ago when they were young.

She shook herself a little and smiled at her fleeting apprehension. Smiled too that she wanted Elisabeth's approval of her plans when her new life was her own. Why should her mother and daughter's approval be so necessary to her happiness? There was really no answer to that. The fact was there, always. She would invite Elisabeth to visit Mellstone as soon as possible and hope for the best.

Maybe one day she could think of expanding but not yet. She took a deep breath of perfumed air and went indoors.

*   *   *

Having at last decided on the guest list for the dinner party Cathy set out to deliver the invitations by hand. A blackbird poured its heart out from the branches of the young birch by the farm gate. The hawthorn hedge bordering the lane was a rich green and dandelion flowers brightened the verge by the school wall. Cathy frowned, suddenly reminded of the first day of her first Summer Term in Mellstone when the police had warned them to keep an eye on young Joe Barden. Karen had stressed the need to be on her guard against more trouble after the loss of the tree and Jenny's part in it.

Her disquiet about Joe Barden was hard to shake off. She had never liked the boy and that had worried her. Wasn't there something likeable about any child once you had taken the trouble to discover it? Ashamed, she had struggled to hide her true feelings. The clatter of crashing milk bottles had her flying to the door at the same time as Karen. Someone had kicked one of the crates against the wall. Joe Barden. She had cringed at the ugly expression on the boy's face. No wonder he had terrified young Jenny and made her life a misery with his taunts.

Cathy unlatched the gate and walked up the brick path to the front door of Marigold Cottage to push the invitation through the letter box. The door opened and Jenny stood there, smiling.

Cathy, taken aback, smiled too. 'I thought you'd be working, Jenny.'

'Coming in?'

'I've more of these to deliver. We're having a dinner party at the farm on Saturday week. I hope you'll come. Saskia, too of course, if she'd like to. But perhaps we'd all be too old for her and she'd be bored?'

Jenny opened the envelope and scanned the contents. 'How kind of you, Cathy. I'll be there like a shot. Saskia works in the pub on Saturday evenings so I'll have to decline for her.'

'We're inviting Tess and Nigel Hartland too, and the vicar, Lesley Bond. And Oliver's home now, our son. Lesley's trying to rope him in to edit the parish magazine on a temporary basis. He'd be good at that. I think he'll do it. Oh, and John Ellis is invited too of course.'

'Thanks, Cathy. I'd really love to come.'

As Cathy turned to go she wondered if Jenny felt lonely here now that the first flush of moving into her new home was over. She knew so little about the great gap of years that had seen Jenny grow and change from the child she had been to the woman she was now. Perhaps she should have been more welcoming, tried harder, introduced her to more people, and been friendlier herself.

Sighing, she closed the gate behind her.

*   *   *

What had become of that young boy Jem? Saskia couldn't help thinking of him each time she turned up for work at The Swan because the pub was opposite the bridge over Mellstone Brook. She hadn't even caught a glimpse of the boy since that first day as he leaned over the stonework looking for otters but she hadn't forgotten him because of his connection with Oliver.

She had liked Jem for himself too, of course, because he had talked to her as to an equal. She liked that. He lived with his father and Felicity, Oliver's sister. So that made him Oliver's nephew. Uncle Oliver, oh dear. It made him sound so old like her Uncle Robbie in New Zealand, Dad's brother. She shuddered. No way. How complicated it all was. Never mind. Jem was definitely connected to Oliver.

Friday was her favourite night, of course, because of seeing Oliver after bellringing practice. Tonight, if she got the chance, she would ask him about Jem.

Conscious all the time of the distant sound of bells, Saskia served the few people who trickled in. She glanced at the clock yet again.

Janis Gedge passed a plate of sandwiches across the bar to a customer and looked at her with a frown. 'What's wrong, love?'

'Nothing, not really.'

'Cheer up then.'

At once Saskia smiled but it was an effort. Was this a warning to her to be cheerful? Decorative, hardworking and happy-looking . . . difficult the way she felt now. She had been working here for two weeks but she hadn't got any further with Oliver. He was pleasant and friendly and always made a point of chatting to her when the bellringers came in each Practice Night. That was all and it wasn't enough. He talked about her enjoying Mellstone and finding more work but not much about the work he was doing in that place in Africa. She wanted . . . needed . . . to be someone sympathetic he confided in. Why didn't those wretched bells shut up?

Tonight she would ask Oliver about Jem. Her heart quickened at the sudden jangling of the bells at last that she knew meant that the end of bellringing practice was near. They were ringing the bells down so that each one, instead of resting on the metal stay ready for ringing, was hanging face down and it was perfectly safe to touch the ropes. Oliver had told her that last Friday.

She straightened the waistband of her skirt, and checked that she'd tucked in her new shirt properly. As it happened, when the bellringers came bustling in talking at the tops of their voices, she was serving someone else. Her face glowed in the consciousness of Oliver's presence but she didn't look at him. Instead she smiled at Melvin Gedge as he wiped the bar and placed on it another plate of sandwiches his wife had made for the young couple in the corner.

It was some time before Oliver left his companions and came to talk to her. She asked at first how the practice had gone. She only mentioned Jem when he had finished telling her about the quarter peal Tom Barnet wanted to organise to celebrate a wedding . . . the couple in the corner? She spared them a glance before looking back at Oliver again. The blue of his short-sleeved shirt was the same colour as his eyes. It suited him. She smiled.

'Jem?' he said when she asked him. 'Haven't seen much of him lately but he'll be around this weekend I should think. Felicity and James are off for a day or two in the Lakes. They like a bit of fell walking.'

'And doesn't Jem?'

Oliver shrugged. 'Maybe. Maybe not. He's with his grandparents anyway. They like to have him. Did I tell you they live in the village?'

'I think so.' She knew anyway because Jem himself had mentioned it.

'Like to see where Jem lives when he's not here?'

Surprised, she stared at him.

'I'm on house duty this weekend, just checking the email and seeing that all's well. I'll be going over in the morning if you're interested, OK?'

Saskia gave a little gulp and nodded. She couldn't trust herself to speak.

CHAPTER SEVEN

Saskia was ready in good time because she had risen earlier than on her last trip into Hilbury job-hunting. Working, of course, was the last thing on her mind this sunny July morning with the prospect of an hour or two in Oliver's company. More, if she were lucky. Her cheeks felt glowing and her newly washed hair seemed to float round her face. She ran a comb through it once more and smiled.

Would Oliver suggest lunch afterwards? Mum, luckily preoccupied with the kiln, hadn't shown any interest in her plans for today, probably presuming another trip into town on the bus. Excellent. She wouldn't enlighten her. Her budding friendship with Oliver must be secret, at least until something more came of it. When it did she would shout it from the top of the church tower, ring the bells, anything as long as the world knew how she and Oliver felt about each other.

She could eat nothing. She made a hasty mug of coffee and drank it scalding hot. With luck Mum wouldn't notice her leaving at a different time than usual this morning when the Hilbury bus wasn't due for another hour. She rinsed her mug at the sink and then crept to the front door to wait hopefully in the lane.

Moments ticked by and then he came. He leaned over to open the car door for her. He looked younger today in T-shirt and jeans. Her heart flipped at his smile.

'All set?'

She smiled back and got in beside him. The sudden tones of 'The Teddy Bear's Picnic' filled the car. With an exclamation of annoyance Oliver pulled out his mobile phone and spoke into it.

'Sorry,' he said as he finished speaking and clicked it off.

'It sounded important,' Saskia said, subdued.

He grinned at her as he put the car into gear and they moved off. 'Work related, that's all.'

But wasn't work important? Would a personal call be more important? It could be if it were someone special. She tried not to let the thought of that get to her but it was hard.

The journey was far too short. She had hardly appreciated his faint whiff of aftershave and the way his hands looked so capable on the steering wheel before it was over in what seemed like breathtaking minutes.

Jem's house, a mile or two south of Hilbury, was on the side of a hill with the bare line of the rounded downs behind it. Oliver drew up in the yard at the back of the house and they got out. Saskia turned to smile at Oliver who was searching for the key beneath a stone container of geraniums.

'Should be here somewhere,' he muttered. He puckered his forehead as he gave up and started to peer beneath other smaller ones that stood about in the brick courtyard. 'Someone's been in and forgotten to lock up.' He tried the door handle. 'I'm right.'

Two black and white cats came rushing out, blinking in the sunlight. Saskia stooped to stroke one of them who twined itself lovingly round her ankles, purring.

'You like animals?'

'Oh yes,' she said, smiling. 'Especially cats.'

'Jem too.'

'Are they both his?'

'Felicity's really but she seems to have handed their welfare over to him now. He

87

does a good job looking after them but then he's keen on all animals.'

Saskia gave them a final pat each and then followed Oliver through the large utility room into the rather gloomy kitchen. Someone had piled farming magazines on the table in the centre. The blinds covering the window made it unnecessarily dim. She wondered why they were down when no one could see much from outside of the property anyway.

The hall was equally dark for lack of windows but the sitting room was bright with sunshine that flooded in from the large window. Oliver pushed open the door in the opposite wall. Through here was another largish room obviously a study. Patches of oil paint stained the bare parquet floor. A large table stood in the window covered with files and containers. Saskia's fingers itched to tidy them into neat piles. The computer stood on another table that took up the whole length of the far windowless wall. There were two printers as well and a photocopier. More box files were piled here too and newspapers.

Oliver grinned. 'They're not exactly tidy as you can see.' He pressed the switch on the computer. 'This won't take long, OK?' He raised his head. 'Listen!'

She heard the thump of footsteps overhead.

'Wait here,' he said, and went to investigate.

A burglar? Saskia hesitated, and then followed him through the sitting room and into the hall in time to see him descending the staircase. He gripped Jem's arm as if he were a potential murderer. At the bottom he let go and man and boy glared at each other.

'You're not supposed to be here,' Oliver accused, his face flushed. 'What the hell d'you think you're playing at?'

'What's it to you?' Jem's eyes flicked over to Saskia and away again.

'Everything to do with me, you little devil. You're supposed to be in Mellstone not here skulking about. Where do your grandparents think you are?'

'Walking about.'

'You must have taken a long time to get here. Too much time for their peace of mind.'

Jem shrugged. He looked unrepentant. His jeans looked new and his sweatshirt had crease marks on it.

'I came to collect this, didn't I?' He held out a DVD and Saskia saw the title *Trees of the World* on a background of green and orange.

Calmer now, Oliver took it and turned it over to read the information on the back. 'Interesting?'

'Could be.' Jem shrugged again and Saskia noticed the withdrawn expression on his pale face. 'They didn't let me take it because Grandma hasn't got a DVD player.'

'So why come back for it?'

'I haven't seen it yet.'

'That's no good reason in the

circumstances.'

'What circumstances?'

'Don't be stupid, Jem.' Oliver handed the disk back 'I can't think what's got into you.'

'I wanted it, that's all.'

'OK. But much good will it do you.' He looked at Saskia. 'Let's get the emailing done. Then we'll get young Jem here back to his worrying grandparents before they panic and alert the police.'

'Right.' She tried to smile. Her sympathy for Jem at this moment was mixed with chagrin that he should be here at all when she expected to be alone with Oliver.

The printing out of the email messages occupied the next five minutes. Then Oliver got on the phone to his sister about them.

Saskia wandered back into the hall. She found Jem in the kitchen, stroking one of the cats. Oliver had pulled the blinds up out of the way and the light reflected from the copper pans on the shelf above the Aga. Kneeling, Jem looked up at her.

She knelt too. 'What's his name?'

'Her. She's called Bella.'

'You could come and view your DVD at my place if you like.'

'I could? When?'

'Tomorrow morning?'

His face clouded. 'I'll be in church then. I have to go with Grandad, worst luck.'

'Not too surprising,' Oliver commented,

90

joining them. 'Your grandfather was vicar of Mellstone once after all. Why the objection?'

Jem looked awkward. 'Grandma makes me go because of Dad not wanting to be a vicar. He won't go to church any more, you see.'

Oliver raised his eyebrows and a smile lingered at the corners of his mouth. Suddenly Saskia wanted to kiss him, to feel those lips warm and soft, to know he felt for her exactly what she felt for him.

'In the afternoon then,' she said to Jem.

His eyes lit up. 'Great!'

Saskia stood up, brushing at the legs of her jeans. 'I'd like to see your DVD myself anyway. I like trees.' It was true, now. She had taken trees much for granted before, enjoying the autumn colours and the fresh greens in the spring but not really noticing them much. They were trees, that was all. But now trees had taken on a new meaning because of Oliver's work in Africa. She might learn something about the parkia tree from the video to surprise him with her knowledge. He had promised to tell her about his work with them hadn't he?

'Why not come too, Oliver?' The words slipped out so easily.

He shrugged. 'I'm off to Southampton then. Sorry.' He frowned at Jem. 'Come on then. We'll get you back to Mellstone before they send out search parties. I'll drop Saskia off first, and then you.'

91

The back door slammed shut.

'They don't care where I go,' Jem muttered.

Oliver locked the door and placed the key in its hiding place. 'Next time I'll tell Felicity to hide it somewhere else where you won't find it, Jem.'

'You won't fool me.'

'Says who?'

Jem looked so knowing Oliver pretended to cuff his ears. 'Get in and behave yourself. We'll be back in Mellstone in no time. Right, Saskia?'

She nodded, her smile fixed on her face as if it had been pasted there. Oliver had parked the car in the deep shade of the conifers and the inside looked gloomy.

Gone was the expectation of more to come and in its place sprang a certainty that anything she might have going with Oliver was in her imagination only. But no way would she give up yet. She got into the car, and seated herself in the back as a sort of penance for wanting more. Jem, in the front, chatted non-stop as if he, too, wanted to prolong the drive back to the village but for different reasons.

*　　　*　　　*

Jenny walked down to lane to Varley's farm for the dinner party. She had been so involved in her work today that she had barely noticed the gentle summer breeze that was dying away now leaving behind pleasant grass-scented air.

Ralph opened the front door and his handshake was warm and firm.

Cathy emerged from the kitchen and enveloped her in a hug as if she hadn't seen her for weeks. 'Come into the sitting room, Jenny. Ralph will sort out the drinks. The others are all here.'

Was she late? Jenny glanced at the grandfather clock in the corner of the hall and saw that it was staring back at her with arrogance. All right be like that, she thought. Smiling, she paused on the threshold of the large crimson-curtained room. At once Nigel Hartland sprang to his feet and then subsided into his armchair at a look from his wife.

'Come and sit by me, dear,' said Tess.

As she did so Jenny smiled at John Ellis. Lesley Bond seated near him looked years younger with her brown hair loose about her face.

'I don't think you've met our son, Oliver, yet,' said Cathy, her voice trembling with pride.

'Hi there, Jenny.' Oliver Varley's eyes crinkled as he smiled. He was like neither of his parents and only a little taller than his mother. His brown hair was short but she could see that it would be curly if given half the chance to grow.

Cathy vanished abruptly. The room was warm, the deep sofa comfortable. For a moment Jenny's gaze wandered to the landscapes of local scenes on the honey-coloured walls. Most of them were watercolours but one of the ancient British hill fort, Larksbury Rings, was in oil. Evening light poured over the sheep-nibbled turf casting a pearly effect over the whole scene. One of Elisabeth's? Definitely. She would recognise that portrayal of shimmering light anywhere.

'You like it too?' said Oliver, his gaze following hers as he seated himself nearby. 'I can almost hear the larks sing.'

'What a lovely thing to say.'

He raised his eyebrows. 'You're into art criticism?'

'My mother was the artist. Is, I mean. We used to go for picnics on Larksbury Rings. Masses of cowslips, I remember. And larks singing. It means a lot to me.'

'And now there's the pleasure of seeing it here this evening when you hadn't expected it?' he said.

'That's true.'

Oliver seemed at ease in his light-coloured cords and green pullover. There was a pleasing warmth about him, a feeling of strength but of peace too. He made no attempt to quiz her further, but leaned back in his seat, a half-smile on his lips.

Jenny had the impression that he was watching her closely as if he had to write a description of her. Not for the parish magazine she hoped. Now what did those initials after Lesley's name stand for, FCA? Football Club Announcer? Friend of Creative Agriculturists?

He lifted an eyebrow. 'You find me amusing?'

'Sorry. I was just thinking. The initials after the vicar's name . . . '

'Frightful Clowning Agoraphobic.'

She smiled. 'I like that. What is it really?'

He told her with laughter in his voice. 'Fellow of the Institute of Chartered Accountants.'

She gaped at him.

'You hadn't thought of that?'

'A well-rounded person, our vicar, in more ways than one.'

Jenny swallowed a giggle as Cathy appeared in the doorway to announce that dinner was served. She had lit pink candles in silver candlesticks. The wall lights were low and dusky shadows hid the corners of the room. The effect of the pink light on the delicate melon and ginger balls was charming.

'Too good to eat,' Tess pronounced as she picked up her spoon and fork.

Cathy looked quickly at Lesley. 'I thought . . . I mean, would you?'

'Say grace? Of course.' The vicar began to speak in the clatter from the utensils Tess dropped hurriedly. 'Bless this food, Lord, and our happy companionship this evening.'

As they finished the first course Cathy,

flushed with pleasure at the compliments, removed the dishes and Ralph poured more wine. Then he helped her carry in the tureens and removed the lids.

'Wonderful, Cathy,' said Tess.

'It's only poached pheasant with celery.'

Lesley smiled as she raised her glass to her lips. John Ellis leaned back contentedly as he listened to Ralph and Nigel discussing the importance of organising people to appreciate all that Mellstone could offer. John had murmured to Jenny that he was here merely to make up numbers but she knew how much the Varleys thought of him. In his dark tweed suit and pure white shirt he looked the most distinguished man there.

After the meal Ralph carried off his male guests and his son to inspect the damp course for his proposed new extension to the small tack room.

Lesley, seating herself near Jenny in the sitting room, leaned forward. The lamplight fell on her broad face. 'I've been meaning to ask you, Jenny. I believe your daughter is looking for employment for the summer and I hear she's good with computers. We need someone in the church office for a week or two. Would she do it do you think? Typing letters, reports, minutes of the PCC. That sort of thing. Oliver's taking over the editorship of the parish mag and might need some assistance with bits of typing. The pay's not high of course. Would she be interested?'

Jenny was doubtful and said so. Saskia still hadn't given up hope of lucrative daytime work but she wasn't sure of her reaction to this idea. She tried to imagine her daughter ensconced in some dark hole in the church typing up minutes.

Lesley smiled in a dismissive sort of way and leaned back in her seat. 'Tell her to come to see me if she feels like it. You never know what might come of it.'

The door opened and Nigel came in ahead of the others, settling himself in the armchair nearest the fire. 'And what have you ladies been talking about while we've been safely out of the way?'

'Technology, modern life,' said Jenny.

'Too highbrow for me,' said Nigel, with red-faced good humour.

Then Oliver was with her again and they talked of the Wayside Arts Association of which Jenny hadn't heard before.

Tess leaned forward, alight with enthusiasm. 'Just the thing for you, Jenny. The Wayside Art Open Weekend's in September. All sorts of people take part, painters, artists, blacksmiths, furniture makers, silver engravers, knitwear designers, potters. The lot. People go round looking and buying. Commissions too.'

'It'll be well advertised,' said Oliver.

Tess raised her voice. 'Have you heard about Jenny's latest ideas, John? Ralph? She needs larger premises for pottery classes and a showroom and that needs money.'

'Hey, wait a minute!' Jenny heard the alarm in her voice.

Tess took no notice and proceeded to tell them all about it, stressing the need for money so firmly that Jenny felt colour flood her face.

To her relief John Ellis put a stop to it by a well-timed question about her husband's Countryside Association. Under cover of the flow of information Oliver smiled at her.

'You have an appreciator, a promoter of your interests.'

Jenny sighed, her face still warm. 'One I could do without.'

'I know, I know. It's the art side that's important to you, the wish to communicate through your creation? D'you read Robert Browning?'

She shook her head.

'There's a piece from his Fra Lippo Lippi that means a lot to me.'

. . . we're made so that we love
First when we see them painted—better to us,
Which is the same thing. Art was given for that;
God uses us to help each other so,
Lending our minds out.'

'Lending our minds out,' Jenny repeated. She hadn't thought of it like that but was that

98

the work of God? If so she wanted nothing to do with it. Browning was wrong, Oliver too if that was what he believed.

'I hope we'll talk some more,' Oliver said quietly to Jenny when it was time to go. 'Could we? Away from here, I mean? I'd like you take me to the site of the oil painting to hear the larks sing.'

'They may not sing there now,' she said. 'Things change.'

Jenny felt John Ellis' eyes on her as they went out into the mild night air. 'Come and see me on Monday afternoon,' he said. 'I've something financial to discuss with you, Jenny my dear.'

She nodded, not sure she liked sound of this. He sounded serious. Too serious. Tess had no business to drop such broad hints.

*   *   *

Later, as she sipped coffee at the kitchen table after her shower, Jenny thought of how once or twice during the evening she had caught Oliver's gaze on her and the obvious way he made sure he sat near her whenever he could. Heady stuff for a woman of thirty nine. At the time she had talked happily about her work, intent only on explaining her satisfaction in creating beauty in her combination of the two crafts. Now she began to wonder. The knowledge of Cathy's son's interest in her work had crept into Jenny's mind only gradually. She allowed herself to dwell on it with a stirring of pleasure.

As well as this there was thought of how it might be if her business began to take off in directions she hadn't at first envisaged. She had assumed that her various contracts, with the occasional craft fair, would keep her fully occupied. Wouldn't taking on anything else mean she was moving too fast? The idea of her own showroom here in Mellstone was merely a beautiful dream whatever Tess said. Pottery classes too. It was something to aim for in the future if she could find the right premises when she was ready. Not yet though. There was much to be done before she even dare think along those lines. Exciting things like winning more contracts through word of mouth with the joy of knowing her work was appreciated. Life was a risk whatever you did but she wasn't ready to take another new step so soon.

And never again would she risk letting a man into her life permanently. There had been one or two since her return to England but nothing serious. She had made sure of that. No way could she live through the break-up of another serious entanglement. She shivered, remembering how it had been when she first discovered Nick's treachery. She loved the peace of mind of knowing she was her own person, making her own decisions.

She put down her empty mug, and ran her fingers through her hair. She thought of Elisabeth's desperate struggle to succeed. Gruelling hard work as well as setbacks had spurred her mother on to win public acclaim and recognition. The very day that the organisers of a prestigious painting exhibition had accepted Elisabeth as an exhibitor she herself had gone down with 'flu. She had become so unwell that wet day at school that the head teacher had asked Cathy to bring her home. Even in that short distance they had got drenched. The brick path was slippery and rain water poured off the thatch to soak them even more as Cathy rang the front door bell. No one came.

By this time Jenny was hot and trembling.

'Where's the key?' said Cathy, shaking herself so that drops flew wildly.

Jenny pointed at the terracotta flower pot. Inside the cottage was achingly cold and smelt damp. 'I can't take you back to school,' said Cathy in despair. 'I'll have to stay here with you until your mother comes.'

Cathy's concern was wonderful, being wrapped in a blanket on the sofa with the bars of the electric fire showing red in the hearth.

Then Elisabeth came, glowing with excitement.

'Flu?' Jenny had felt Elisabeth's hand on her hot forehead and heard the panic in her voice.

No kind and sympathetic sponsor had come forward to provide much needed financial help for Elisabeth. She had to rely only on herself and had to ignore all setbacks if they were to survive.

Now, in her bright kitchen, Jenny thought that it sounded like a betrayal to have things made easy for her.

CHAPTER EIGHT

Saskia, raiding the bookcase in the sitting room on Sunday afternoon, found only one book on trees. She was sprawled on the floor with it open in front of her when Jenny came in from her kiln. Rain or not, there was work to be done out there.

Jenny pushed back her wet hair. 'What on earth are you doing, Saskia?'

'Is it the only tree book we have?'

Jenny wrinkled her nose. 'I think so. Isn't it good enough? And why is the DVD player hanging open like that? We haven't any DVDs of trees.'

'Someone's coming with one. A boy. I said he could watch it on ours.'

Jenny sank down on the window seat and looked at her, obviously amazed. 'You've met someone else? Who is he? Oh Saskie, I'm so pleased. You'd better tidy up the room a bit then.'

'Oh Jem won't mind. He won't notice.' Saskia leapt to her feet, the book in her hands. 'And I haven't met anyone, not in the way you mean, so don't get excited, Mum. Jem's just a kid. I thought I'd get to know a bit about trees before he came but these are all British ones.'

'I can't help you there, I'm afraid. Wait a minute. New Zealand trees! We must have something somewhere.'

Saskia snapped shut the book. 'Not New Zealand, Mum. Never mind. Jem'll be here soon. His grandparents haven't got a DVD player.'

Thank goodness Mum didn't question her. Jem was connected in a big way with Oliver and she didn't want to speak about Oliver. He was a glow about her heart and too precious to discuss with anyone. Except perhaps Jem.

'Oh, by the way,' said Jenny. 'The vicar, Lesley Bond, was there last night. You know I had dinner at the Varley's?'

Saskia stared at her mother, wondering if she had heard correctly. 'At the Varley's? Was Oliver there?'

'Oliver? Yes, of course. Why shouldn't he be? You could have come if Saturday wasn't one of your working evenings at the pub.'

A feeling of sheer envy swept over Saskia. 'Did you talk to him?'

'Saskia, what is this?'

'You didn't tell me you were going to the

103

Varley's.' Just as well really. Last night would have been a nightmare if she had known.

'Listen to this, Saskia. Lesley Bond asked if you'd like to work part time in the church office. You're to go and see her if you're interested.'

Saskia, her thoughts on Oliver, mumbled a reply. She glanced at the rivulets of rain on the misted window and then at the clock. 'I thought Jem would be here by now.'

Jenny gathered up the magazines on the chair and thrust them into the rack. 'I'll make some lemonade. Or don't boys drink that nowadays?'

'Great.' Saskia jumped as the telephone rang. 'I'll get it, Mum.'

Jenny heard the desolation in her daughter's voice as she dragged herself back into the room and sprawled on the sofa. 'He's not coming.'

'Too wet to venture out?'

'It's not that. His grandmother won't let him come here. When he said he was coming to Marigold Cottage that was it. Definitely not. No way. Kaput.'

'Who's his grandmother?'

'Someone called Mrs Moore. D'you know her? Her husband used to be vicar in Mellstone years ago.'

'My old head teacher.'

'Really? Sounds as if she hates you, Mum.'

Jenny shrugged. 'I was never her favourite

104

pupil.'

'But that was eons ago.' Saskia sat up and looked at Jenny in concern. 'It's not fair. Jem only wants to see his DVD on our player because they haven't got one. Where's the harm in that? You can't take your feelings out on a young boy.'

'Oh I think you can, Saskie. Poor Jem. I'm sorry.'

'I'll phone her myself.' Saskia sprang off the sofa.

'No, Saskie, wait,' Jenny said, alarmed. 'It'll only make it worse for the boy. 'Tell me about Jem,' she added gently.

Saskia did so, concentrating on how she had first met him and discovered his love of the natural world. 'He knows a lot about otters,' she said at last, cheering up a little. 'But the DVD was about trees. I'll ask to borrow it.'

'Will you see him again?'

Saskia smiled. 'He's often here in Mellstone, down by the brook. I'll see him.'

She sounded convinced that she would. Jenny sighed and wished things could have been different.

* * *

After her frustrating morning in Wernely a visit to Nether End Farm seemed to Jenny the best way to spend the warm July afternoon.

The alstroemerias from the florist in

Hilbury hadn't been the shades of apricot and peach that she had wanted. Having planned her colour schemes carefully this was disconcerting. Should she drive the eight miles beyond Wernely to Stourford to see what the florists there had to offer? It was that or a re-think. She chose the re-think.

So her work today hadn't entirely satisfied her even though the manager seemed pleased. She had bought extra flowers with John Ellis in mind, some deep bronze iris that caught her eye because they were perfect for the creamy yellow container she had already made for him. It was the least she could do to show her appreciation of his intriguing invitation at the end of Cathy's dinner party.

Her gift delighted John and the arrangement looked well on the low table in his charming room.

'Mrs Horlock's making tea,' he said as he invited her to take a seat. 'Ah, here she is.'

He lifted out a small table in readiness and Mrs Horlock placed the large wooden tray on the table and smiled at Jenny. 'You won't remember me,' she said. 'I used to see you about the village as a little girl when I worked in the post office, a young slip of a maid myself.'

'Of course I remember you, Mrs Horlock,' Jenny said, delighted. 'Meeting people I knew then makes me feel part of the place now.'

As well as the tea things the tray held a

plate of buttered scones and a dish of strawberry jam. They ate and drank leisurely and then John suggested a walk up his beloved hill. Jenny, knowing how much it meant to him, agreed with pleasure. His black and white collie, Lassie, sprang up to accompany them.

To Jenny's surprise John walked as swiftly as ever. What had she expected, a slow gait with John leaning on a stick and stopping for frequent rests and they trod the soft turf of the hillside? Lassie, at John's side, seemed to throw her a look of reproach for thinking such a thing.

At the top John paused to look back at the view over his home and land to the mistiness of the vale beyond.

Jenny was glad of the rest too. 'It's beautiful.'

John smiled. 'I think so. I hope I'll never have to leave, to sell eventually.'

She was horrified. 'Sell?'

'Thinking aloud, that's all,' said John apologetically. 'I'm not as young as I was, you know.'

'You? Nonsense. You nearly left me behind on this hill. It's steep.'

His eyes twinkled.

Jenny took deep breaths and looked at the view of hills and trees. She couldn't see the village from here because the rising land to the left hid it from view.

'So you feel well settled in Mellstone now,

Jenny my dear?' he said at last.

I needed to find some roots, you see and to put down some new ones. It's helped knowing Cathy of course. She's a good friend.'

'Tell me about the ideas you have for expanding your original plans.'

'Not for a very long time,' Jenny said, smiling. 'Tess Hartland seems to think I should surge ahead at once but it's far too soon.' They started to walk down the hill. The clear air seemed to stretch for ever. Jenny told John of how the idea of classes had cropped up and taken her by surprise. 'One day I would like my own showroom too.'

'Of course nowadays a lot of people appreciate that sort of thing,' John said. 'Handicrafts and so on. There's a ready market.'

Jenny nodded. She saw that Mrs Horlock had removed the tray from the sitting room. 'So you would really like to branch out?' he said as they seated themselves in the deep armchairs once more. The room, subdued and comfortable, felt welcoming. Lassie heaved a deep sigh and settled down for slumber.

'I like the feeling that I'm creating something that wasn't there before, making use of the natural world to make something beautiful to please other people as well as myself'

'A noble venture, my dear. It would give me great pleasure to be allowed to help you financially.'

She looked at him in astonishment.

'You'd actually invest money in me, John?'

John smiled his slow smile. He didn't speak for a moment but the withdrawn look in his eyes told her volumes. She couldn't help remembering the hurried flight from Mellstone, hers and Elisabeth's, and her mother's obvious unease until they were well away from the village en route to relatives in London long since dead. For years she herself had lived with her guilt about her own childish efforts to keep John and Elisabeth apart. She couldn't quite believe, even now, that the responsibility for that hadn't been hers. She looked at John thoughtfully. A lonely man now, he was still agile and with a mind as sharp as ever. He was handsome too with his white hair and slow smile.

I think your idea of a workshop and showroom is a good one,' said John. 'I have reason to believe that the Old Bakery is coming on the market at long last. It would be an ideal location for you in the centre of the village. That's why I'm raising the matter now. It seems an opportunity that might not repeat itself. I can offer you an interest free loan to be repaid at your convenience, in years to come if you like. What do you say?'

Jenny gasped. 'You're serious, John?'

'As serious as I'll ever be. You know the building I mean?'

'Opposite the church?'

'A prime position. It's been empty for some years. All things being equal I'll be happy to advance the money for the purchase and for the work needed to be done on it.'

Jenny was silent as she considered John's offer. She had thought it too soon to expand, that she needed time to work her business up slowly but with John's offer of finance might it not be worth considering now? Her very own showroom and workshop, large enough to hold pottery classes . . . the thought was tempting. Jenny knew in her heart that whatever Cathy said she herself had been partly responsible for Elisabeth's decision not to marry John. By accepting his offer of finance now which he was anxious to give might help to assuage her guilt about the part she had played all those years ago.

'I'd have to think about this very carefully, John,' she said. 'You understand, don't you? I hope I don't sound ungrateful but I've got to be sure I can do it.'

'I must remind you that there's some urgency. Others might well be interested. Why not take a look at the place?' He smiled. 'Your dreams are part of you, Jenny. You should be allowed your dreams.'

She was reminded suddenly of the Browning poem that Oliver had quoted to her. It was so easy to fall under the spell of being understood. But she was being ridiculous.

110

What possible reason was there for craving Oliver's understanding? She allowed herself, for a warm second, to wonder how it would feel to have it always.

'So you believe that what I'm trying to achieve is worth investing in?' she said.

But John, his eyes on the Turner painting on the wall by the window, didn't answer. Was he thinking of Elisabeth? His sadness was almost more than Jenny could bear. Later, when he opened the back door to let Lassie out for her late night run, John thought of Jenny's sensible reaction to his offer of help. He respected her natural reluctance to jump straight in even though he had expected otherwise. He hoped she would allow him to finance her for as long as she needed it. Indefinitely, as far as he was concerned. He had known that offering money to Jenny as a gift would not do. A loan was the next best thing. There was a deep need in him to invest in the future and what better way was there than this?

He took a step or two outside and breathed deeply of the mild air. He liked the feeling of things settling down for the night, the events of the day finished and done with. Nowadays a continuous sadness seemed to pervade everything, but not tonight. He felt the years drop away. He pulled his shoulders back, breathed yet more deeply.

A gnat landed on his forehead and he

flicked the insect away. He thought suddenly of the swathes of flying insects when he and the young forestry student had walked up the hill long ago. They had gone over the other side because he was considering introducing conifers to some of his land and wanted advice. Arnold Bronson, that was the young man's name. A brash young fellow if ever there was one.

'It's a question of size,' Arnold had said. The smaller the plantation the higher the cost of establishment per acre.'

'You mean the comparative increase in the amount of rabbit netting required?' John had been proud of a remark that showed he'd done his homework.

Young Bronson poured out a mass of information about the mixture of trees resulting in their roots not competing with each other because they were at different depths. 'Deciduous trees are better for the soil, too. Conifers are highly inflammable. They make good growth with hardwood because they give them protection in the early stages. Go in for it in a big way, and make something of it. There's all the land this side. Get it all covered in trees.' He waved his arm at the sloping fields. 'Something for your children, your grandchildren to fall back on.'

John had felt an ache of regret that he had no one to inherit his life's work and his beloved home.

112

Jenny phoned Elisabeth as soon as she got home. 'John Ellis invited me out to Nether End this afternoon,' she said breathlessly. 'He's come up with a business proposition he wanted to discuss.'

Elisabeth sounded surprised. 'He has?' Her voice seemed a long way away.

Jenny hadn't as yet told Elisabeth about her idea of starting pottery classes. Now she did so, beginning with the interest generated by her talk and demonstration. 'John has suggested where I can do this,' she said. 'Do you remember the Old Bakery?'

'Opposite the church?'

'Apparently it's just the right size for what I have in mind. It'll need work done on it of course.'

'But . . . can you afford it?'

Jenny hesitated. Now came the crunch. 'John's offered to lend me enough money for me to put in an offer and for the alterations.'

There was silence on the other end of the phone for a long moment. 'Couldn't you get a bank loan, Jenny?' Elisabeth asked at last.

'This would be interest free and no deadline for repayment. No collateral either. A lot of advantages.'

'And will you accept?'

'I'm still thinking about it. It's tempting.'

113

'Oh Jenny, be careful.'

'I will, I promise. There'll be enough money to convert the place into a suitable room for pottery classes as well as a showroom if I decide to go ahead. There's a lot of interest in pottery. I'll think about it some more before I give John an answer. He wants me to take a look at the building and I think I will.'

Only after she put the phone down did Jenny realise, with a stab of shame, that she hadn't asked how her mother was. She hadn't mentioned, either, about Elisabeth's plans for visiting Mellstone. Maybe it would be better to get things settled before Elisabeth came to stay. There would be a lot to do if she accepted John's offer. At least Saskia seemed happy enough with her evening work and with the prospect of helping out in the church office.

Jenny shrugged as she went into the room downstairs she used as her workshop. The shelves of glistening pots were depleted now after the success she'd had with recent orders. No hardship in making a start on more immediately.

Pummelling clay, she let herself imagine how it would be running classes in pottery and flower arranging. Evenings would be the best time so that they didn't interfere with her contracts. She could advertise in various places, the parish magazine for one. Oh yes, there was a lot to think about.

114

*   *   *

Elisabeth noted the excitement in her daughter's voice on the phone with disquiet. Was it wise for Jenny to take on so much extra when she had only been in Mellstone a few weeks? And to borrow the money from John Ellis!

Replacing the receiver, Elisabeth gazed at the photo of the young Jenny on the bookcase. In it the child's face looked pensive, her sensitive mouth on the brink of a smile. John had been a young man himself at the time the photo was taken. What was he like now that Jenny was a grown woman who knew exactly what she wanted and seemed to be going to great lengths to get it?

There was something about the whole business Elisabeth found disturbing. She picked up her stick that had fallen between the telephone table and the wall and decided to take a walk through the narrow streets of Down-Along as far as Porthmeor Beach.

Sparkling light slid across the wet sand where the tide had gone out. Elisabeth stood by the bars edging the road, savouring the crispness of the afternoon. Then, breathing in the salty air, she went down the steps to the beach and looked across the shining hard sand to the island where gulls whooped and screamed. There were notices now warning

115

against feeding them because of their nuisance value. The gulls soon learnt to help themselves, swooping down on unsuspecting holidaymakers and stealing food from their hands.

Elisabeth strolled across the beach keeping to the hard sand. She climbed up the steps to the path that led to the steep grassy Island. On the seaward side the yellow lichened rocks gleamed. The scent of wild thyme pleased her.

Memory was a strange thing, bursting into one's mind without warning. That long ago day when she and the young Jenny had visited John at Nether End. How often that vivid memory had taken her unawares! Now Elisabeth let it come. She needed to re-examine her feelings and to lay the ghosts conclusively because soon she would be visiting Mellstone and probably Nether End too.

When Elisabeth had followed after Jenny that day across the lawn to the track up the hill she found John beside her. His skin looked warm and there was a softness in his eyes she hadn't seen before. She felt a glow in her heart that he had come to find her.

He smiled. 'I saw you from over there, Elisabeth. You were deep in thought.'

'I'm looking for Jenny.'

'She's up there, picking primroses. There's no need to worry.'

'I'm not worried.' She quickened her pace.

'I'd better find her.'

Amusement flickered in his eyes. 'Can I come with you?'

She flushed, ill at ease. His kind friendliness surprised her after his unkind criticism of her way of life the last time they had met. He looked comfortable in his old clothes with the sunlight on his fair hair.

They paused by the field gate that gave views of Larksbury Rings against the pale sky. She liked the bareness of it and the feeling of space and freedom. Sheep grazed the hillside, tiny in the distance. John was silent as he filled his pipe. Then he began to tell her of his plans for the fields below them. The smoke from his pipe rose in the still air. His obvious love for the place moved her.

After a while he said, 'I don't think I could bear to lose all this, and I very nearly did because of someone I cared about.'

The closed expression on his face didn't invite comment. 'Divorce is a kind of death,' he said at last. 'At the best it left me with a sense of failure.'

'But you care for all this, John, I can see how much. And you have it still. It's your life, just as mine is painting.'

He gave her a brief smile and then looked down at the pipe in his hand as if wondering what it was doing there.

'I wish I could convince you how much my painting means to me, John.'

117

'You could try,' he said gently.

'It gives me a surging sense of release, of well-being, of completeness. Don't you feel the same when you look at your land? All I know is I'm happy when I paint.'

'Happy?'

'Content is a better word perhaps. When I'm not painting I feel a terrible urge to be working again.'

'And everything else is a waste of time like your visit here today?'

He didn't understand. She turned away and stared up the track that disappeared into the trees. A sudden weariness filled her. She needed action to dispel it, and pulled out her pad and pencil from her pocket. 'D'you mind if I sketch this?'

He leaned on the gate, watching her swift pencil strokes. 'May I see?'

She shook her head. 'It's only a rough sketch to help me paint it in oils in the studio. Perhaps I'll show you the finished painting one day.'

She hadn't needed the sketch to remind her. The smallest twig and the tiniest blade of grass of that particular place were etched on her mind for ever.

She had snapped shut her sketchbook, and started to walk up the track.

'Not so fast,' John said from behind her. 'Don't run away from me, Elisabeth.'

She was breathless for no reason at all.

'Jenny . . . I must find her at once.'

They had discovered the child soon afterwards. She appeared suddenly on the track ahead, her red hair awry and her green gabardine coat bright against the leafless hedge.

'Have you been picking flowers for your mother?' John asked.

Jenny had stared at him, wide-eyed, pulling at Elisabeth's hand. 'Let's go back. I don't like it here.'

Now, all these years later John's willingness to finance Jenny was worrying. Was there more to it than just a business arrangement? John was years older than Jenny.

Suddenly Elisabeth knew that she must accept Jenny's invitation to Mellstone very soon. The sun had gone now and the grey sky pressed down on her. The gulls cried mournfully as she walked back through Down-Along.

CHAPTER NINE

Jenny leaned forward and removed a thick pamphlet from the coffee table to make room for the tray Cathy was carrying into the sitting room. The deep window seats hidden by red velvet curtains on the night of the dinner party still had the red flowered cushions she remembered from long ago. The material must surely be new otherwise some of it would look worn by now with a few stains of tea or coffee or something? She thought of the welcome Ralph and his son had given her. Oliver especially because he seemed on the same wavelength as herself.

Cathy smiled. 'Throw it on the window seat out of the way, Jenny. That's the result of some of Oliver's work in Africa.'

Jenny did so and then accepted a cup of coffee. 'Tell me about it.'

Cathy picked up her own cup and looked at it thoughtfully. 'Farming methods out there are changing, you see and Oliver and his group give advice among other things. In the past the parkia trees were part of the natural forestation but the land's gradually being cleared. The idea now is for the trees to continue to grow among crops. But there's a snag. The shade. They also have wide-spreading surface roots and that's not good for the root crops beneath them either.'

'Yes, I see.'

'But the good news is that parkia trees help prevent soil erosion.'

'Aha. So what does your son actually do, apart from encouraging the growth of these wonder trees?'

'Research. Experimenting with what grows best beneath the trees. You know that he's home in order to lecture and publish articles in

120

the hope of raising more money?'

'You said.'

'Ralph's pleased he's involved with this sort of thing. Says farming's in Oliver's blood and this is the way it's coming out in him at long last. He felt betrayed when Oliver didn't want to take up farming here when he left college. He's happier about it all now.'

'I like enthusiasm in any shape or form. Good luck to Oliver.'

Cathy smiled. 'That's what Oliver has always admired too, genuine enterprise. He was so supportive when I started up with the Bed and Breakfasts. I couldn't have done it without him egging me on. And now look how successful it is. Even Ralph has to admit that now.'

'I should think so too,' said Jenny. 'You always seem to have strange cars parked in the yard.'

'He's a good boy, Oliver,' said his mother. 'Sadly, he and Ralph have never seen eye to eye. It would never have done for Oliver to come back here after agricultural college with that sort of atmosphere. I think he was glad to escape. He's been lucky to find his metier out in Africa helping to set up these various schemes. He's grown up quickly in a short time. The climate suits him and he came home this time looking so confident. He's matured, I suppose. Ralph says it's about time at twenty eight but I wonder if parting from Linda had something to do with it.'

'Linda?'

'A mismatch if ever there was one and he's well out of it. Ah well. I gather she was too clinging and he got tired of it. A pretty little thing apparently. I never met her. Ralph's eager for him to settle down and have children but I tell him there's plenty of time.'

'Plenty,' Jenny agreed.

'It's wonderful that he'll be editing the parish magazine while he's at home. Ralph's pleased about that too as he's helping the church. Lesley said Oliver can use the new equipment in the church office. There's a copier there and he can make use of it for his own work. And what about you, my dear? How's your business going?'

Jenny looked at Cathy's pleasant face and kindly eyes. 'That's what I wanted to talk to you about, Cathy, to ask your advice.'

'Mine?' said Cathy, surprised.

'In confidence of course.' Jenny hesitated for a moment and then told her about John's offer of financial help and his idea of purchasing the Old Bakery for her showroom and pottery classes.

Cathy looked astonished when she had finished, even disbelieving. 'That's an extraordinarily generous offer.'

Jenny paused, not sure now whether or not she should have told her. Perhaps not. John might have wanted it to be confidential. But he hadn't said so and she needed impartial advice. Elisabeth had been heavily involved with John once. It was bound to reflect what she said about it now. 'You don't think I should accept?' she said.

'Oh I didn't mean that. John doesn't do things lightly. He's obviously certain you have talent, Jenny. It's a compliment, my dear.'

'Yes, I feel that too.'

'You'd be silly not to consider accepting. But you think it's too soon?'

'If I'm sensible I know it is.'

'What a shame the Old Bakery's come on the market now and not in a few months time.'

Jenny sighed. 'My thoughts exactly.'

'But you say you have several contracts already and have started really well?'

'Seasonal mostly, but two have promised to renew and I'm hopeful I'll get others. And there's the Christmas market.'

Cathy leaned back in her chair. 'Things don't always pan out as we want them, do they? Why don't you just take a look at the building? No harm in that. It may not be as suitable as John thinks. That way you'd know and it might help you come to a decision. As I see it John's money would be at risk not yours if you couldn't make a go of it.'

'But I'd have to pay it back.'

'Didn't he promise to give you years to do that?'

'But he may not have years.'

'John's what, sixty five? I don't suppose he plans to leave us yet awhile.'

'I certainly hope not,' said Jenny with fervour. 'And not just because I'll owe him money.'

'So you've almost decided then?'

'Well, maybe.' Jenny leaned back in her chair and smiled. 'Thanks, Cathy. I'll make an appointment to view and then see what I think. You've helped me to see things a lot more clearly.'

Cathy, pink with pleasure, smiled.

*   *   *

Robert Moore leapt up at the prolonged ringing of the doorbell at Lynne Cottage. He opened the door quickly, breathing fast. 'Hilda!'

Hilda Lunt pushed her way past him into the dim hall. 'Have you heard? The very idea!'

'An emergency?'

Enraged, Hilda glared at him. 'I'll say. Does Karen know about the Old Bakery? It's going on the market.'

'Is that all? I expected it to be burnt down at the very least.'

She gave him a look of withering scorn. 'I expected more support from you than that, Robert.'

He was immediately contrite. 'Sorry Hilda. We can hear the door bell perfectly well you know. Indeed, a short press is all that's necessary.' He stood aside to let her barge into the sitting room and collapse, uninvited, into an armchair.

Karen Moore, half-risen in her own seat, now sank down again. 'Whatever's the matter, Hilda? You look . . . strange.'

Hilda's puce face deepened in colour. 'The cheek of it, the sheer bloody nerve! A newcomer thinking she can just waltz into the village and take the ground from under our feet.'

Robert seated himself opposite her and looked at her intently beneath bushy eyebrows. 'What are you talking about, Hilda?'

'The Old Bakery is coming on the market at long last. It's the perfect place for the new village hall. The Village Society has got to purchase it. Common sense. And now this.'

'You mean the Village Society wouldn't be the only prospective purchaser?'

'You've hit the nail on the head.'

'May we ask who else is interested?' said Karen.

'Remember that red-haired woman we got as speaker, pottery and flowers? Some of the fool members want her to do pottery classes. She wants the Old Bakery for her showroom. Can you believe it? Yes, I see you can. You wouldn't support her, I hope.' She stared at both belligerently.

Karen shook her head, speechless.

Robert looked at his wife anxiously. 'Indeed the Old Bakery is in the perfect place for a new hall. Near the centre of the village, opposite the church. What could be more suitable, as you say?'

Karen leaned forward. 'Do you know the asking price, Hilda? Can the Village Society afford it?'

'And how did you know all this?' asked Robert.

Hilda looked at him with contempt. 'Ways and means, Robert. Ways and means. It'll be in the *Hilbury News* tomorrow.' She smashed her right hand down hard on the arm of her chair. 'We've got to have it'

'Of course we've got to have it,' said Karen.

'There'll be trouble, real trouble, if we don't.'

'So how did you know there was someone else interested?'

'That I can't say.' Hilda looked triumphant. 'But believe me it's true. Someone making enquiries, not a million miles away. Strange, I thought, he's got that place at Nether End . . .'

'You can't mean John Ellis?' cried Karen, aghast.

'Surely he doesn't want the place for himself?' said Robert.

'Evidently not if the idea is to set up a pottery workroom. He's hand in glove with her.'

Karen gasped. 'You're talking about the
126

person who gave the demonstration at WI?'

Robert smoothed his chin in an attempt to calm his anxiety. The village had used the old school building as a hall since it closed. What a dreadful day it had been when County Hall notified Karen that the village school would close. He had gone into school to see her when the children had gone home. Alice Pengold, at her cleaning work in the Infant's room, had banged her broom against the skirting board and then pushed open the door in the partition and backed in with her cleaning paraphernalia clutched to her like a shield. Alice's reaction was typical. 'What do they want to go and close the school for? What about my money? No one thinks of that. It'll be the pub next, and the church. It's the fault of them as made them hack down our Tidings Tree.'

He was aware that Karen had taken a long time to convince herself that the proposed closure of the school was not her fault and that it had nothing to do with Jenny's accident. If she ever had. His wife's bitterness over Jenny had deepened in the past weeks. At times he had even wondered if it was affecting her mind. But he thrust that disloyal thought away, ashamed of having entertained it even for a second.

'Then we must do something positive about it,' said Karen. 'Hilda, we'll rely on you to pass the word round.'

Hilda struggled to her feet, looking

purposeful. 'We won't let anyone take the Old Bakery from us from us as long as I have breath left in my body. The village needs that building.'

*   *   *

In the Church Office, a small room partitioned off the vestry, Saskia sat at the computer. The vicar had been and gone, busy on some parochial business. Now here she was alone in this cluttered room whose high window hardly let in any of the sunshine outside. Only a single shaft reflected off the brass jug someone had stuffed among the papers on the top shelf of the bookcase.

At first Lesley Bond's suggestion that she should work part time had flattered Saskia. In any case no other work, apart from her bar work at the Swan, had been forthcoming. Now she wondered what she had let herself in for.

Her brief this afternoon was to set up some databases. Working on this latest machine was a pleasure. Lesley wanted her to take a small group for basic computer skills and that would be no problem. Most members of the PCC were computer-wise already but the treasurer was new and needed assistance in getting the accounts sorted out and on to computer.

Saskia leaned back in her seat, humming and twiddling a strand of her hair. The treasurer would be here soon. Here he was now. As the footsteps in the church came nearer she sat upright again, prepared to rise.

The door opened, and Oliver came in. She stared at him, open-mouthed. 'You're the treasurer?'

'I may look like it with all these papers but no, sorry.' He looked round, and then pushed aside a pile of books on the table beneath the window and placed his papers there. Out of the pocket of his jeans he produced a memory stick. 'I want to save stuff from this on another. I understand there's a spare one for me in the drawer.'

'Well yes,' she said, pulling the drawer open.

He smiled. 'Lesley said you'd be here. You finish at four thirty don't you? I'll be back before then to do what needs doing.'

Bemused, Saskia stared at him. Her heart was thumping so hard she thought he might see the movement beneath her thin blouse. Totally unexpected, his appearance here at this moment was hard to take in. His presence made the small room brighter, full of joyful anticipation.

'Hadn't you heard? I'm the editor of the parish mag, the new boy. I'll be popping back and forth at intervals, OK?'

Very much OK. Saskia beamed back at him, feeling suddenly warm. 'Great.'

He left, closing the door gently behind him. Saskia sprang up from her seat and twirled around joyfully. Oliver would be back and forth every day with luck. Incredible. This was more than she could possibly have hoped for. He'd be back very soon. Wow, wow and yet more wow!

Her light jacket was hanging on a hook by the door. She went at once to rummage in the left hand pocket. No comb! Oh heavens, she'd left it on the shelf by the bathroom mirror. What an idiot. Frantically she ran her fingers through her hair, wishing she'd taken time to wash it this morning. But how could she have imagined that anything as wonderful as this would come out of a job that had sounded boring when Lesley talked to her about it? It just showed you should be ready for anything that life threw at you. She wouldn't make that mistake again.

She glanced round the room and saw the brass plate on the wall opposite listing people who had been generous with something in some way or the other. She went across to peer into it, hoping it would give back enough reflection to check she didn't look too much of a scarecrow. But it was no use. The brass cleaner hadn't done much of a job this week. The rota was on the wall behind her, and she glared at it. Twenty black marks at least. The only thing she could do was to smooth back her unruly hair and hope for the best.

When at last she heard sounds of returning footsteps Saskia pinched her cheeks hard to bring some colour into them. She opened her eyes wide and smiled.

It took only few minutes for Oliver to finish what he needed to do. He removed the second memory stick. 'I'd better keep this here, I think,' he said. 'OK with you, Saskia love?'

'Here, let me.' She took it from him, brushing her fingers against his hand. A rosy glow made her fingers tremble but he didn't appear to notice. 'This drawer's empty. I'll label it as yours, shall I? It'll be safe here.'

'I'll take your word for that.' He smiled, and turnd to go.

'Quick, stop him! 'Oh Oliver, I've been meaning to ask. How's Jem?'

'Jem? OK as far as I know. Why?'

She frowned. 'He wasn't allowed to watch his tree DVD at our place. D'you know why?' Oliver wouldn't know of course, but she had to ask. 'It's his grandparents. I know it is. But why should they mind?'

He shrugged.

At once she was afraid of boring him but couldn't seem to help herself. If only she could think of something really riveting to say. 'I had a feeling . . . Jem doesn't like staying with them, does he? And what did he mean by having to be like his father and go into the church? They can't mean it, surely?'

Oliver sighed, and perched himself on the edge of her desk. She leaned back in her chair and looked up at him hopefully. She'd like to help Jem, and if it meant seeing more of

Oliver in the process so much the better.

'There's always been a bit of a problem there. You see James, the Moores' son, was to have followed his father into the church but changed his mind at the last minute. It nearly finished them. Don't look so amazed. It happens.' His mouth twisted a little and then he smiled.

'I wish I could help him, Jem I mean. He always looks so . . .'

'Lonely? I know, I know.'

'Well yes, but . . .'

'Felicity tried, my sister. When she and James moved in together they fell over backwards to help Jem. He'd had a bad time when his mother died. Not easy for any of them. But there you go. And his grandparents stepped in and helped a lot by having him at weekends.'

'Every weekend?'

'Most, anyway.'

'And now they want to decide Jem's life for him? Doesn't his father have any say in the matter? You'd think he'd be on Jem's side.'

'It'll sort itself out, OK?'

Saskia felt herself flush. None of her business? That's what Oliver meant. She stood up so quickly some papers fell to the floor. Oliver slid off the desk and bent to retrieve them. For a second she gazed down on the crown of his head and noticed, with a pang, that his hair was beginning to thin. She wanted

132

to reach out and touch it and her fingers burned with longing. Then she sat down again, feeling foolish.

An outside door thumped shut. Saskia looked up, surprised. 'Who's that? The treasurer?'

Oliver held his head to one side, listening, as someone came stumping through the church and into the vestry.

The office door crashed open and a head appeared followed by a body clad in a voluminous green anorak that did nothing for the broad figure it covered.

Oliver leapt to attention. 'Miss Lunt? Not the treasurer after all.'

'Vicar not here?' The interloper's disapproval deepened as she took in Saskia at her desk and Oliver nearby. 'I want her opinion.'

'Can we help?' Oliver winked slightly at Saskia and made her smile.

Hilda Lunt frowned at him, her thick brows almost meeting. 'Someone's after the Old Bakery. We've got to stop it. Newcomers . . . the very idea! Useful, I'll admit, stepping into the breach when we needed a speaker. But that doesn't give her the right, pottery or no pottery. A take-over of Mellstone, that's what it'll be, you mark my words. And you, young man, can tell your mother I said so.'

With that she departed in a flurry of crashes and bangs. The silence was stunning.

133

Oliver let out a long whistle and perched himself on the edge of the desk again.

Saskia gazed up at him, bewildered. 'Does she mean Mum?'

'She obviously didn't register who you are.'

'But what was it all about?'

'The Old Bakery's coming on the market. The village want it for a hall but haven't the money. Has your mother mentioned anything about it to you?'

'Well no. D'you think Miss Lunt made a mistake?'

'Got hold of the wrong end of the stick?' Oliver grinned, and then was serious again. 'Unlikely, knowing Hilda. Don't take any notice of her manner. That's just her way.'

'Not a good way.'

'I've known her all my life, poor Hilda. When she was young the boys never troubled her, that's what I've heard people say. I used to imagine those words engraved on her tombstone. *Here lies Hilda Lunt whom the boys never troubled.*'

'And the sooner the better,' Saskia said with feeling.

He laughed. 'Good heavens, girl, what harm can poor Hilda do?'

'She'd better not try to harm my mum, that's all.' Saskia gathered up her papers, and shuffled them, tight-lipped.

'Come on now, Saskia love, ease up. From what I've seen of your mum she's an independent lady, OK?'

'Well yes, I suppose.'

'There you are then.' He smiled and got to his feet.

If only she could delay Oliver for longer, but what good reason was there? In any case the advent of the dreadful Hilda had spoilt everything. No boys had ever troubled Hilda . . . ha! If Hilda Lunt was as overbearing as this in her youth she didn't wonder at it.

CHAPTER TEN

St Andrew's Church looked welcoming on Sunday morning as Jenny and Saskia walked through the gate into the churchyard. The bells rang joyfully. Jenny glanced at Saskia and saw that her daughter was smiling with her head held a little to one side. She felt like smiling too because she had made the effort at last to attend a church service and Saskia was, surprisingly, with her.

'Hurry up, Mum,' Saskia urged as the measured tones of the bells changed to a swift jangling. 'They're ringing them down already.'

'Ringing what down?'

'The bells of course. They do it at the end of ringing.'

'How on earth do you know that, Saskia?'

'Can't you hear them?'

135

Jenny glanced at her watch. 'There's plenty of time yet.' She paused and looked back at the building across the lane where the black lettering *For Sale* stood out in stark contrast against the yellow on Hatchet and Drew's board. Definitely a suitable place for a showroom. Hopefully there would be ample space behind for a pottery workroom. Her fingers itched for notepad and pen to jot down a few ideas.

'Come on, Mum.'

Jenny followed her daughter into the church where the rich tones of the organ music flowed over them. Somehow she had expected the broad figure of the vicar to be there to greet them and present brownie points for effort. Jenny's inward smile made her lips twitch, but she sobered immediately at the sour expression on Hilda Lunt's face as she handed her three books and a leaflet.

Jenny knelt beside her daughter in a pew near the back. Someone had spent long hours making the tapestry kneelers, all colourfully different. She squinted at them as she thought a brief prayer. The rest of the congregation had scattered itself about the church. Did the vicar, Lesley, mind the people being seated like this instead of in a compact group? Maybe she understood that they felt too embarrassed, perhaps, to be directly beneath her gaze in the front when she mounted the steps to the pulpit.

A small door opened in the corner and several people emerged, among them Cathy and Ralph Varley and their son. Beside her she heard Saskia give a relaxed sigh and settle back in her seat. Outside the windows shadowy figures flitted past. Obviously the escape route for the rest of the bellringers who had decided that the sunshine out there was preferable to the dimness within. There were other Sunday services, of course. No one could expect them to attend every one.

The service began. Jenny joined in the prayers and hymns, feeling a sense of peace creep over her, engendered perhaps by Lesley's calm tones and the confident responses of the congregation. Afterwards there was coffee.

Hilda Lunt, bearing a tray, headed straight for Jenny. She looked like an angry bear in her voluminous brown jacket. 'You won't get away with it,' she growled as Jenny took a cup and saucer.

Jenny, startled, moved back a little and spilled some coffee in her saucer.

'More sense to use a mug,' said a voice behind her.

Turning, Jenny recognised the treasurer from the WI. 'What does she mean? Get away with what?'

'Hilda? She's on about the Old Bakery. Take no notice.'

None the wiser, Jenny looked round for

137

Saskia. She saw that her daughter was a pew or two away not far from Oliver Varley. Seeing Jenny looking in his direction, Oliver smiled at her. Then he gulped his coffee, placed his cup and saucer on Hilda's tray and made a move in her direction. But someone else stepped in the way, a tall well-built man.

Jenny was aware, with a thrill of pleasure, that she knew him from long ago. This was surely the one-time vicar of Mellstone who had married her ex-head teacher? The years between had whitened his thick hair and stooped his broad shoulders. When he came into school to take the service when she was a little girl she had always liked Mr Moore. There was still warmth in his brown eyes and his smile was friendly.

'Mr Moore?'

He looked delighted. 'Jenny! How are you? I heard you were back in Mellstone. Settling in well, I trust.'

Jenny smiled. 'Very well, thanks.'

He looked at her in a friendly way, bending his head a little 'Indeed, my dear, it's good to meet you at last.'

'And you remember me?'

'I do indeed.' Clattering crockery mingled with the voices all around them and the scent of coffee filled the air. 'It's a little different from the old days, I'm sure you'll agree. I've been thinking of the first Christmas you and your mother spent in Mellstone. You attended

138

the carol service, if I recollect.'

'Ah yes,' said Jenny, remembering too. The church had been packed. A horde of people pushed into their pew, and she smelt the cabbagey smell of that awful Mrs Barden. One of the accompanying boys trod on her foot deliberately and made her gasp.

'I trust your mother is well?'

Jenny nodded. 'You know she's in St Ives? She has several exhibitions a year now.'

'Splendid. Splendid.'

'I'm hoping to get her to Mellstone for a visit before long.'

'You are? Indeed, that's good news.'

Jenny finished her coffee. Now Oliver Varley reached her side. 'Let me.' He took her empty cup and saucer from her, looked round for a handy tray and seeing none placed them in the nearest pew.

'So,' said Oliver. 'What brings you here on this sunny summer morning?'

Jenny laughed. 'Call it curiosity if you like.'

'Come outside. I've got something to show you.'

She followed him to the church door. Lesley who was obviously trying to have a word with everyone had got stuck with Hilda Lunt.

'This way,' Oliver said as they emerged into the sunshine.

Someone had been cutting grass recently and the sweet summer smell hung on the air. Behind the church the gravestones leaned

139

drunkenly. Most had been placed against the outside wall. From their tilted positions they seemed anxious to be back in their original positions.

'This one,' said Oliver.

Jenny looked closely at the headstone he indicated. The stone was darker than the others and mottled with a hint of white. A faint sheen of crimson made it stand out from those on either side. She ran her fingers over the surface. 'It's beautiful.'

He looked pleased. 'Inspiration?'

'Definitely. I love it. I'll have a try at getting that same effect in my next lot of glazing. Thanks for showing me.'

Oliver grinned. 'I aim to please.'

'Plenty of possibilities here. I'd never have thought of it for myself. I'll be able to nip over the road to the churchyard for ideas quite easily. I'll get my students on to it too.'

'You have students?'

'Well, not yet,' she admitted. 'A bit of wishful thinking. I've been imagining myself ensconced in the Old Bakery you see. If it came to pass I'd have a showroom, hold pottery classes. That sort of thing. Flower arranging too.' They were walking back to the other side of the church now. Jenny glanced at the building opposite.

Oliver looked too. 'I heard you were interested.'

'You did?'

'From Hilda Lunt.'

'Really? How did she know?'

Oliver grinned, and shrugged. 'Breathes it in from the air I expect.'

'So that's what her cryptic remark meant?' Jenny looked thoughtfully at the estate agent's board. The words *For Sale* seemed like a challenge she ought to be taking up if she wasn't being sensible. She had leapt in at once with the purchase of Marigold Cottage but the money was there and she was looking for a property as soon as her course finished because she needed somewhere to live and work. But this was different.

Oliver kicked a stone from the path. 'The woman's mad. Take no notice.'

'She's not the sort of person I'd like to fall foul of.'

'Did your daughter say anything?'

'About Miss Lunt? Not a word.' Jenny ran her fingers along the top of another headstone. 'I'll keep well out of her way.' She couldn't imagine why Hilda Lunt should have it in for her. You won't get away with it, she had said. Why should she possibly mind her interest in the Old Bakery? Unless she wanted it for herself.

Oliver grinned at her. 'You do that.'

'I was thinking of making an appointment to view.'

'Good luck, then.'

The rest of the congregation were emerging

from the church now. Some stood about in groups and others wandered off down the path.

Saskia joined them. 'Oh there you are,' she said, looking at Oliver.

Jenny, looking across at the Old Bakery, mumbled a reply. If Hilda Lunt knew about her interest in the property someone must be talking about it. Hilda couldn't have plucked the knowledge out of the air whatever Oliver said.

*　　*　　*

'You go on, Mum,' said Saskia. 'There's something I have to do.'

To her relief Jenny went, smiling a goodbye to Oliver.'

He laughed. 'She's a busy lady your mother.'

'Me too,' said Saskia firmly. She wondered at herself taking events into her own hands. Making things happen. Hopefully. She smiled at him, putting all she had into willing him to respond to what she had in mind. Most of the congregation had gone now and the sun was warm on her face. 'Oh, Oliver, I've been meaning to ask. How do I set about learning bellringing? Would I be strong enough?'

He looked at her speculatively. She had his interest now. She glowed, liking his gaze targeted on her like this. 'You don't need strength, Saskia, just determination.' He hesitated.

'Oh I've plenty of that.'

'And a head for Maths.'

She looked at him in surprise.

'Just joking. It helps though. But why are you keen to learn?'

Here was a tricky one. She hesitated in her turn. How to explain her sudden resolve? All she wished, of course, was to be with Oliver. She wanted him to show her how it was done, to be involved in her progress. Was he picking up on some of this?

'It's an old country craft,' she said, tilting up her chin. 'I like hearing the bells. I'd like to learn while I'm here.'

For a moment he looked solemn but then his face lit up with a warm smile. 'Have a word with Tom Barnet the Tower Captain, OK? He'll put you in the picture. He's a good teacher.'

Only afterwards did she remember that she worked at the pub every bellringing practice night so that was out. She would have to drop that idea and it had seemed such a good one. Her dismay felt like a load of lead. Oh well, she'd tried. Something else would come up.

*　　　*　　　*

Saskia, in deep thought, moved about the kitchen preparing the evening meal. Up on the back lawn on her sun-lounger beneath the blue

143

and white parasol her mother rested for once. It was good to see Mum like that. Late afternoon shadows darkened the lawn in the corner by the roses but it was still hot.

In a minute she would join her while the vegetable lasagne was browning in the oven. She ran hot water into the sink and began to wash the utensils she had been using. Then, when everything in the kitchen was tidy, she put knives, forks and a bowl of green salad on a tray and placed it ready on the table. Then she went out into the warm air.

'Ready in about half an hour, Mum,' she called as she climbed up the steps to the lawn.

Jenny's eyes shot open and she sat up.

'Don't move,' said Saskia. 'Nothing to do now but wait for the lasagne to cook.' She felt happy and relaxed as she removed her shirt and shorts and sat down on the grass in her bikini. 'Mmn . . . bliss! I thought we'd eat out here. I'll bring that little table out in a minute. The weather's too good to miss. They say it'll rain tomorrow.'

Jenny pulled up the back of the lounger to lean on and settled herself comfortably.

'There's something I'd like to talk to you about, Saskia,' she said. 'I need to get your reaction.'

'Sounds interesting.'

'I'm thinking of expanding my business. I've been thinking it all out now. I could have a showroom and a place to set up some

144

equipment for teaching pottery classes here in the village. A good idea, d'you think?'

Saskia wrinkled her nose, considering. 'Could be. Can you afford it?'

'If I take out a loan.'

'From the bank?'

'An old friend. You've heard me speak of John Ellis of Nether End? He wants to back me. And there's a property for sale that could be suitable for a showroom and workshop, the Old Bakery.'

'That old place? Oh, Mum, it's a ruin. Haven't you got enough to do here?'

'I know it's a bit soon but it's a golden opportunity to expand my business.'

"OK, Mum, go ahead if you're really sure and you can get the money. Who am I to stop you? Sounds like he fancies you, this John Ellis. You're not thinking of getting together permanently?'

Jenny laughed. 'With John? Heavens, no. It's not like that at all. He's years older than me.'

Saskia was silent. Was that such a disaster? Oliver was a lot older than her. When she was Mum's age Oliver would be nearly fifty. Impossible to imagine. Oliver was Oliver. He would never grow old.

'So you don't think it works, having a big age gap?' she said at last. She tried not to let the hurt sound in her voice. What did it matter what anyone thought, even Mum?

'It wouldn't work for me,' said Jenny.

'Not even if you fell in love?'

'Saskia, what are you saying?'

'But for some people? It might work for some people, having a big gap in age between them?'

'Possibly. Anyway John was interested in your grandmother years ago.'

'Gran?'

'More of an age, don't you think?'

Saskia couldn't get her mind round that and wasn't going to try. With only half her attention she listened to her mother talk of estate agents and surveys and the need to get in quickly. Wayside Arts Weekend was coming up. With luck she could get organised by then and take part.

'I still think this John Ellis's keen on you,' she said when Jenny finished. 'I wouldn't mind if you got together, honestly.'

'Get away with you,' said Jenny. 'I've no intention of getting together with anyone.' She glanced at the brick wall encasing her kiln and smiled.

Saskia leapt up, grabbing her shirt and shorts. 'I'll check on the lasagne.'

In the kitchen she lifted the dish carefully out of the oven. Perfect. The smell was gorgeous. She had a sudden vision of herself preparing such a meal for Oliver.

*　　　*　　　*

Jenny was forced to curb her impatience until the next morning. Even then she had commitments to carry out before she could get to the Old Bakery. She had taken the precaution of phoning the estate agent to make an appointment to view at twelve o'clock.

Driving back from Wernely she felt a surge of excitement. A showroom of her own in Mellstone . . . wonderful! She was making mind-plans already. With luck there would be ample space left over for a room devoted to demonstrations and classes in pottery. She could see it now . . . waist-high units lining the walls with ceramic tops of her own design. Pale blue possibly because the background was suitable for showing off students' work. A huge table in the middle of the room, of course, and room also for two or three turntables. The ideas thrown at her after her talk at the WI back in July were definitely taking shape.

She parked the car outside Marigold Cottage and glanced at her watch. Nearly time.

The young man waiting for her at the Old Bakery looked familiar. He stood with his head thrown back staring up at the yellow *For Sale* board as if he had never seen one before.

'We've met already,' said Jenny. 'You sold me my cottage here in Mellstone back in the spring.'

He smiled back at her uncertainly. 'Miss Finlay?'

147

'That's me.'

He appeared not to recognise her. He looked down at his clipboard.

'Something wrong?' she asked.

'No, oh no. Very much all right, actually. We've had one or two enquiries. Things are definitely looking good.'

Jenny frowned. Other people's interest in the place wasn't good for her. She would have to act swiftly if she decided to go ahead.

He unlocked the door and stood aside for her to enter. She understood his surprise that anyone should consider buying this run-down, broken-up place. But she could see the potential at once. No doubt others would, too, if they had imagination. Money would have to be spent on it but in the end she would have a place to suit her purposes admirably. She concentrated on looking like an intelligent prospective purchaser, poking into corners and examining the floor.

The young man stood watching her with the greatest of interest, clutching his clipboard to his chest and making no attempt to point out the advantages. Obviously he could see none and wasn't going to pretend an interest he was unable to feel. She admired his honesty.

'I'm definitely interested,' she said.

He nearly dropped his clipboard. 'You mean you'd want to buy it?'

'Subject to survey, of course. I'd like to make an offer,' she said, and named a figure that was five hundred pounds lower than the asking price. John had insisted she be sensible though her instinct was to offer the full price and more.

'I'll put it to the vendors when I get back and see what they say. I'm not too sure at the moment what the position is concerning the other interested parties. But we'll let you know as soon as we can. We've got your phone number?'

Jenny nodded. She must get on to John now and let him know what she had done. Deep in thought she walked slowly up the lane to the Tidings Tree.

A car pulled up alongside her and stopped. Oliver Varley wound his window. 'Hi there. Any news?'

She smiled at his eagerness. 'Not really. Only that I like the building because there's masses of space. And want it, I think. I've been making plans.'

'Tell me about them.'

'What now?'

She jumped as a car horn sounded behind her.

'Hang on' said Oliver. He pulled over to one side so that the other vehicle could pass in the narrow lane. Then he leaned across and opened the passenger door. 'Can you spare an hour? Jump in.'

Jenny did so, marvelling at herself. 'Where are we going?'

'You'll see.' He smiled as they set off and joined the main road.

She leaned back in her seat, ridiculously pleased at the interest Oliver was taking in her work. She would telephone John when she got back.

CHAPTER ELEVEN

'We'll have lunch,' Oliver said. 'I won't be long at the reference library in Hilbury. You don't mind?'

Jenny didn't mind in the least especially when forty minutes later she found herself seated beneath the overhanging branches of a sycamore tree in the scented garden of a pub. Beyond their table the ground dropped steeply away and the view across the sunny vale faded into misty distance. They ordered what turned out to be the largest Ploughman's Jenny had seen. She smiled when the waitress placed her dish in front of her on the wooden table. 'You expect me to eat all this?'

Oliver laughed as he spread butter on a gigantic granary roll. 'I know, I know. Not for the faint-hearted. But somehow I don't think you are faint-hearted, Jenny.' His eyes twinkled at her though his expression was serious.

They talked of the Old Bakery as they ate.

Jenny had only vague recollections of the building when it had been the village bakery. Once or twice she had gone there after school to collect bread hot from the oven.

Oliver, obviously enjoying himself, told her as much as he knew. 'The business was in the Horlock family for years. Then when the last of them wanted to retire the place was sold and used as a hay store for a long time and then left empty. Someone bought it and used it as a storeroom. Then someone else wanted to change it into some sort of dwelling but the plans came to nothing. That was three or four years ago. It's been empty ever since.'

Jenny bit into her roll and ate slowly. 'And now there's a lot of interest apparently.'

'That's what I need to tell you about. You won't be downhearted, OK?'

Jenny laughed in an attempt to lighten the atmosphere. 'Do I need to be?'

'The village needs a new village hall. They've got their eye on the Old Bakery.'

Jenny saw the implications at once. She looked down at her hands in her lap. 'I see.'

Oliver nodded. 'Sorry and all that. I had to tell you, OK?'

'Thanks for warning me.' She sighed. 'I must admit it seemed too good to be true.'

'I know, I know. I wouldn't worry too much, OK? Raising that sort of cash is pretty well impossible in the time. Rumour has it that the owners want it all to go through quickly now they've made up their minds to get rid of it. Go for it, Jenny.'

She smiled at the enthusiasm in his voice and looked up in time to see a sympathetic gleam in his eyes.

'You think I should?'

'You owe it to yourself. That's how I see it.'

'Thanks, Oliver,' she said. 'For that and for the meal. It's great having someone take an interest.'

The notes of a familiar tune came out of the pocket of his jeans. At once he pulled out his mobile and switched off. 'Coffee, Jenny? You're not going yet surely?'

She stood up. 'I've an important phone call to make and other things to do too.' She wished she hadn't. It was hard to tear herself away.

Oliver placed his hand briefly on her arm. The pleasure of it lingered for some time. He followed her out to the High Street and was silent until they reached his car.

'How about doing this again one day?'

Jenny smiled. 'Maybe.'

*   *   *

Tess Hartland tripped down her path to the gate. In her own front garden Jenny was dead-heading the roses, deep in thought. A bumblebee droned nearby.

'Jenny!' Tess called.

Jenny jumped and looked up.

'Have you a minute, dear? I want to show you something, d'you mind?'

Snapping shut the secateurs Jenny placed them on the grass and sighed. 'Coming.'

Each time she went into Ivy Cottage she expected to be in the cosy cluttered room it had been when it had been the home of John Ellis' aunt and had smelt of lavender and beeswax. Now there were radiators against the bright walls and flowery cushions on the window seats.

'You're looking well, dear,' said Tess.

'I am?' Jenny said. Perhaps her pleasure that a young man should seek her company was showing on her face. Refreshing at her age.

'Sit down for a minute, dear,' said Tess. 'Coffee?'

Jenny shook her head as she perched on the window-seat. 'I'm in a bit of a hurry. I was just allowing myself a few minutes off to tidy the front garden before my mother sees it. She's coming for a visit next Friday.'

Tess' eyes shone. 'How she'll love seeing the old place again and reviving old memories. Such a shame that there aren't many of the old people left.' She looked sad for a moment. 'We can't help it, you see, being new. It seemed perfect when we found this cottage and Nigel's so able. It's just a pity that people don't seem to see his qualities. They laugh at him, you see.'

'Take no notice,' Jenny said. 'I wouldn't.' Easy to say, but could she manage to ignore village opinion? She might soon have the chance to find out.

'Of course there's Cathy and Ralph,' said Tess, brightening. 'Your mother will know them, won't she? Not the son, of course, Oliver.'

Jenny smiled. Strange that Tess should mention Oliver at this moment when her own thoughts dwelt on him more than was good for her.

'I hear you're interested in the Old Bakery, Jenny. The Wayside Arts people will be pleased. So convenient in the village centre not far from the Tidings Tree. It'll look well in their brochure. And that's what I need to ask you about. I said to Nigel . . . Jenny's a good friend. I expect she'll let me put up a little stand for the sale of my books.'

Jenny's mouth fell open. 'Your books?'

Tess picked up some thin volumes from the table and held them up. *'Mellstone Magic, Wernely Ways.* They're little guidebooks of the area, so suitable for visitors who come to your showroom. There'll be a commission for you of course.'

'So you're Therese de Poissièrre?'

'The very person.'

I had no idea. How clever of you, Tess. No

154

one's ever said it's you who wrote them.'

Tess' smiled faded. 'So sad. No one round here wants to know. A prophet in her own country sort of thing. Except of course this isn't my own country.'

She looked so woe-begone that Jenny leaned forward and pressed her hand. 'I posted my copy to my mother only yesterday. She'll love knowing it's one of yours. And of course we'll have a display of them in the showroom, Tess.'

'Thank you, dear. You're so kind.'

Jenny left her, feeling respect for Tess that hadn't been there before. She had been back in her garden for at least five minutes before it occurred to her that she had spoken as if the proposed showroom was up and running.

*   *   *

Cathy and Oliver sat on a wooden bench in the shade against the barn. Cathy leaned back, a mug of coffee in her hands, glad to rest for a minute or two in the company of her son. There was so little time to talk since Oliver's return. She had asked him about his work out in Africa, of course, and the way his lectures were going in this country. Soon he would be off to London and other places to raise money and there would be even less chance of it.

'You're quiet, dear,' she said. 'Nothing wrong?'

155

For a moment Oliver didn't answer. Then the smile he gave her was the warmest she had seen for a long time. But the vulnerable expression in his eyes seemed at odds with the confident way he had about him these days, and she wondered. Once or twice she had seen this as he was growing up each time some girl was becoming difficult. She hoped it wasn't the case this time. She had been half-expecting to hear that he'd met someone else in Africa, perhaps a girl in his group doing the same kind of work. So good to have similar interests if you were going to spend the rest of your lives together. She and Arnold had had bellringing in common, and walking. She had tried to like trees and ask intelligent questions about them so he wouldn't despise her ignorance, but . . .

'What's up, Mum?'

Recalled to the present moment, Cathy flushed. 'You'd tell me wouldn't you, Oliver, if something was bothering you?'

'Now why should there be anything bothering me, Mother dear?'

The vulnerable look had vanished now and Cathy smiled as she sipped her coffee.

*   *   *

Elisabeth was glad to be on her way at last. Once in the train she leant back, closed her eyes and tried to imagine present day Mellstone. The tree was different, a small

156

thing now but small things grew.

She smoothed her fingers over her lips and smiled as she thought of the wintry day when she set out to paint outside with her canvas bag swinging at her side. There had been rims of frost on the fence posts and on the tractor wheel marks across the field. The muddy smell from the banks of the brook pleased her. The swinging hazel catkins made interesting patterns against the wintry sky and the stone roof of Nether End farmhouse showed clear and bright between them.

Such a good remembered feeling. If only all her memories of Mellstone had been as pleasant. As usual Elisabeth's mind had shied away from one of the worst. But now, as the train hurtled towards Plymouth, she dwelt deliberately on that terrible autumn afternoon when she entered the school building from which Jenny had run out into the cruel wind the previous day. In her grey suit and with her dark hair pulled back from her face, the head teacher looked pale and hollow-eyed. 'It was Jenny's own fault,' she snapped. 'No child has ever done such a thing before. I can't understand why a normal nine year old would even think of it. We don't like that sort of behaviour in Mellstone.'

Elisabeth had come to reassure Jenny's teacher for her own sake, and hadn't expected to be attacked. 'I'm prepared to say to anyone you like that the accident was Jenny's own

157

fault and I don't hold you responsible.'

The head teacher's face hardened as she frowned but her relief was obvious. Not to have made this plain would have been cruel even though the dislike of Jenny was unnecessarily obvious. Suppose it still was? Jenny had told her that Karen had come back to Mellstone. With Robert of course. She could well make things difficult for Jenny now.

Elisabeth blinked. How sharp the past was sometimes. How bitter the thoughts she had tried to bury. The village was a different place now inhabited by different people. Or mainly different people. Cathy was still there and Ralph. And John was still farming at Nether End. How different her life would have been had they settled down together as he had wanted. Jenny's too. Her decision not to marry John hadn't been taken lightly and she'd had many moments of acute emotional strain when she left Mellstone behind her. Once settled in St Ives she'd put it all behind her and she wasn't sure that she wanted to meet John again.

*   *   *

Jenny glanced at her watch and then at the three empty pots on the wooden table in the room set aside for her on the ground floor of the Vale Hotel. The room seemed damp and dreary even with the overhead light on. The

158

sooner she was out of here the better.

The manager had looked at her apologetically when he had first shown her round. A challenge, she had told him confidently. Now, already behind schedule, she wished she had more time to give of her best. The arrangement for the largest room must be eye-catching enough to disguise the fact that the view consisted only of a row of dustbins near several brown garage doors. She decided to go for a mass of colour to draw the eye away from the non-view beyond. These deep pink and red roses were perfect. There were more for the bedside tables of the smaller rooms in low white containers with just a hint of swirling blue in the glaze.

She worked quickly and then stood back for a moment to check the effect. The arrangements looked good once she had them in position. Then she gathered together her floristry scissors, the spare foam and the tape, said goodbye to the receptionist and went out through the side door to the car park.

*   *   *

'This is nice,' said Elisabeth, looking round the Hilbury tearoom with pleasure.

She and Jenny sat at the table in the window overlooking the busy High Street. Behind them china rattled, and the tinkle of teaspoons accompanied the muted conversations of the other customers.

'I was starving,' Jenny said. 'I thought it best to stop here on the way back to Mellstone in case I passed out with hunger.'

Elisabeth smiled. 'I can wait just a little longer to see Saskia. I'd have to anyway, wouldn't I, as you say she's working this afternoon?'

Jenny finished her cottage cheese and watercress sandwich and took another. 'You can say that again. She's really keen. The church office job seems just the thing for her. She'll try to leave early today as you're coming. She wants to see your reaction to the village and to Marigold Cottage.'

'Me too.' Elisabeth laughed but she looked at Jenny in concern, noting the lines of fatigue around her eyes. Her light navy jacket couldn't quite conceal the loss of weight. 'You've been working too hard, my love. Don't deny it. Business going well?'

'Wait till you see what I've been doing. And now there's the Old Bakery and the plans I've got for that if I get it. I'm so grateful that I'll have the money to go ahead. John Ellis seems happy about it all.'

Elisabeth stared at the cup in her hand and said nothing.

Jenny cleared her throat. 'But all that can wait for the moment.'

Elisabeth replaced the cup in the saucer. 'I'm looking forward to hearing about your work, Jenny, and the commissions you've got. It's those that are your bread and butter. You know where we are at this very moment, don't you, my love? This used to be the Art Shop years ago. The proprietor gave me my first chance, got me going, in fact. Don't you remember, Jenny? I had to produce fifty paintings quickly for his exhibition. I was so excited. I'll never forget waiting at the bus stop afterwards, clutching my precious sample paintings to my bosom. I hardly noticed the sleeting rain or a car stopping to offer me a lift.'

'I hope you took it.'

'Oh yes.' Elisabeth smiled, remembering John's anxious expression as he glanced at the parcel she carried. The sodden brown paper covering of the top painting fell apart, showing the track up the hill at Nether End. She had told him in excitement about the exhibition, expecting his encouragement but not getting it. 'I don't know much about painting,' John had said in disapproval. 'It seems an extraordinary number to do in a short time. There'll be no chance of a normal life for you now.'

'Normal?' she had cried. 'It's as normal to me as breathing.'

He was unconvinced, condemning. She had looked down at the top painting in her lap, knowing in her heart how precious it was to her because it she had planned it at Nether End.

Elisabeth blinked, and saw that the café was filling up fast now. Around them the murmur of conversation rose. With all her heart she hoped that Jenny's success would continue and grow into something really worthwhile. After her disastrous marriage her daughter needed fulfilment and peace of mind. She was glad that Jenny had John to back her even though he had failed her when she needed his moral support.

Jenny was beginning to fidget.

Elisabeth smiled. 'Come on, then, my love. Let's go.'

*   *   *

'Gran!' Saskia rushed to Elisabeth to hug her. 'I wanted to be here when you came.'

'You're a working woman now I know,' said Elisabeth, laughing as she extricated herself. She was a little shaky in her balance these days and feared a fall, but Saskia, in her bright young exuberance had forgotten that. She wouldn't remind her.

They were in the garden admiring the purple clematis that grew so abundantly against the fence. Jenny had placed white plastic chairs on the shady patio and a low white coffee table. She had wondered, in the train, how the garden would look without the cedarwood building where she had once worked long and hard. Now she found she

162

liked the extra space.

They sat down. Jenny, bearing a tray, came up the steps towards them. 'Tea, Saskia? A cold drink?'

'Lemonade, please,' said Saskia. 'Tell me what you think of the cottage, Gran. Has it changed much? D'you like it now?'

Elisabeth accepted a cup of tea and gave a happy sigh. 'It's lovely. I certainly approve of the changes. And all so fresh and spacious-looking. It seemed dark when we lived here.'

They talked of Saskia's job in the church office and of Elisabeth's work in St Ives and of how she was managing the steep street up to her small terrace cottage. Insects murmured in the grass and a bright admiral butterfly hovered over the blue flowers of the plumbago.

'I haven't looked at the village properly yet,' said Elisabeth. 'It whisked by so quickly in the car. Fancy an expedition?'

Saskia sprang up. 'Great. Let's go. Mum?'

'Go on, the pair of you, enjoy yourselves.' Jenny stood up and picked up the tray. 'I've things to do here. But remember, Saskia, Gran's not as young as she was.'

Elisabeth laughed as she got up. 'Speak for yourself.' To prove her agility she went quickly down the steps ahead of her grandaughter.

As the front gate clicked behind them she paused to glance along the lane at the cottages round the triangle of grass and the Tidings

163

Tree. That area hadn't changed, thank goodness, outwardly at least apart from the tree. She hoped that smoke would still emerge from the chimneys on winter days. What a hypocrite she was. She wanted the dwellings of others to remain in a time warp, at the same approving of the changes to the inside of Marigold Cottage.

They walked towards the tree. 'One day the leaves and branches of this young thing will cast their shadows over the thatch just like the old one,' said Elisabeth.

'Don't be sad, Gran.'

'I'm not sad. Nostalgia needn't be sad.'

'Doesn't it make you think of all the years that have gone for good?'

'Profitable years one hopes. And I'm content now, my love.'

Saskia smiled at her. 'As well you might be with all the success you've had. I hope Mum does as well.'

'She'll go far, your Mum. It's a lovely thought, isn't it Saskia, the sunlight rippling through the leaves? You'll see it, or your children will. I like the thought of that.'

Saskia's bright face flashed for an instant into a mischievous smile. 'So you imagine me here with a crowd of kids?'

Elisabeth laughed. 'Three at least.'

Her grandaughter looked suddenly sad. 'I don't think there's much chance of that now, Gran, kids of my own.'

164

Elisabeth glanced at her anxiously 'Don't look so anguished. It spoils your pretty looks. Last time we spoke you were telling me about a nice young man.'

'Ash?'

'Another tree?'

Saskia's brief smile didn't quite reach her eyes. 'Ashley Lovell. It's finished now. He's at uni with me. Did Mum tell you? Ash was supposed to come and stay and then he didn't.'

'And you're upset about it.'

Saskia shook her head. 'No way. It's over. I don't think about him anymore. Not much anyway. No, it's not him.'

'Someone else?'

Saskia nodded. 'But I don't think he cares about me at all.' Her voice shook a little. 'I like him a lot you see. He's friendly, very friendly, but that's all. He doesn't understand how it is with me. He smiles and makes jokes, but . . . '

'And it hurts?'

'It hurts.'

Elisabeth felt at a loss. There was little she could say that would be of help. This was something her beloved grandaughter had to work out for herself. Obviously the best self-help was to throw herself into her work in the church office and at the Swan Inn . . . but Saskia understood that. She was an intelligent girl. She didn't need telling.

Elisabeth put out her hand and touched the slim trunk of the new tree.

'Are you making a wish, Gran?'

'The trunk feels so cool and firm. I can feel its optimism that one day it will be tall and strong. If I did make a wish, my love, it would be that you find your true love and your true vocation in life so that you grow into happy old age.'

Saskia smiled. 'That's lovely, Gran. 'I hope you do too.'

'Find my own true love? A little late for that, I think.'

Elisabeth expected Saskia to laugh but instead her grandaughter gazed at her with an unfathomable expression on her young face.

CHAPTER TWELVE

'Our aged parents are hard at it at home, reminiscing like mad. I thought I'd escape.'

Jenny smiled. Cathy would hate being thought aged. Elisabeth too, for that matter.

'You're laughing at me again.' Oliver's eyes twinkled at her in a way she found immensely attractive. 'Can I come in? You once said you'd show me your work. Is this a good time?'

'Of course, Oliver. Come in.'

For a moment, as they went in from the front garden through the open French windows, her workroom looked dim. Facing north as it did the light was good for her purposes but Jenny wished that the sunshine poured in to show her work to more advantage. Aching for Oliver's approval, she was uncertain about his reaction. Even to her eyes the room looked messy, stacked as it was with all the paraphernalia of her working life.

Oliver placed his papers among the tools on the workbench, and began to circle the room. As he went he took time to examine everything in detail and ask questions. He reached the shelves containing her finished work. Totally absorbed, he gazed at each pot in silence.

Watching him, Jenny was enchanted. That he was treating it all with such seriousness was wonderful. She had known that what she was doing interested him in a general sort of way. He had made that clear from the first and she was glad of it. But this intent examination was different.

She watched him as he picked up a few of the pieces for a more careful scrutiny. He held each piece with reverence before replacing it. This was balm to her soul, an appreciation of her creative powers she had come to expect from few people. She felt a lump in her throat, and knew that in a minute if she wasn't careful, she would dissolve into tears.

Oliver put down the blue and silver dish he was holding, and turned to her. 'I'd like to take you in my arms, Jenny.'

She looked at him in wonder. Could this really be happening to her, this extraordinary feeling of tremulous delight? He had spoken quite simply as if what he said to her was the most natural thing in the world. She felt as if she had left her untidy, dusty workroom and was on a higher idyllic plane where such amazing words could be said and understood.

He made no move towards her but stood gazing at her. She felt devastated by the deep devotion in his eyes. He was a young man, some years her junior, whose life was totally unimaginable to her. Africa, the parkia tree, research . . . what could that tell her about this man whom she had, so inexplicably, attracted?

'Jenny? Is that such a strange thing to want, my love?'

'Not now,' she said quietly. She wanted more than anything to relax against him, to feel loving arms round her, something she had never imagined feeling again. But she felt reluctant to rush into something as serious as this promised to be. Sensible or cowardly? She hardly knew.

'Then when?' His voice was husky.

'I don't know . . . I can't say. I need to think.' Jenny's hand shook. She walked to the open French windows and stepped out into the warm afternoon. She couldn't cope with this although she wanted it most desperately.

And Oliver? When he followed her she saw he held his papers under one arm again. He looked businesslike but his expression was sweet as he gazed at her. 'I want to see more of

168

you, Jenny, OK?'

She could only turn away so that he shouldn't see in her face this feeling of unbelievable happiness was almost more than she could bear. She was singing inside but for the moment she needed time to assimilate what was happening to her. Standing out here among her flowers was the last place for this sort of conversation. The wonder of it was that no one had come walking past already.

He smiled. 'I'll see you soon then Jenny my love, very soon. We'll arrange something away from here.'

He didn't wait for an answer but moved swiftly to the gate. Placing one hand on it he sprang over into the lane. Jenny laughed as he turned and waved.

Only immediate action could subdue Jenny's turbulent thoughts now. She felt her face glow as she locked the door and set off along the lane to the bottom of Hodman's Hollow. She began to walk to the top of the hill.

She brushed her hair away from her forehead, remembering the exciting stir of fear that had drawn her up here one long ago day on her own when Elisabeth had been busy in the studio. She had dared herself to walk all the way to the top. At first it was exciting to see the leafy branches above her head that almost cut out the blue sky. Invisible birds sang. Then, turning a bend, she saw a dark figure some way ahead carrying a black shopping bag that jerked against her side. Mrs Pengold! She had stopped, horror-stricken, as the figure plodded on. Jenny couldn't break her dare or something horrible would happen so she couldn't run back the way she had come until she reached the top.

Soon Mrs Pengold was over the brow of the hill. To get her dare over with quickly Jenny ran and arrived at the crest out of breath.

Her terror on seeing the old lady nearby picking feathery heads of cow parsley was so great she could only stand and stare.

Mrs Pengold turned. 'You didn't ought to be up here all on your own, a young maid like you with your red hair all over the shop. It don't do no good to wander about like some wild thing.'

With a gasp Jenny ran back the way she had come. Seeing a small gap in the hedge, she shot through. On the other side a body lay face downwards on the grass. She screamed and the person on the ground sat up and was immediately familiar.

'I thought you were dead, Miss,' Jenny said.

Cathy sat up, rubbing her eyes and scrunching a letter in her hand. She thrust it in the pocket of her cardigan.

Aware that the teacher was unhappy Jenny tried to help. 'This would be a good place for a Nature Walk,' she said. Then she had told Cathy about her own best place, Brooklands that was really a secret. She trusted her because Cathy was kind.

Jenny blinked now as she walked up that same track so many years later. Oliver was Cathy's son. How would she feel about his interest in a woman so many years his senior with a grown-up daughter? Regarded like that it was totally out of order.

But deep inside Jenny a soft warmth persisted. She had been unusually reticent so far and had held back from Oliver in her wish to consider the implications. But where was the harm?

She turned as she reached the brow of hill and hurried down the track again. She needed to do something positive to release all this new-found energy inside her. She would go into Hilbury immediately and confront the estate agent about the Old Bakery. She had been kept waiting long enough.

Action, action, action!

Hatchet and Drew's office in Hilbury was deserted when Jenny entered. Immediately one of the doors opened in the wall opposite. She was pleased to see the same young clip-board man who had shown her round the Old Bakery a few days ago. Seeing her, an evasive expression flitted across his face.

'Please be seated,' he said.

He shuffled some papers but before he could say anything else the outside door crashed open. Startled, he rose to his feet to greet the woman who came marching in.

171

Hilda Lunt glared. 'Take me to the manager, young man.'

'I'm sorry, madam. He's out at the moment.'

'Out?'

'Showing more clients round the old property in Mellstone.'

'Then he's wasting his time. The Old Bakery must be removed from his books immediately. I'm here to tell him so on Mrs Moore's orders. And what are you doing here, Miss Finlay?'

'But . . . ' The estate agent looked so browbeaten that Jenny was moved to protest.

'I think you'll find he can't do that without the vendor's instructions,' she said.

Hilda Lunt turned slowly to face Jenny. 'I'll not be told. He knows our views and that's the end of it.'

'I'm here to make enquiries about the Old Bakery too.' Jenny smiled, though her heart was quaking. 'I'm here to check on my offer.'

'Over my dead body. We can't be doing with all this underhand carrying on.'

'Underhand?' Jenny felt her colour rising. 'The property's on the open market.'

The young man cleared his throat. 'That is so, Miss Lunt, I'm afraid.'

'Afraid?' Hilda looked as if she had never been afraid of anything in her life. 'So what are you offering to give for the place, if I may ask, Miss Finlay?'

'You may not,' said Jenny with spirit. 'I

intend to have a private interview about the matter and then I shall go.'

Hilda Lunt drew herself up. 'It's no good looking at me like that, Miss Finlay. If you get the Old Bakery your life in the village won't be worth living.'

'Don't threaten me, Miss Lunt.'

'A warning, that's all, for your own good. You'll do well to take heed.'

The phone rang. The young man answered it with obvious relief. As he replaced the receiver the manager returned.

At once Hilda, all smiles, allowed herself to be led off to an inner sanctum. The young man, brightening as he re-seated himself, told Jenny all he knew about the state of affairs concerning her offer for the Old Bakery. This amounted to nothing she didn't know already. She was wasting his time and her own.

Disappointed, she stood up and found she was trembling. Hilda Lunt's angry reaction had had more of an effect on her than she realised.

*   *   *

Talking to John Ellis on the phone when she got home, Jenny relaxed a little. His calm tone of voice was reassuring. He was fairly sure that her cash offer would be accepted if she were patient.

He had said this before, of course, but she hadn't waited. She had seen the enmity in

Hilda Lunt's eyes and knew that even if the village couldn't have the Old Bakery Hilda and Mrs Moore would see to it that she didn't get it either.

Hilda Lunt had looked a forlorn figure standing by the bus stop and so Jenny, against her better judgement, had drawn up by the kerb and wound down the car window.

Hilda glared at her. 'It's the hospital I'm off to now to see old Bill Gedge. He'll back me up and no mistake. The Moores are angry too. Karen'll be on the war path. I wouldn't be in your shoes for all the tea in China.'

Her expression meant business. And there was Elisabeth to consider, too. Jenny's dread that her mother and Karen Moore would come face to face now seemed an even more chilling prospect.

But were Hilda's bullying tactics to go unchallenged? Definitely not.

Hilda leaned as far into Jenny's car as she could without toppling in. 'Lived in the village all his life, old Bill. He'd want the Old Bakery to belong to us. And now Bill's at death's door what happens?'

About to offer to drive Hilda to the hospital, Jenny thought better of it. She waited until Hilda withdrew her head and then, chastened, drove home.

*   *   *

174

The breeze ruffled the top branches of the ash tree in the lane opposite the Swan Inn as Jenny drove across the main road to the high-banked lane to Nether End the following afternoon. She had heard the delight in John's voice when she changed the subject of her phone call yesterday from the Old Bakery and talked about her mother's visit to Mellstone instead. At once he had suggested Elisabeth should visit Nether End. She supposed John wished to be on his home ground when they met again after all these years. Or maybe he wanted Elisabeth to see what she had lost? But no, John wasn't like that. His pleasure in Elisabeth's suggested visit was too genuine to imagine that it could be anything else but pure friendship.

Beside her in the car Elisabeth seemed subdued. At first her mother had demurred at the idea of visiting Nether End on John's invitation.

'I'm not sure I'm ready for this, Jenny,' she had said in dismay. 'I need more time.'

'But you've been here a few days already and it has to happen sometime. Isn't it better to meet at Nether End rather than in the lane or the Post Office? At least you'll be alone, two friends talking over old times.'

'Very old times and not happy ones at that.'

Jenny sighed. It was all so long ago and John was insistent that she should bring her mother to visit him. 'Would it be so very terrible?'

'Ah well, it's as well to get it over with I suppose,' Elisabeth said. 'You've persuaded me, Jenny, but it'll be your fault if the meeting's a disaster.'

'Call me on my mobile if it is and I'll down tools and come to the rescue.'

Elisabeth had smiled at that but had looked anxious too.

Since this was a working afternoon Jenny had arranged to drop her at John's home and then return to collect her later.

John came to the door at once to help Elisabeth out of the car and to usher her inside. His handshake lingered a little and Jenny was relieved to see that Elisabeth was smiling.

*   *   *

'Your hand's cold, John,' Elisabeth said as he released it. 'You're keeping well?'

His smile was as slow and attractive as she remembered. He hadn't changed much, still the same straight figure. His hair was white now, of course. It suited him. He was a good-looking man.

'Perfectly well,' he said. 'And I can see you are too, Elisabeth. I'm glad you have come.'

They went inside. The hall seemed wonderfully familiar. She had been apprehensive about meeting John after so many years, afraid they had both changed and would meet as strangers. But John seemed far from that as he ushered her into his sitting room at the back of the house.

'Mrs Horlock has laid a tray for us on the terrace,' he said. 'I think it's warm enough. Shall we see?'

The walnut tree created enough shade to make the area a pleasant place on this warm afternoon. Elisabeth found herself relaxing in John's company as they drank their tea and enjoyed the chocolate biscuits of which John was so fond.

'Tell me about your work in St Ives,' he said, leaning forward a little.

He appeared deeply interested as she talked of the exhibitions of her paintings planned for later in the year.

In front of them the lawn stretched to where the ground began to rise. This interest in her work was different from the old days when John had criticised her way of life to such an extent she could stand it no longer. He had tried to shatter her dreams and that had been unforgivable. She couldn't quite reconcile herself to his changed attitude now.

'I have one of your watercolours in my room upstairs,' John said as he placed his cup and saucer on the tray. 'Do you remember the one you did of the track up the hill?'

Surprised, Elisabeth nodded. She remembered only too well the day she had sketched the scene. She had been young then and it was early spring. Actually February but it felt like spring because the primroses were out.

'Do you feel like a stroll?' John asked now.

Elisabeth was glad to walk with him across the wide lawn to the beginning of the track. They didn't go far along it, turning back at the first field gate after standing for a moment to gaze at the view across to Larksbury Rings where sheep still grazed the olive-green slopes.

'So unchanged,' she said. 'So beautiful still in the afternoon sunshine.' She was unutterably moved, so glad she had overcome her scruples about visiting John this afternoon. He had shown her nothing but kindness.

*　　　*　　　*

They were in the sitting room when Jenny returned. To her disappointment nothing was said about further visits.

They got into the car, John careful of Elisabeth's comfort. Jenny drove in silence for a few moments. Something held her back from questioning her mother.

'You're not saying much, Jenny,' said Elisabeth as they reached the end of the drive. 'Are you all right, my love?'

'Tired, that's all,' said Jenny.

'A busy afternoon?' Elisabeth sighed contentedly. 'We had a lovely time after all,

John and I. You were right. We had to meet again sometime. What a treasure he has in Mrs Horlock. So good to see her again. John showed me his collection of old maps after we'd had a short walk. Fascinating but depressing too in a way to see how much some of these places have grown in the past twenty years or so. Oh, and he told me some sad news. An old man called Bill Gedge died today in hospital. The funeral's on Thursday at eleven. He was in his nineties, John said. But it's sad. A sudden illness, I think. A good way to go, I suppose.'

Elisabeth smiled a little sadly as they arrived at Marigold Cottage. There had been no hint of censure from John this afternoon as he asked about her life in St Ives. He had mellowed over the years. 'I'd like a closer look at your latest batch of work, Jenny,' she said. 'I haven't seen any of it properly.'

Jenny smiled. 'Easily done. I'll bring the pots into the sitting room to show you.'

Almost speechless with admiration, Elisabeth looked carefully at each of the five containers that Jenny carried in. She picked up each in turn, holding it up against the light. 'All so different.'

'I've been experimenting with a different mingling of glazes.'

'And it's certainly paid off. They're beautiful. The best you've ever done. Mellstone is obviously good for you.'

Jenny smiled. 'I've been working hard for this Open Weekend, Wayside Arts it's called. I hope I do well.'

'You will if these are anything to go by.' Elisabeth placed the last one carefully on the table at her side. Suddenly she noticed a new glow about Jenny. 'You seem to have some sort of strength about you that wasn't there before,' she said. 'If I didn't know you better I'd say you were in love.'

Jenny was still for a long second, her head bent as she gazed at the vase in her hands. Then she looked up, smiling. 'In love with Mellstone more like.'

Elisabeth smiled too, glad that her daughter had found life here so much to her liking.

CHAPTER THIRTEEN

Tess Harding wore a sleek black outfit and such spike-heeled shoes to Bill Gedge's funeral service on Thursday that Jenny thought she would topple over as she tottered up the church path ahead of her.

Cathy and Ralph Varley were near the front of the church and Jenny expected Oliver to be in the same pew. She glanced round the crowded church and saw him to her right. At the same time he saw her and smiled. He looked taller in his dark suit and strangely

180

solemn. She hoped she looked suitable in her dark clothes too.

She felt uncomfortable among these sombre people because she had hardly known the old man. Would he have minded her being here on this solemn occasion? Probably not. She had heard a lot about Bill Gedge though couldn't remember him clearly. It was Cathy's memories rather than her own that had made her think she had known him. Or maybe her own subconscious coming up with the knowledge that as a little girl she had seen him in Mellstone. It was said that all the past was there inside you. But where exactly? So perhaps it was all right for her to be here because of that. Anyway Oliver had asked her to come so that he had someone to talk to afterwards.

The notes on the organ faded away. The congregation stood up as the funeral entourage entered and made its way slowly up the aisle with Lesley leading the way, proclaiming the solemn words from the service.

From the pulpit Lesley looked solemnly down at the congregation. 'Bill recognised subconsciously that God calls us to be his people. He had the inward knowledge that's denied to most of us these days with the image bombardment through the media. Nowadays the community has broken down. We need to rediscover it. Bill worked hard for his family

181

and the community. He never lost touch with his roots. Everything that happened here through the years was important to Bill. He had satisfaction in humble jobs. Bill knew, perhaps unconsciously, that we live by the results of our actions. His memorial is the ongoing life of Mellstone, an invisible atmosphere that touches us all who live here. I am proud to have known Bill Gedge even for a short time.'

Jenny gave a little sigh. She hadn't had much experience of funerals though she remembered Elisabeth coming to John Ellis' uncle's funeral in this church. Jenny smoothed back a loose strand of hair from her forehead, remembering how she had run out from school in the dinner hour that day, upset by the suddenness of it all and thinking that Mrs Pengold had made it happen because she was a witch. She had only just got back in time for afternoon school.

Jenny smoothed her hair again, thinking of Mrs Pengold? Would Lesley give her a glowing report to take into the next world when the time came . . . *Alice Pengold, a pillar of society, frightener of small girls?*

As she left the building ahead of Oliver Jenny saw Cathy leave her husband's side and walk towards her.

'The family are very keen for everyone to join them at the Swan, Jenny. They've set aside a special room and laid on a bit of a spread. You'll come?'

Jenny hesitated. 'I hardly like to. I didn't really know him. Or them.'

'They want a crowd, that's all,' Cathy said apologetically. How could she refuse? Jenny nodded, and then walked with Cathy and Ralph down the church path. At the gate there was a hold-up as a dark blue Peugeot drew up and the passenger door opened wide.

'Someone's managing to escape,' said Oliver's deep voice in Jenny's ear.

She felt herself flush at his nearness. They watched while an elderly lady was helped into the passenger seat and the car eventually drove off. Jenny had the feeling she should know her. Deep down a memory stirred and was gone.

Inside the Swan Inn the family stood about looking awkward while a tray of sherry was circulated by a girl no more than ten. Or so it seemed. Jenny smiled at her and took the nearest glass. She could hardly ask the girl how old she was but she would like to know. She looked for Saskia and saw her behind the bar, neat in her white blouse. Busy, of course, but that's why she was here.

Oliver, at Jenny's side, glanced round the low room with interest. Sipping the sweet liquid in her glass, Jenny followed his gaze. It was far too warm in here and the passing traffic darkened the small windows every now and again with a swish of noise. The clock on the shelf chimed with a sweet rippling sound.

The room was filling up fast. Jenny saw Hilda Lunt in a magnificent hat talking to a couple she didn't know. Newly retired, she thought . . . anxious to please, uncertain of their welcome, wanting to soak up local atmosphere, to belong. Knowing nobody except Hilda, the woman looked grateful and drank her sherry too fast.

'Want some more?' the girl asked her, pushing her way through the crush.

'No, oh no. Really.'

The man took his wife's empty glass and placed it on the tray. Nigel moved to his side and they began to talk. Jenny smiled. Roping him in for his Saving the Countryside gang?

'Why are you smiling?' asked Oliver.

'Was I? Oh heavens, it's hardly suitable at a time like this.' Jenny took another sip of sherry and then placed her glass on the windowsill as Saskia appeared with a tray of sandwiches. Her cheeks were flushed and her eyes bright. She smiled at Oliver and avoided looking at her mother.

Jenny took a ham sandwich. Oliver took four and was rewarded by a conspiratorial look from Saskia. 'I'll come back again soon,' she promised.

Oliver turned to Jenny. 'What a crush. I only came to be with you.'

'I don't believe you.'

'OK, OK. You win. I was fond of the old

chap.'

A group that seemed perfectly at home were clustered round the man Jenny knew as Tom Barnet, Tower Captain.

More food came, this time a dish of sausage rolls carried by a short woman in royal blue who smiled kindly at Jenny. 'My old dad were one of they bellringers,' she said. 'Mr Moore'll tell 'ee. Fell out with him, he did, over ringing in the New Year. They don't do that no mwore.'

'Why not?' asked the new man with interest.

His wife looked disappointed. Another old custom down the drain and before they had time to enjoy it? Jenny saw Hilda Lunt, hat askew, moving to the woman's side again obviously about to fill her in on a few more things. Hopefully not about the Old Bakery.

'She's Bill Gedge's daughter,' Ralph said as the royal blue woman moved on with her sausage rolls and was lost in the crush.

Oh ah, old Bill,' said Tom. 'An old character if ever I knew one.'

'Remember that debacle in the Tower one New Year's Eve,' someone asked.

'I'll say.' Ralph drained his glass. 'Not that we did ring it in properly, did we Tom?'

'It were that home-made rice wine Bill brought up to the ringing chamber. We got started on it a bit too soon. And you started swinging on them ropes, Ralph.'

A slow smiled spread across Ralph's rugged

185

features. 'It was safe enough with all of them except the treble because they weren't pulled up. And like a fool I caught hold of the treble's rope by mistake and all hell was let loose. The rope lashed round and round and the bell made a gigantic din. The rope caught me and knocked me flying. There was I face downwards on the floor until it was safe.'

Now in the warmth of the Swan Inn Ralph laughed easily. Oliver came carefully towards him with a refill. Ralph took the glass and raised it high. 'A lot of water's flown under the bridge since then.'

Ralph looked at Jenny and saw her smiling at his son. There was something in her expression that gave him pause. For a moment he stayed motionless, watching carefully. He knew he wasn't observant, leaving that sort of thing to Cathy. But this time he had seen something for himself and he wasn't sure he liked it. He glanced at his wife who seemed unconcerned. Had it he imagined it, that loving look cast by his son at a woman old enough to be his mother, give or take a few years?

*   *   *

Jenny raised her glass to her lips but someone behind jogged her arm and sherry flowed down the front of her jacket. She dabbed at it with a tissue as Hilda Lunt, minus her hat, came pushing past to position herself between Ralph and his son.

She glared at Jenny. 'Never mind water flowing under the bridge but what about the Old Bakery, I say? You heard what the vicar said back there in church. Bill cared about the village all his life. We owe to Bill to do what's best for the village now.' She looked round triumphantly, confident of the agreement of all.

Jenny tried hard to press herself back against the wall out of sight. Oliver's face was flushed and she could see he was holding himself back with difficulty.

'Come off it, Hilda,' said Tom Barnet. 'Now's not the right time.'

Hilda Lunt bridled. 'Right time? Any time's the right time.'

Lesley moved towards Hilda, looking businesslike in her black cassock. 'There's someone over here you should talk to about it, Hilda,' she said. 'Come along.' With one hand beneath Hilda's elbow she bore her off.

'Bill were a grand old chap,' said Tom Barnet. 'They don't make them like that no more. He saw a good few come and go in Mellstone. Some of them still here. Others passing through, here for a while and then gone.'

Jenny nodded. Gone, like the tolling of a bell, gone, gone, gone. So much had gone from Mellstone. Outwardly the village hadn't changed but the atmosphere was different now. Tom Barnet smiled at her. 'Aye, old Alice should be here. You remember Alice?'

'Alice?'

'Lived opposite you. Alice Pengold.'

Jenny looked at him in surprise tinged with nervousness. The old woman had been much in her thoughts lately. She glanced towards the door, half expecting Alice Pengold to burst through with her mop and bucket and start a thorough cleaning job as had once done on the school.

Tom Barnet took a swig of his beer. 'Alice Gedge as was. Bill's sister. Another strong un. You never get the better of old Alice. Aye, she should be here somewhere.'

Jenny tried not to shudder. The old lady would be over ninety. More witch-like than ever? Grow up, she told herself. What was the matter with her?

Jenny glanced at Oliver and saw his lips twitch a little at one corner. 'Those dark colours suit you, my love.'

'You look rather distinguished yourself.'

'Let's get out of here.'

'How can we?'

They were both wedged in to a corner with others pressing close. Oliver downed the last of the liquid from his glass. 'Excuse me,' he said, his voice firm.

Space was made for him to slip through. Jenny, attempting to follow, was held back by several women who had come in late and blocked her way. When Oliver looked back to see if she followed him, she shrugged, smiling. Short of appearing rude she was unable to budge. In any case she didn't wish to make her interest in Oliver obvious to everyone. She saw him pause at Tom Barnet's side and knew he was content for a moment or two. She was content to wait too.

*   *   *

Cathy felt disturbed as she intercepted the look that passed between Oliver and Jenny and saw the expression on her son's face. There was something there that was more than friendship. How could that be possible? She must have been mistaken.

They had parted now, Jenny and Oliver. He paused among another group of people. Jenny, remaining where she was, shrugged and smiled in his direction and then turned away and began to talk to someone Cathy didn't know. Imagination, it must have been. And yet . . .

All at once Cathy wanted to be at home where there was much to be done. She opened the door and went out into the lane, relieved to feel the fresh air on her face although her unease about Jenny and her son still troubled her. She thought back to the end of the church service. Oliver had made his way down the path behind Jenny and reached her at the gate.

They stood near each other as the Moores got into their car and drove away.

Cathy paused and looked back down the lane at the sound of running footsteps. Saskia, Jenny's daughter, bent double as if in pain and with one arm across her body, came stumbling towards her, gasping.

'Saskia, my dear, what's wrong? Are you ill?' Cathy asked in alarm.

Saskia raised a desolate face to her. 'No, no, not ill.'

'But what's wrong? You look dreadful. Let's get you home quickly.' Cathy put out a sympathetic hand to her but the girl shook it off. She seemed not to know what she was doing.

'No, please, I . . . I can't go home.'

Saskia's desperation alarmed Cathy. 'But you can't stay here, my dear. Come home with me for a while until you feel better.'

Saskia sprang away from her as if she feared she would strike her. She did however straighten a little and walk along beside her, averting her eyes from Marigold Cottage as they passed.

Cathy ushered Saskia into the farm kitchen and sat her down at the wooden table. For one thing the kettle was handy and Saskia looked in need of a hot drink. The room was warm but Saskia was shaking and Cathy looked at her in concern. She wanted to question her but knew it was futile and that Saskia would tell her what was troubling her in her own good time. Forced confidences often did more harm than good.

Cathy made tea as swiftly as she could and then seated herself beside Saskia. She began to pour and pushed the sugar basin forward.

Saskia shook her head and sipped her tea scalding hot. Cathy was glad to see the colour return to her cheeks. She drank her own more slowly. When she had finished she glanced at Saskia and then away again, waiting for her to speak.

'It's kind of you, Mrs Varley. I'm sorry to be a nuisance. You'll have things to do.'

'Nothing that can't wait, my dear. My husband'll be a while yet, I shouldn't wonder, and Oliver.'

'Oliver,' gasped Saskia. She gulped and her lips trembled. She put up a hand to disguise it but Cathy saw the tears in her eyes.

'Oliver's upset you?'

'No. He, I . . .'

Cathy got up to busy herself replenishing the teapot with more hot water, not looking at Saskia to give her some space.

'I . . . I'm sorry. I didn't mean to . . . And you're his mother.'

'But not too besotted to criticise him if needs be.' Refilling Saskia's cup, Cathy sat down again. 'What's Oliver done? Can you tell me?'

Saskia shook her head. 'It's nothing really,

191

except that . . . I liked him, you see. I thought he liked me. I really hoped . . went out with him . . . once. He asked me to go with him to check the email at his sister's place. Your daughter's I mean. But Jem was there too and . . . ' She broke off, shuddering.

'Drink your tea,' Cathy said in sympathy. She was beginning to see what really troubled the girl. Oliver, yes, but something else painful as well. She herself had caught that smouldering look that passed between her son and Saskia's mother. Might not Saskia have seen it too and been shocked? With all her heart she hoped that she and Saskia had jumped to the wrong conclusion for all their sakes not least Oliver's himself. Ralph would be livid if he ever got a whiff that his son was interested in an older woman, especially one whose childbearing years were in the past.

And her own reaction? A slow rising anger that she had somehow been betrayed. How long had it been going on between the two of them? She hated the thought even though she found difficulty in taking it in properly. Oliver and . . . Jenny? With great effort Cathy pushed it to the back of her mind and tried to concentrate on Jenny's daughter in her pain and bewilderment. Her own distress must not show by the slightest flicker.

'I thought . . .' Saskia began, her lips trembling again. 'I'll have to get over it, I've got to. You won't say anything will you? It's just that . . . I don't usually do this.'

'No my dear, I'm sure not.'

'And it was nothing really.'

Cathy sighed. 'I understand.' She knew too well the agony of unrequited love. Just like herself with Arnold. In her pain she had wondered how it was possible to go on, day after day, knowing Arnold had stopped loving her, had perhaps never loved her in the way she had loved him. She had dreaded the pitying and curious glances, the derision because Arnold had discarded her.

If what she feared was true Oliver couldn't have given Saskia the least bit of encouragement. Just because she had fallen for him didn't mean he was obliged to reciprocate. Not that this made it any the less painful. Cathy's heart was sore for the young girl who looked back at her in such misery. But Oliver was her son. He needed space to make up his own mind. Love was cruel.

Saskia took another deep trembling breath. 'He's never given me any reason to . . . I mean, somehow I just hoped. He seemed to like me. You won't tell him? You won't tell Oliver of me being such a fool? Oh please, not that!'

'Of course I won't,' Cathy promised, heartsore for this girl she could have welcomed as a girlfriend of her son if Saskia were a little older and Oliver had more sense.

Saskia picked up her cup again and began to drink. Then she stood up. 'You're very kind,

193

Mrs Varley. I'll go now. It's best.'

'You're working in the church office this afternoon?'

Saskia shook her head. 'I've got it off because of helping at the funeral lunch.'

Cathy watched Saskia go with a feeling of sadness. The girl would cope, just as she had done, by hiding her pain from the eyes of the world. Saskia was proud and pride had a place here in helping her to get on with her life.

CHAPTER FOURTEEN

'Any chance of you being free for the rest of the afternoon?' Oliver asked as he and Jenny stepped outside the Swan into the warm sunshine of the lane. 'I'm due at Hilbury Townswomen's Guild at three. Fancy coming along with me?'

Jenny smiled. 'Townswomen's Guild . . . you?'

'I know, I know. But I'm not a member, honest. I'm the speaker, that's all. Three quarter of an hour's talk with slides and then questions. We'll be away by four. OK?'

'You forget I have my mother staying. Not possible, I'm afraid.'

'You don't sound exactly disappointed.'

'Oh, but I am.'

Oliver grinned. 'Truly? How long is your

mother with you?'

'A fortnight. One more week now. I can wait.'

'I can't.'

Jenny smiled, loving the moment. They began to walk up the lane towards the Tidings Tree.

'I'm off to London in twelve days time,' Oliver said. 'One of the organised money-raising events. Fancy coming too?'

'For the day?'

He nodded. 'And then on the way back we'll stop at a place I know in the New Forest.'

Jenny took a deep breath. She wasn't sure if she was ready for this. There had been one or two occasions during her sojourn in Chester when she had accepted invitations to dinner or days out in North Wales but she had never wanted anything more. Until now.

This needed thinking about. Why not just enjoy Oliver's interest in her? And it was genuine interest, incredible as it seemed. The way he gazed at her with such warmth proved that. He seemed so much in earnest. Why not bask in his wish to seek her company on his jaunts about the countryside? No harm, surely? With some careful thought she could re-adjust her work schedule without too much difficulty. At least she could try.

She smiled. 'Maybe.'

'That's my girl. But don't hide yourself away from me in the meantime will you, OK?'

'OK.'

They reached Marigold Cottage.

Jenny hesitated. 'Coming in to meet my mother?'

'Just for a moment then, OK?'

Elisabeth was in the garden. Jenny climbed the steps ahead of Oliver to the lawn and saw the remains of her mother's lunch on the small table in the shade with Elisabeth seated nearby, reading.

'I've just been down to make a pot of coffee,' said Elisabeth when Jenny had introduced them. 'Get some more cups, my love. There's plenty here for three. Sit down by me, Oliver. It's good to meet you. I've heard a lot about you from your mother.'

The two of them were getting on well when Jenny returned. Oliver was filling Elisabeth in on the funeral service in some detail. He wrinkled his forehead in an effort to remember some of the older people present he thought she might recall. Now Elisabeth, fascinated by Oliver's work in Africa, questioned him closely about living conditions and how he had become interested in the project in the first place.

At last he glanced at his watch and sprang up. 'I'm giving a talk this afternoon in Hilbury. I invited your daughter to come to hear it. Why don't you come too?'

Elisabeth was delighted.

Jenny, carrying the tray down to the kitchen, smiled to herself. She had to hand it to Oliver.

196

She liked the way he adapted without fuss to anything that came up. Probably the result of his training in Africa. She had the feeling that he had himself well in control.

She wondered how much John Ellis would have minded if she had gate-crashed his tea party with Elisabeth the other day. Maybe not at all.

*　　　*　　　*

As soon as Saskia left, Cathy went upstairs to the bedroom. Sitting on the side of the double bed she pulled open a drawer in the bedside table. At the bottom her fingers touched an envelope containing the only letter Arnold had even sent her and one that she kept hidden away. She opened it out to read now. It hadn't occurred to her when she received it that the flamboyant handwriting looked as if Arnold had tossed it off in haste, perhaps even as an afterthought.

'*My dear Cathy,*

As you know, I've felt for some weeks that I've been wasting my time here in Mellstone work wise. Now I think it's time to get out. And of course, there's us. I expect it's been clear to you as well as me that it couldn't last much longer. I'm putting it baldly but do try to understand. There's no time to see you as I'm off

*tonight. Someone I know thinks he can
land me a job on the Halland Forest Estate
if I get up north right away, so keep your
fingers crossed. I'll be in touch when it's
fixed.*
    Yours ever,
    Arnold.'

Arnold hadn't been in touch, of course. She
had known instantly that this was an empty
promise.

How thankful she had been at the time that
she had taken the letter upstairs to read in
private, away from the prying eyes of her
Mellstone landlady. For a moment the words
on the white paper had failed to register. Then
their impact hit her like a jet of cold water.

The clock downstairs had struck half past
eight, time for school. She folded the letter,
and put it in her pocket. Then, picking up her
bag and jacket, she went downstairs.

Her mind was numb and it was a great
effort to thrust aside the fog that enveloped it.
At school some of her children ran up and
accompanied her into her classroom where
they started crashing the chairs down from the
tables, talking and laughing. Ordinarily she
would have quietened them, but not now.
They were being helpful. She had the strongest
urge to gather them to her and to hug them.
The strain of trying to smile was so great that
she felt she like a gargoyle with fixed open lips

198

in a stone-white face.

The whistle blew outside and the children lined up to start the school day. Then followed the usual bustle of the register and the lining up by the partition wall for the service with the big ones, all the usual daily things that stretched ahead of her for ever.

And eventually she had married Ralph Varley and been happy.

Cathy raised her eyes and saw the mobile phone on Ralph's side of the bed, his book and reading glasses. Ralph always kept a spare pair of glasses here for reading in bed though he always fell asleep immediately.

She looked down at the letter in her hand. Why had she bothered to keep it through the years? A flimsy piece of nothing, that was all. She tore it into pieces, and threw the whole lot into the waste paper basket.

Later, when Ralph came into the kitchen Cathy looked at him with concern. She noted the twist to his mouth and the way he wouldn't look at her as he sat down in the grandfather chair at the table to remove his best black shoes. She found his slippers and handed them to him.

'Oliver back yet?' he asked as he put them on and stood up. 'I'd best get upstairs and change out of this lot.'

'Ralph?'

His expression was smouldering. 'A load of rubbish!'

'Oliver and Jenny?' Cathy sighed. She wished she'd kept the knowledge of Jenny's hysterectomy to herself.

'You saw it too? Just wait till I get my hands on him.'

We can't interfere, Ralph. Oliver's a grown man with his own life to lead.'

'How can you say that, woman?' He flopped down in his chair again and bowed his head. She had never seen him so deflated and she didn't know how to comfort him, aware of the depth of his passion for family traditions, the passing down from generation to generation of land that had been the Varley family's for a very long time. But no longer if their son formed a relationship with Jenny Finlay. Their daughter's moving in with the Moore's widowed son had hit him badly but time had softened his angry reaction. He had even accepted Oliver's experimental work in Africa because it was connected with agriculture. But this was a different matter. For Ralph to have picked up on their son's interest in Jenny surprised her but it meant that the implications of that passionate glance must be true.

Cathy stood beside him and placed a hand on his shoulder. 'It may blow over, Ralph.'

'You think so?'

She didn't know what to think. She loved Oliver. To love someone meant you had their best interests at heart. She wanted her son to

200

know true happiness but if that lay with a woman so much older than himself unable to bear children, what then? She gave another deep troubled sigh.

Ralph sprang up. 'Where is he? Gone off somewhere with her, I suppose. Well, his home's no longer here. You can tell him so.'

'And have him move straight into Marigold Cottage? No, Ralph. That's the best way to throw them together. I won't have it.'

'Either that or he can clear off back to Africa. Why should I care?'

'Of course you care. And so do I. He's our son. He stays here as long as he likes. We've got to be sensible, Ralph, and stand back. I know it's hard, but we've got to do it.'

He went to the door. 'I'll take a shower.'

'Ralph? Oliver's our son, a grown man. I don't want to lose him and we will if we're not sensible. I love him, Ralph. Whatever he does, I love him.'

'And what about me?'

'O Ralph! Of course. But what else can we do?'

Ralph, muttering, opened the door and let it crash shut behind him.

*   *   *

The following afternoon Saskia's eyelids drooped as she sat at her desk in the church office. She jerked herself upright and yawned.

Then she stared with dislike at the board on the wall opposite that told her information she didn't want to know about the weight of the eight bells in the tower and the date each was cast. She saw that two of the dates were in the sixteenth century. Interested now in spite of herself she got up to look at the board more closely. Amazing, she thought. Just think of all that's happened in the world while the oldest bell has been hanging here being rung every Sunday by a succession of Mellstone bellringers.

Lesley Bond's voice startled Saskia out of her reverie. 'I'm here at last, Saskia. Did you think I wasn't coming?' She placed a pile of papers on the desk, and looked at her in concern. 'You're looking pale today. Everything hunky-dory?'

'I didn't sleep much last night.'

'Problems?'

'Sort of.' Saskia, seated now, looked at Lesley's calm face. An impulse to confide in her was strong but no way could she mention Oliver and confess her own stupidity. She couldn't mention her suspicions about Mum, either. She had no real proof that anything was going on though it was fairly obvious. When Mum and Gran had returned from a lecture in Hilbury or something she gazed at her mother long and hard. She had seen nothing in her expression out of the ordinary but she had known with painful deep certainty.

202

'I'm here to help if you need it,' said Lesley. 'But not if you don't.'

Saskia smiled, feeling her skin tighten about her mouth. 'How do you know the right thing to say?'

Lesley laughed. 'Trial and error I suppose. Training, maybe.'

'What made you want to be a vicar? You don't mind?'

'Not at all. Ask away. I had this growing conviction that it was the right thing for me to serve the Lord in this way. The Moores' young grandson was questioning me about it the other day.'

'Jem?'

'Poor lad. Jem needs befriending by someone.'

Saskia smiled. Herself . . . why not? She'd like to and she had nothing else much to think about. A startling flash of freedom surprised her. It vanished, though, and she was back to pain. But it had given her a slight hint that things wouldn't always be as black as they now seemed.

She smiled again, and picked up the top sheet of paper. 'Are these the things you want photocopied? How many copies? I'll do them now.'

'Right.'

Lesley gave her a swift glance and then composed her face into a smile. 'Twelve of each, please. Could you drop them off in the vicarage sometime? Have a coffee or something?'

'OK,' said Saskia, already busy with the photocopier.

*   *   *

Saskia returned to Marigold Cottage to find it, thankfully, empty. She had dreaded seeing her grandmother whose sensitive eyes might well pick up on her suffering. She dreaded, even more, her mother.

Suddenly anger shook Saskia with such force she had to clutch hold of the banister rail to stop herself falling. She took deep, shuddering breaths until she was calm again

Work tonight would be agony when Oliver came in with the other bellringers after their practice but she had to get through it. She would be strong. She'd get to the pub extra early to make up for rushing out yesterday when she saw Mum and Oliver close together and had known instantly what they were up to. But for how long, oh how long? The pain was terrible.

In the event the evening's work wasn't as bad as she feared. In quiet desperation she pulled pints, replied to friendly banter and did everything that needed doing. All the time she listened for the church bells that tonight were strangely silent.

'No bellringing practice tonight,' Janis told

her when she asked. 'Because of Uncle Bill dying, see. They don't practice this week out of respect.'

Relief. Deep, thankful relief. Saskia felt the tension seep out of her. But how hardhearted to be relieved an old man had died! Had Bill Gedge still been alive there would have been no funeral and she would still be in ignorance of the true state of affairs.

For a moment Saskia allowed herself the dream that this was so, but what good was that? Suppose she hadn't known until it was out in the open, what then? She at least had warning and could try to get herself together, agonising as the effort was.

*   *   *

Jenny's hand strayed towards the telephone in the hall at Marigold Cottage. Should she check with Hatchet and Drew again while her mother was over the road at Ivy Cottage? The last time she had contacted the estate agents had been a few days ago after Bill Gedge's funeral. By now the vendors might have made up their minds.

She lifted the receiver.

Unfortunately not, it seemed. 'There's been a hiccup,' the manager said. 'Just a moment and I'll put you through to my assistant. Mr Callow is dealing with the sale.'

Clip-board man? Or had they taken on

someone else more dynamic to stand up against the awesome Hilda?

'Keith Callow here.' She would recognise those diffident tones anywhere. 'Good afternoon, Miss Finlay. I was going to phone you later with some rather disturbing news.'

'They've accepted another offer on the Old Bakery?'

'No, no, nothing like that. Not yet anyway. Someone's organised a petition, you see. I'm sorry. It all sounds most unpleasant. There's a lot of feeling. I haven't seen it myself but the vendor's solicitor informed me this morning that his clients are a bit concerned. I'll get back to you, Miss Finlay, as soon as I know more.'

Jenny replaced the receiver, sick at heart. Did this mean the end of her hopes? For a moment she gazed thoughtfully at the telephone, trying to think what to do next. She needed to talk to someone about it, someone with her interests at heart. But not John. How could she admit that she was doing a bit of fussing about the Old Bakery, unable to wait patiently as he advised?

A moment later she was tapping on the door of Ivy Cottage.

'Oh well done, Jenny,' Tess greeted her. 'Your mother and I are having a lovely chat. I was hoping you'd come. Now you'll join us in a glass of sherry, won't you, dear?'

As Jenny followed Tess inside her gaze

206

wandered to the carriage clock on the mantelpiece. Then she caught Elisabeth's expression and swallowed a giggle. Her mother, seated comfortably near the window, seemed perfectly at ease with a glass of sherry in her hand. She gave the impression that drinking sherry in the middle of an afternoon was something she did every day.

Jenny sat down and took the glass her hostess offered. 'I need this, thanks. I've just heard about a petition someone's got up about the Old Bakery. I bet Hilda Lunt's behind it.'

Elisabeth looked alarmed. 'But I thought you said the village can't afford the purchase?'

'I'm so sorry, dear,' said Tess. 'I thought it best not mention the petition to you, not wanting to upset you,' she said. 'Actually Karen Moore's played a huge part in organising it so they told me at the Post Office just now.'

Jenny glanced at her mother and saw that she looked horrified. Her hand shook and a drop of sherry spilled on her skirt.

'Wasn't she your school teacher once?' said Tess. 'It's odd her stirring things up against you like this.'

Nigel Hartland came in at that moment. 'Are we discussing the Old Bakery?'

'Sit down, Nigel, and listen to what Jenny has to say about this wretched petition. I told them in the Post Office we'd refuse to sign.'

Nigel leaned back in his seat and crossed one long leg over the other. 'How exactly was

207

this petition worded?'

Tess wrinkled her nose in an effort to remember. 'I didn't really look. I was too incensed. Does it make a difference?'

'I'm wondering, that's all.'

'But a petition is a petition. Can't you do something, Nigel?'

Jenny sighed. She expected him to look at her kindly and to shake his head but he did neither.

'Leave the problem with me, Jenny. I'll enjoy having a go at it.'

'Of course.'

John would have told her that knowing about the petition could do her no good at all. She would have done better to leave well alone since she could do nothing about it. He would be right, of course.

CHAPTER FIFTEEN

John stood on the grass at Nether End with Lassie at his side and watched Saskia and Jem's antics with pleasure. They made a delightful picture, the attractive girl and the earnest young boy. For a moment he allowed himself the fantasy that they were his grandchildren and he a loved grandfather whose pleasure was to indulge them. The only indulgence Jem required was to poke among the grasses at the side of the brook with a captive audience. John knew himself too old for that. Last night's rain had soaked the ground and Jem would get cold and muddy. Saskia would, too, though she didn't appear to mind. The girl looked pale, as if she'd been indoors too much. Perhaps the open air, chilly as it was, would bring the roses back into her cheeks and the sparkle to her eyes.

Saskia was good for Jem, throwing herself into the fray with every appearance of enjoyment. He was glad he'd had the idea of inviting her along to lunch as well as Jem and his grandparents. Making use of her, he had explained, but she hadn't minded that in the least. Jem was a lad to be proud of, intelligent, single-minded, intense. Karen and Robert should think themselves lucky.

The sound of a car turning into the gateway made John look up. He walked across the lawn and arrived at the front door at the same time as his guests. Robert helped his wife out. Karen looked frailer than when John had last seen her and now walked with a stick.

John, calling Lassie to heel, greeted them. 'Come inside. Too cold to linger out here.'

'Where's young Jem?'

John glanced at where he had seen him last. 'He was inspecting the brook over there a minute ago. Gone up to the lake I expect.'

Karen looked alarmed. 'Alone?'

'Don't worry, Karen. He's not alone. I've

got another visitor I'd like you to meet.'

They were in the hall now, divesting themselves of jackets. John ushered them into the sitting room and arranged the seating before he explained who Saskia was. The ensuing stunned silence surprised him.

'You've actually invited that girl here to meet us?' said Karen.

Robert looked anxious. 'It's all right, my dear, she's a pleasant enough young lady. I spoke to her in church.'

'And that makes it all right, does it, that you spoke to her in church? Never mind who she is, the grandaughter of that woman or that she's a bad influence on our grandson, encouraging him in his mad ideas. But what do you expect, given her parentage?' Karen's voice, charged with venom, rose to a crescendo.

Both men looked at her in alarm. Karen gasped and clutched her throat. 'Isn't it bad enough that the mother wants the Old Bakery and you hand in glove with her, John? I'm surprised at you. Oh yes, we're well organised. Over two hundred signatures already. Something's being done, no thanks to you.'

'You'll make yourself ill, Karen,' Robert remonstrated.

John moved to the door. 'I'll bring in some refreshment.'

Neither of them answered. Robert, concerned with his wife, leant towards her and held her hands in his own. Escaping, John called himself all kinds of fool. Was it really possible that Karen's bitterness against Elisabeth and Jenny had lain dormant all this time and still rankled? As head teacher of the school Karen had been held responsible for Jenny's truancy and accident that stormy day and had been in deep trouble because of it. Even so her reaction to Saskia's presence seemed . . . unbalanced? He hadn't seen his old friend like this before.

It was important to do something at once to relieve the situation. He must explain to Saskia, ask her if she minded returning home before lunch but the task was awkward in the extreme. This was to have been a pleasant Sunday spent in the company of friends. Jem, let off church on this occasion, had arrived early and Saskia a little later. He must find those two immediately even if it meant a trek across wet grass and muddy paths. Perhaps on his return emotions would have calmed and they would be able to discuss the outcome with a degree of good sense.

As he suspected Jem and Saskia had moved on to the lakeside. A ripple stirred the surface of the expanse of water. Jem, swinging his arms about, was jubilantly explaining something to Saskia. They both looked pleased to see him.

He stood for a moment in silence, drinking in the scene. The pearly calm was pleasing.

211

The misty downs faded into a background of grey sky, the chillness had quite gone. Lassie, panting at his side, looked up at him enquiringly with wagging tail.

'Now for it, Lassie,' he said.

Jem came running to join him. Saskia, turning suddenly, tripped and fell. She slid down the slimy bank to the water but scrambled up at once, laughing, plastered in mud and wet from the thighs down.

John rushed forward. 'Oh, my dear, are you all right?'

Saskia rubbed her muddy hand across her face. 'One born every minute. Isn't that what they say? I'm fine.'

John smiled, relieved. He admired the girl at this minute more than he could say.

'You should have looked,' said Jem.

Saskia grimaced. 'Sorry I'm in such a mess. I think I'll have to go straight home. Would you mind?'

John shook his head. 'Of course not, if you're sure? I'll drive you.'

'No way. Imagine the state of your car. I'd rather walk.'

'The car doesn't matter. It'll clean.'

'So will I after a good brisk walk. I don't mind, really.'

John was relieved to see that the girl looked better now, not as wan and haunted-looking as when she arrived at Nether End earlier.

They walked back together to the front of

the house. He tried to remonstrate further about Saskia getting herself home but to no avail.

'You like her, don't you, Jem?' said John as she left them.

Jem shrugged. 'She's all right. Quite sensible, really.'

More sensible, perhaps, than her elders. Thoughtfully John rejoined his guests. He was glad to see that Karen seemed calmer and Robert less worried. Supplying them with sherry, he spoke of other things. No one mentioned Saskia. It was as if she had never been.

John, thinking about this later, failed to understand exactly why the girl's presence at Nether End should have upset Karen so much even though Saskia was Elisabeth's grandaughter. He had found the way Karen referred to Elisabeth quite shocking.

He thought of the sweet expression on Elisabeth's face as they sat talking outside on his terrace a few days ago. He had found the afternoon of her visit immensely satisfying. He wanted her to come again. If he was honest he wanted her here with him always.

But Elisabeth was a successful artist living an interesting life in St Ives. They had talked of her work and of her plans to experiment with pastels, a medium she hadn't used much before and was beginning to appreciate. It was this quality of looking ahead and trying out new things that no doubt helped to keep her mind so young.

*　　　*　　　*

Having the cottage to herself was a definite bonus. For a short while Saskia had no need to pretend that everything in her life was normal.

After a leisurely shower she pulled on her best cream top and slinky skirt. She slid her hands over her hips, finding the smoothness soothing. Her face glowed and that was comforting too. A new Saskia, one who could cope easily with everything life threw at her. If only! She walked backwards and forwards in her tiny bedroom under the eaves, imagining the swish of her clothes at each turn. So elegant, so sophisticated. Perfume! Not her usual flowery stuff but something suave, refined. But she had none, and she wouldn't use Mum's. She shied away from that thought and went downstairs to scavenge for lunch.

She wasn't hungry really but she must make an effort. A yoghurt and a banana were just the things. They were soon eaten, too soon. She went back to the fridge and cut off a hunk of brie, rummaged in the cupboard for biscuits and opened a can of coke.

The empty afternoon stretched before her. She wandered into the sitting room with the can in her hand. What was Jem doing now? Would he return to the lake and start building the hide he had planned? But she was glad she wasn't there with him, pretending Jem wasn't a relation of Oliver's. Thinking of their connection was too painful, and she couldn't forget it when they were together, she and Jem, however hard she tried.

She thought suddenly of her filthy clothes discarded on the bathroom floor. Let them stay there, witnesses of her earlier humiliation when she had slithered into the water uselessly grabbing handfuls of grass that grew on the slippery bank.

She returned to the kitchen, and opened the fridge door. She pulled out butter and eggs. An afternoon's baking would occupy her mind and please her grandmother whose sweet tooth was often ignored by Mum.

*   *   *

They still hadn't come. Saskia prowled round the cottage to give herself something to do now she had finished her baking and tidied everything. She had even dealt with her dirty clothes and they were now on the washing line after a turbulent time in the machine. A Victoria sponge, sandwiched by masses of raspberry jam, lorded it beside the scones on the rack on the worktop. The pineapple cake nearby looked mouth-watering but she resisted the temptation to dig into it.

Should she try Mum's mobile? It was now

past six o'clock and the bells were ringing for evening service. Oliver would be there. But suppose he wasn't and he and Mum were together somewhere . . . gone off for a day out? Mum had said something about Tyneham and the Purbecks. Suppose her phone call interrupted something?

Saskia removed a can of lager from the inside of the fridge door, snapped the can open and took it into the sitting room. She stood at the window and looked out at the lane. She was almost tempted to go along to church to see if Oliver came down with the others from the ringing chamber. But what would she do if Oliver wasn't there . . . create a scene in church? The pain would be overwhelming.

It was agony imagining them together. Worse than when she and Ash split, much worse. Gran had been sympathetic about that. Gran! Mum wouldn't go off with Oliver with Gran in tow. So where were they?

Saskia drained the last of her lager and carried the empty can to the bin in the kitchen. She stood deep in thought. If Ash was here now he'd say *'Don't worry. And if you can't help worrying list some plans of action to keep yourself occupied.'* He'd be calm, sensible. For a second she wished Ash were here with her making her feel safe they way he had at first before she saw him with that girl. He hadn't admitted anything of course. But suppose

216

there hadn't been anything to admit?

The phone rang.

Saskia jumped and leapt to answer it.

'Oh you're back, Saskia.' Her mother's voice was breathless with relief. 'I tried your mobile but got no answer. We've got held up.'

Who has?'

'Saskia are you all right? You haven't been worrying?'

Saskia shook her head and then remembered that her mother couldn't see her. 'It's all right.'

'Gran's had a bit of an accident and she's broken her wrist. We'll be a while yet. Could you get the meal started? Something simple that won't spoil.'

Saskia replaced the receiver, her mind reeling. Her concern was deep and genuine but she knew to her shame that her first reaction was of relief that Mum and Oliver hadn't gone off together. So what did that make her? Completely selfish, that's what.

*　　　*　　　*

'You can't go back to St Ives in this state,' Jenny said. 'Think of all those steps up to your studio and the stairs too.'

Elisabeth, seated in a high-back chair in the living room with her plastered wrist resting on the wooden arm, looked at her in concern. 'It's no good, Jenny. I can't do this to you. Not at a

217

time like this.'

Jenny froze. 'A time like this? What d'you mean?'

'Your Wayside Arts work.'

'Oh that.' Jenny sank down on the window seat. 'We'll talk more about Wayside Arts later.' She had almost forgotten Wayside Arts in her worry about how this latest development would affect her meetings with Oliver.

'So stupid not to have been more careful. I should have known the pavement was wet and slippery.'

'At least it was only your wrist,' said Jenny as she reached for a cushion Elisabeth obviously didn't want. She put it down again. 'I was afraid for your hip.'

'Me too. But this is bad enough. It could be weeks before I'm fit to cope on my own. I'm so sorry . . .'

'I'll make up a bed for you downstairs here. The office'll make a good bedroom.'

'But how will you manage?'

'No problem. There's room here in the living room for the computer and the desk too if I move the sofa up a bit. Don't worry, please. It'll be all right, I promise.'

Elisabeth moved a little in her seat. 'Wayside Arts is such a wonderful opportunity but I know only too well what it entails. Weeks of planning and hard work. And now I'm an obstacle and I can't bear it.'

An obstacle to more than she realised,

218

Jenny thought in despair. Her anguish as she thought of Oliver was almost more that she could bear. How could they find a way round this? She struggled to think only of Elisabeth who prided herself on her independence but needed her help now.

'Oh Jenny, how can I do this to you?'

'Please, don't think like this. Everyone needs help from others sometimes.'

'But the timing is all wrong.' Elisabeth leaned her head back against the headrest and closed her eyes. Her face was pale and she was obviously still in shock.

'You're staying here with me for the foreseeable future,' said Jenny. 'I shall work just as hard as if you weren't here, I promise.'

Elisabeth opened her eyes and smiled. 'You're a good girl, Jenny. I hope you'll always be as blessed in your daughter as I am in mine.'

Jenny, humbled, gazed down at her hands. Elisabeth was a fighter. She had found success in the end and now she was determined her daughter would too. For her part she would never let her mother suspect her true feelings about her being here at this time.

*   *   *

During the next few days Jenny marvelled that Oliver was able to stand back until she could manage to see him again. Brief meetings between jobs only of course. Sometimes, as today, it wasn't worth going home for lunch. She had got up earlier than usual so she could leave Elisabeth's lunch prepared. All she had to do was pop it into the microwave herself if she wanted to be independent and eat before Saskia got back from Hilbury. Otherwise she would do it for her. No problem there.

'Come,' Oliver said, laughing at Jenny. 'What are your strengths then? We've talked about mine, such as they are. Now it's your turn.'

Jenny took a sip of iced water and put the glass down. They had seated themselves at a small table in the café in Hilbury where she and Elisabeth had lunched the day her mother arrived. Today, though, the sun wasn't shining, and a fine drizzle misted the windowpane. She and Oliver had arranged to meet here for a swift lunch between her appointments. The place was convenient but Jenny wished they had found somewhere less cramped. She thought with longing of that pub garden with the wide and distant view across the vale where she had first lunched with Oliver. She had thought, then, that he was merely interested in her work. Now she knew differently.

Oliver sat grinning at her, his head held a little to one side as he waited for her answer.

Jenny smiled. 'You tell me what my strengths are. Well no, on second thoughts,

220

don't. I'm not sure I'll agree.'

He reeled off attributes she knew were pure fiction. There was no stopping him. She thought he would be put out by her talk of her mother's accident and Elisabeth's prolonged stay at Marigold Cottage. To her surprise Oliver had accepted without question that she wasn't free. She had felt a little hurt.

Jenny finished her drink. Time was passing and she had to be in Stourford at three. First she had to pick up her order from the florist a few doors away. She glanced at her watch, loath to bring this snatched time with Oliver to an end.

Oliver drained his glass and stood up. 'Come on,' he said. 'I'll be your flower boy.'

Jenny was glad of his help as she had parked her car some distance away. They walked so close together she smelt the sweetness of the lilies of the valley and knew, with sudden clarity, that the memory of the scent would stay with her for a long time.

They reached her car. Carefully she laid the flowers on the back seat, and then turned to face Oliver.

He leant towards her, his eyes shining. 'I've never felt this way about anyone before,' he said. Then he took her in his arms and kissed her.

She melted against him, the sweet lily scent lingering about them. As he released her the loving words he murmured were bliss to hear.

She stood quite still, savouring them and wishing she were free for the rest of the afternoon.

'So, Jenny, when?'

'Oh Oliver, I don't know. I have responsibilities. My mother . . . '

'I know that, my love.'

Jenny sighed. 'I shouldn't leave Mum too much on her own. She's still a bit shocked. It's bad enough me being out of the house so much. And then there's work to be done in the workroom and on the computer. I can hardly give her any time. I feel so guilty. She doesn't complain which makes it worse. You do see?'

Oliver's smile was warm and the expression in his eyes tender. 'Of course I see. I'd be a brute not to, wouldn't I?'

'Perhaps you should give up on me.'

'I'm not about to do that, Jenny. I want to be with you but I can wait. Not too long though, promise?'

'Promise.' She smiled. 'I'm torn, Oliver. I need time. I can't have my mother thinking she's a nuisance because she's not. It's such a strain getting her to believe it.'

'I know, I know.' He tilted her face towards him and kissed her lightly on the lips again.

'Until next time,' he said.

* * *

Saskia hurried up the lane to the church, late

for her afternoon's session in the church office. To her dismay she saw the bulky figure of Hilda Lunt in the gateway carrying a bunch of roses. A smaller figure dressed in black was with her.

'Let a body get past,' muttered Hilda's companion.

'We've plenty of time, Alice, don't worry. I think you knew this young lady's mother as a child when she lived in Marigold Cottage?'

'That I did. A red-headed li'l maid jigging about here and there and no shame on her.'

'This is Mrs Pengold,' Hilda told Saskia. 'She's going to do the flowers on her husband's grave.'

'Husband's?' said Saskia.

'Dead, of course.'

'A great storm it were then,' said Alice Pengold, gazing at the churchyard wall as if seeing the past emblazoned on a rugged screen. 'And the maid running about over them graves. I told her straight she'd no business here. She came with me meek as a lamb and then down come the branch from the Tidings Tree.'

Saskia had heard the tale from her grandmother and knew that it was the beginning of Gran's disenchantment with Mellstone. And no wonder.

'And then what happened? I'll tell 'ee. The young maid injured and the school mistress in trouble.'

223

'Everything turned out all right in the end, though,' said Saskia.

Hilda Lunt looked at her darkly. 'I've seen a thing or too lately I'd rather not know. You tell that mother of yours to lay off. Folk won't like it. It's his mother I'm sorry for and his Dad.'

Saskia flushed. 'Please let me pass,' she said with dignity though her eyes stung and there was a lump at the back of her throat.

CHAPTER SIXTEEN

To have someone attracted to her was life-enhancing. Jenny went about her work at Marigold Cottage, dwelling on Oliver's words with wonder. He was prepared to give her all the time she needed. Their brief meetings were all the more valued though it was agony to part. Even the thought of the petition seemed less ominous to Jenny now. Her designs became more inspired, her glazes more beautiful. She tried to see herself through Oliver eyes each time she caught sight of her reflection in the glass door of her display cabinet in her workroom. The features of her face softened and her hair felt springy. He said she had freshness and vigour and that he loved her for it. He loved her for the faint aura of mystery surrounding her and the way a dimple came and went in her cheek when she smiled.

This last one especially came from a vivid imagination as did the others, she had told him. But he would have none of it.

Now, a week after Elisabeth's accident, she moved about in her workroom as if floating on air. In a minute or two she would go out to the kiln, open the door and discover the results of her last batch of pots. This was always her best moment.

Humming softly, Jenny put down the one she was holding and went out into the dewy morning. The grass on the back lawn was wet and the scent from the stocks almost overpowering.

She had left Elisabeth reading in the sitting room, glad that she seemed content now that she had stopped worrying that her presence would ruin her daughter's career. Elisabeth provided welcome inspiration. Oliver too, though she had never told him so.

Jenny wished that Oliver, away in London, were with her now so that she could share with him the wonderful moment of opening the kiln door. His deep disappointment that she couldn't accompany him had worried her because she couldn't bear his sadness. Her own feelings about it were more complex. Her disappointment hadn't equalled his and that was disturbing. She missed him though, most desperately.

As she hoped, the glazes were pleasing. The

familiar wonder and pride swept over her as she lifted out the vase from the kiln that Oliver's interest in trees had inspired. Sunlight shimmered the deep green to a wonderful sharpness and the ultramarine that mingled with it was enchanting.

With great care Jenny carried her precious vase down the steps into the cottage. Elisabeth, imprisoned in the sitting room, would appreciate the mixture of colours and the sense of rightness about it. Surprised, Jenny heard the murmur of voices as she pushed open the door. John Ellis, standing with his back to the empty fireplace, was looking down at Elisabeth in concern.

'Is anything wrong?'

They both looked at her smiling.

'Far from it,' said Elisabeth. 'Oh Jenny, you've opened the kiln. That vase is beautiful. Look, John, how the colours blend.'

John smiled at her enthusiasm. 'Reminiscent of the sea, Jenny. You won't go far wrong if you can produce work like this.'

'You like it?'

'It's wonderful,' said Elisabeth. 'Listen, my love. John's invited me to stay at Nether End for a week or two.'

'It seems the best thing for your mother in the circumstances,' said John. 'Don't you think so, Jenny? There's a bedroom and bathroom downstairs. The terrace and lawn are flat and easily accessible and Mrs Horlock will be delighted to have someone to look after.'

Elisabeth looked anxious. 'What do you think, Jenny? My absence will free you to concentrate on more work like this.'

For a moment Jenny was afraid to speak in case she was unable to disguise her relief. Then she smiled. 'A change of scene, why not?'

'That's settled then.'

'I'll help you pack?'

'Saskia kindly offered, dear. I thought it would save you trouble.'

'Already?' So her daughter was in on this too? These arrangements going on without her were slightly disquieting. Saskia, so anxious for her grandmother to stay at Marigold Cottage, now seemed willing to be rid of her to the first taker. There was something going on here she didn't understand.

John smiled. 'We've got room for your daughter too if she'd like to come. She seemed happy enough at Nether End last week,' said John. 'Why not ask her?'

Jenny thought for a moment. Maybe it would be a good idea for Saskia to keep her grandmother company some of the time and to see to her needs. John was obviously happy about it. 'Where is she? In your room, Elisabeth?'

Her mother nodded, still smiling.

Saskia was at the window, looking out into the lane. There was something about her hunched shoulders that spoke of deep unhappiness. Not even when she arrived from Exeter at the end of term on her own did she seem as vulnerable as she did now. 'Saskie . . .' Jenny began.

Saskia spun round. Her expression of intense misery was shocking. 'What d'you want?'

Jenny, speechless, put her green and blue vase on the chest of drawers and sank down on the bed.

Turning her back again, Saskia stood with her forehead pressed against the glass. 'The sooner I get away from here the better. I loathe this place.'

'John said . . . '

'It was my idea to go to Nether End. I asked him.'

Jenny was silent, trying to take in the scene before her and to make some sort of sense of it. Saskia was blaming her for something. To her dismay she saw her shaking shoulders and knew she was crying. Saskia didn't cry easily. Not since she was a little girl had Jenny seen her in tears. She wanted to leap up and go to her weeping daughter but something held her back. In agony she sat on the bed knowing that whatever she did in the next few minutes was incredibly important.

'Can you tell me what it is?' she asked gently.

'That awful Lunt woman was right.' Saskia gave a shaking sob.

'Has Hilda Lunt been upsetting you about the Old Bakery business?'

'Not that. I don't care about the Old Bakery.'

'Then what, Saskia?'

'I know it's true and I can't bear it.'

Jenny leapt up and strode to the window. 'Saskia, tell me.'

'Go away!' Saskia spun round. Her arm caught the edge of the chest of drawers. The vase, near the edge, toppled and fell.

Jenny gasped. A glint of sunshine highlighted a fragment of cerulean blue among the rest of the shattered pieces. She gazed at it, mesmerised.

'You think you can have your own way about everything,' Saskia burst out. 'It's not fair. Oliver's years younger than you. Why can't you leave him alone?' Turning, she presented a face ravaged with tears. Her mouth worked uncontrollably.

Aghast, Jenny stared at her. 'Oliver?'

'Oliver!' Saskia moaned.

'But Saskia . . . '

'Hilda Lunt said she's seen you. You can't deny it. Oh Oliver . . . '

Jenny was silent. She could have said she had no reason to deny anything because she had done nothing wrong but there was something here she recognised as profoundly serious. She was completely out of her depth.

'Is everything all right?' she heard John call

from the passage. 'We heard the crash.'

'It's nothing,' Jenny called back rather shakily. 'It's OK, John. We'll be with you in a minute.' She took a deep breath, knowing she could say nothing more to her daughter at the moment. She needed to think and to work out the implications of Saskia's agony.

Saskia's gasping sobs stopped suddenly. She grabbed a handful of pink tissues from the side of the bed and scrubbed her face. Then she rushed to the door.

'Leave me alone!' she cried though Jenny had made no move to touch her.

*　　　*　　　*

Jenny collected the dustpan and brush to take to Elisabeth's room to clear up the glittering shards that had been so briefly her beautiful creation. Saskia hadn't known that the inspiration had come from Oliver. Her action wasn't deliberate. Tears welled in Jenny's eyes and slid down her cheeks. Oliver, oh Oliver . . .

Jenny was thankful that John had seemed oblivious of the undercurrents in the atmosphere before Elisabeth and Saskia left Marigold Cottage. Calmly he waited for Saskia to pack a few things and then escorted both of them down the brick path to his waiting car. Elisabeth had been smiling, happy no doubt to be going where life would be a little easier for her until she recovered from her fall. Saskia's

230

carefully averted face spoke of deep private pain.

Jenny longed to rush to her but held back. Her daughter didn't want her. Saskia might never want to be near her again. Helpless in her distress, Jenny watched them leave.

She stared down at the jagged pieces in the dustpan. Then she returned to the kitchen and flicked open the cupboard door with her knee to clatter the pieces into the waste bin. Her loneliness of spirit was devastating. She longed to be in Cathy's untidy home full of the warmth of friendship. But this was out of the question because of Oliver. She wasn't strong enough at the moment to face his mother, not knowing how Cathy felt. Hilda Lunt would have told her by now. Tess prattling on about the Countryside with a capital C was more than she could bear either. Where then? Jenny glanced out of the window to the kiln that stood small and square on the back lawn. Not there, not yet. Later she would finish unpacking the kiln and start another batch, but not yet. She thought of the church, but that would be empty and echoing at this time of day apart from the odd visitor wandering about, guide book in hand. Questions on the antiquity of the building of which she knew nothing were not her scene now or ever.

Could she go on seeing Oliver, knowing that a rift as wide as Africa had opened between herself and her daughter because Saskia was in love with Oliver too?

She needed some sort of action to counterbalance these unprofitable thoughts. Minutes later she shut the front door of Marigold Cottage and headed down the lane past Varley's farm and away from the village.

*   *   *

She had hardly been this way since her return to Mellstone though she had described to Saskia the place she had loved as a child. Brooklands was the name of the field that sloped steeply down to the banks of the brook. She had loved the secrecy of it and the small hidden waterfall and the widening of the brook into a small pool of water she named Piper's Pool. Now she longed to be there, to return to a past that had held precious moments of joy.

The sloping field looked just the same and the thicket of undergrowth at the bottom by the hidden brook. Moles had been at work halfway down the field and the earth hillocks were dark among the grass. The wooden sleepers that formed the bridge down below looked old and worn. The same ones as long ago? They looked like it.

Jenny stood on the bridge to lean on the rickety wooden rail and gaze down into the water. Little eddies swirled among stones at the shallow edge where the cows came to drink. She wrinkled her nose at the muddy smell that mingled with that from the cow pats where the cattle had left their hoof prints in the sticky earth.

She remembered with pain Saskia's joy at landing the job in the church office every weekday afternoon. Cathy had told her about Oliver's connection with the parish magazine and how he liked to use the church computer. It wasn't hard to see the connection. Oliver had mentioned it himself once or twice. They had talked of the family likeness that Oliver saw and she didn't. Once he had teased her about her red hair and Saskia's luck in not inheriting the gene from some common ancestor.

So what was more natural than for Saskia to fall for Oliver on the rebound from Ash? Jenny understood only too well what Oliver's warmth and understanding could mean.

The tragedy for Saskia was that Oliver didn't return her interest in the way she wanted it. Instead it was Saskia's mother who held it. For Saskia this was intolerable. No one could blame her for lashing out.

Jenny moved slightly and the bars creaked. To be the cause of anyone's pain was unbearable, especially to someone as close to her as Saskia. There must be something about herself that caused harm to others, some flaw hitherto unsuspected. Her mother's decision not to marry John all those years ago? She could have a vast guilt trip about that in spite

233

of Cathy's reassurance that she wasn't responsible. Now, as she watched the ripple of the water, Jenny began to wonder if at some deep level she had been responsible however indirectly.

The business with the tree hadn't helped any of them. Not long after the decision was taken to fell the Tidings Tree they closed the village school and careers changed direction. Because of the part she had played? It was easy to think so.

At last Jenny turned to go, retracing her steps to the lane and back to the village past Lynch Cottage where the Moores lived. Cathy's black Fiesta that Oliver used when at home wasn't in the yard at the Varley's place because he was away in London. And that was something else . . . the reaction of his mother and father to what might happen between Oliver and herself. In Jenny's present state she thought of it with the dismay she might otherwise have grown to ignore. Cathy had never made any secret of her husband's dogmatic views about the passing down from one generation to the next of family land. If she and Oliver continued their relationship there would be no Varley grandson for Ralph and Cathy.

*   *   *

Saskia's relief in escaping to Nether End was

overwhelming but she still had her work in Mellstone to think about. Should she just up and off? But no. Tempting as the thought was she knew she couldn't do that because she had commitments she couldn't break without damaging her self-esteem that was low enough anyway. What reason would she give for not showing up . . . that the man she was in love with had eyes only for her mother, a woman almost old enough to be his? The shame of it! Work in Mellstone at the pub and in the church office was better than that. Anyway she needed the money. When she had saved enough she would be off. Back to Exeter? Probably not. Somewhere a long way away. But not Africa. Definitely not Africa.

So, unpacked and lunched, Saskia set out along the lane to Mellstone. John, of course, had offered to drive her but she wasn't having that. She owed John Ellis enough already for rescuing her from Marigold Cottage and not questioning her about her obvious wish to get away.

To find Oliver waiting for her was devastating. He stood in the nave, with his head thrown back, reading the inscription on the brass plate above the pulpit. She had never noticed it before, but now she looked. The words made no sense because her eyes watered.

'Leave what you want me to do, and then go,' she said.

'What?' He took a step back in the aisle, and gazed at her in surprise. 'Saskia? Are you OK?' His voice was deep with concern.

'Leave my mother alone,' she burst out. 'Why d'you have to mess about with her? Everyone's talking about it.'

Oliver's eyes blazed. 'What the bloody hell business is it of yours or of anyone else?'

Shocked, Saskia recoiled. Her hip thumped against a hard pew end but she felt no physical pain for the anguish in her heart. 'She's my mum.'

'And are you her keeper?'

She gasped. 'Leave her alone, that's all.'

His sudden anger frightened her. Sobbing, she rushed to unlock the door into the office. She crashed the door shut behind her and leaned on it, gasping.

She hated him but she loved him too. She gave a little groan.

To her relief he made no attempt to follow her. She supposed he had left his work in one of the pews for her to pick up when she was ready. Later she would investigate and steel herself to touch the paper that he had touched. For the moment she had enough to do in concentrating her mind on the work in hand.

*   *   *

Oliver threw down his papers in the front pew

and strode from the church. The sunny air outside did much to cool his flushed face but he still seethed inside. But by the time he reached the gate into the lane he felt a good deal better. Saskia had her mother's interest at heart, that was all. Obviously she thought they didn't include him. But that wasn't for Saskia to decide, worked up about as she was about her mother and himself finding a little happiness together.

He stood still for a moment before going down the steps to the lane, thinking of the girl's flushed face and dewy eyes. There had been a certain beauty about her today, a hint of hidden depths. Jenny, too, gave the same impression of there being much beneath the surface. In her case there was detachment too. He found that intriguing.

He set off up the lane, whistling softly now. Let the busybodies go hang. They couldn't hurt anyone with their nasty tongues so why take any notice?

*   *   *

When the phone rang Jenny was in the hall, wiping a greasy mark from the silver platter that hung on the wall above the telephone table. Oliver? She had been expecting to hear from him all day. She picked up the receiver.

'Nigel's been successful at last,' Tess said joyfully.

237

'Successful?'

'The petition's not against you at all,' came Tess' jubilant voice. 'All it says is the undersigned wish to have the chance to buy the Old Bakery for the village.'

'But we knew that already.'

Tess sounded triumphant. 'Exactly. Nothing sinister about that.'

For a moment Jenny said nothing. What did the Old Bakery matter now when her mind with filled with Saskia . . . and Oliver?

'Are you feeling all right, dear?'

With a huge effort Jenny replied. 'Thanks, Tess. Tell Nigel he's a pal.'

Later, lying flat on her back in bed and unable to sleep, Jenny knew that when Oliver got back from London they must talk.

CHAPTER SEVENTEEN

The thatched riverside pub near Stourford Oliver had chosen for their meeting this Wednesday lunchtime was new to them. At any other time Jenny would have enjoyed the view from their table on the raised terrace of the meandering river through trees heavy with summer. Today she felt too exhausted to care. Even Oliver, returning with a half of scrumpy cider for her and a pint for himself, seemed strangely remote.

He handed her the menu. 'There's more on the board, OK? What do you fancy?'

'Nothing for me, thanks. I'm not hungry.'

'You've got to eat.'

'No, really. I've got some crisps in the car for later. I won't starve.'

He puckered his forehead as he decided on his own choice and then got up to go inside to order at the bar.

Jenny leaned back in her seat and closed her eyes, grateful that Oliver hadn't insisted on ordering any food for her. The peace of the scene began to get to her but she knew it wouldn't last. Bees buzzed among the marguerites in the flowerbed nearby, and the scent of mignonette wafted across to where she sat. She wished the moment could be frozen in time, that she need never open her eyes and start on painful explanations.

She heard Oliver's footsteps on the path. He carried a plate of sandwiches. He sat down and gazed at her, an expression of deep hurt in his eyes.

'I see in you all I want or will ever want, Jenny my love. Why should that matter to your daughter?'

'I can't forget the way she looked at me. Saskia is desperately shocked and I can't bear it.' Jenny hesitated. She couldn't tell him of her suspicions of the true state of affairs. She owed her daughter that at least. Saskia's pride was important in this situation. 'The age difference upsets her,' she said. 'I need her approval, her understanding.' She looked away from him, breathing deeply in an effort to remain calm and in control. She felt his left hand close over hers and the warmth from it was comforting. She left it there for a moment before withdrawing it gently and looking at him again. His face was paler than usual and the collar of his turquoise shirt was turned under on one side. This was very nearly her undoing. She clenched her hands to prevent herself adjusting it for him.

'I'll have to go very soon,' she said, picking up her glass with fingers that trembled. 'I'm due at Hilbury. I can't let them down.'

'I know, I know.' His voice was deep with emotion.

He was aware of where she should be this afternoon but not that she now had the cottage to herself. Thank goodness she had kept that from him. She marvelled at her strength. Meeting here in the circumstances was far easier. She knew that had she told him Elisabeth and Saskia were staying at Nether End she would have been tempted to invite him to Marigold Cottage to talk over their future. And that wouldn't do. The wonder of it was that word hadn't got out yet. Tess might have spied John's car driving off with Elisabeth and Saskia but she wouldn't have known they weren't coming back an hour or so later. Except for the suitcases, of course. But

240

Tess hadn't seen and Jenny hadn't told her.

'Please, Oliver, I need time to think.'

He gazed down at the glass in his hand, his sandwiches uneaten. His bowed head looked vulnerable and she longed to touch it. He was due to go off again soon on another lecture tour, meeting up with some of his colleagues in the Midlands. Jenny hoped she would be able to hold out until then.

She finished her drink and put the glass down with great care. 'The flowers I ordered were beautiful. Roses, pale pink and lemon. I must ask what variety they are. I'd like to grow them. Delphiniums too, those deep blue ones.' She knew she was filling in the silence with trivial chat to avoid the deeper issues because she was afraid of them. She couldn't stop herself while she sat opposite him at this small table. She got up and moved to the balcony rail.

'Jenny?'

'Yes?' She gazed at the clump of trees on the top of the hill, planted there perhaps by some long ago farmer to provide shelter for his livestock. Standing out starkly from the azure sky, they reminded her of sentinels guarding a precious citadel. They never did get to Larksbury Rings portrayed in Elisabeth's painting as they had once planned. She swallowed hard.

'Jenny, please.'

She wouldn't turn round. If she could get

241

through the next few minutes without contact she might survive. 'I have to think. I *must* think. You too, Oliver. Where do we go from here? I don't know. I really don't know.'

He stood silently at her side, a little apart. A distant sheep bleated in the far distance. One movement on her part and she would be in his arms. She shivered. *Oh please don't let him touch me. Please.. .*

'You know how I feel about you,' he murmured at last.

'Well yes . . . ' How could she not know?

'I'm not going to change, Jenny. I'm here for you. You know that. OK, OK, there's your life too. Let's not complicate things at the moment. I have two months left in this country, that's all. Unless . . . '

Unless he gave it all up and stayed in Mellstone? Jenny couldn't get her mind round that at the moment. To have Oliver give up his life's work for her? Impossible, impossible. This was another example of how she caused pain to others.

She knew now that this was a deep defect in her and she was still in shock from her recent realisation of that truth. She wondered that it hadn't dawned on her before. Now she could think of little else and her heart was sore.

'I need my own space, Oliver. For a little time. Please? No more lunches or anything else. Just a little time.'

She knew she had hurt him but she had to

242

do this. She dare not look at him as she collected her bag from the back of the chair and walked ahead of him down the steps to the car park.

*　　*　　*

'I didn't mean to come inside the building,' said Jenny.

Lesley Bond's surplice billowed round her in the draught from the door. 'It's a fine place this church of yours.'

'Mine?'

The vicar laughed. 'You live in the village, Jenny. The church isn't an exclusive club. Everyone's welcome.'

'I didn't think you'd be here.'

'Things aren't working out too well for you this afternoon then are they? Give me a minute and I'll divest myself of this. The vicarage is the best place for a coffee. You look as if you could use one.'

Lesley's cheerfulness raised Jenny's spirits a little. She had never been inside the vicarage before, not even into the large hall. Flower prints covered the white walls and a bowl of scented freesias looked good on the small lace-covered table beneath the window. Surprising that Lesley, stout and sensible-looking, should choose to surround herself with delicate things.

'The sitting room I think,' Lesley said.

Books lined the walls and deep armchairs clustered round the empty fireplace. Here too was the scent of flowers, sweet peas this time. For the first time Jenny wondered at this woman living alone in a house that could house a battalion with ease.

The tray that Lesley carried into the room looked heavy. Jenny leapt up to remove a large manila envelope from the small table between them.

Lesley smiled her thanks. 'Have you heard of the plans for the new vicarage? I've been looking at a few ideas. We don't need a vicarage as huge as this.'

Jenny leaned on one arm of her chair and put her hand to her mouth. So their vicar was a thought-reader? She must be careful to keep her mind blank. But how could she when Oliver filled her thoughts to overflowing?

She hardly listened as Lesley talked of her love of gardening. Jenny's wandering mind dwelt only on the lunch on Wednesday that had turned out to be not a lunch at all. She hadn't been able to eat anything. And now she had chosen not to see Oliver until she had sorted out her thoughts and desires and everything else. Yes, and how she was going to cope with Saskia and other people too. Her head ached with the enormity of it.

'Prayer's the answer of course, as always,' said Lesley.

Pulled up short, Jenny stared at her.

244

Lesley pushed the plunger down into the cafetière. 'The parish is pouring money into this place. But we need to know the way to go forward. There's been bitter trouble about it in the past. Before my time but it left an aftermath. Now we need to work it all out on a sensible basis. God specialises in turning wrong to right and redirecting false pathways. Have a look at the psalms, why don't you? Have you ever thought that the psalms are a remarkable prayer diary?'

Jenny gazed at her in silence. She had never thought about the psalms at all. They had learnt the twenty third one by heart at school. She could still remember the first bit . . . *The Lord is my shepherd: I shall not want. He maketh me to lie down in green pastures.* She hadn't time to lie down in pastures, green or otherwise. Green pastures sounded so restful, so calming. The knowledge that everything was right. Her longing for that brought tears to her eyes. She wiped them away hastily with the back of her hand.

Lesley poured coffee into china mugs, added milk, and handed one to Jenny. 'A leaving present from a parishioner in my last place. Nice, aren't they?'

Jenny smiled. 'Someone had excellent taste. Such a delicate design. The water in the pool looks so real, even the rippling of the surface as if someone's tossed in a stone.'

'Ripples on a pool,' said Lesley. 'The

245

someone in question was clever to find these. We'd been discussing how everything we do affects others in some way. True, of course, good and bad. So when he produced these I was delighted.'

'Yes, I see.'

'Anyway tell me about yourself, Jenny. You're working hard I believe. Wayside Art is becoming a big thing in the area. We haven't had anyone in Mellstone taking part in it before. How are you getting on?'

Jenny elaborated on the commissions she had acquired from hotels and guesthouses. Refusing more coffee, she felt warmed by Lesley's interest and calm for the first time in days.

'And you've more plans, I hear?'

'I'm hoping to find somewhere bigger to exhibit. I'd like to hold classes too, in pottery and in flower arranging. I'll need more space for that. You know about the Old Bakery? It's all so slow. The Wayside Art Open Weekend is next month. I'll have to exhibit at Marigold Cottage after all. I hope to set up tables on the front lawn if it doesn't rain.'

'What about the old school?' said Lesley. 'It's handy being next door to you. I can give you the number of the bookings secretary.'

'Well yes. Why not? Thanks.'

Lesley's round face was alight with enthusiasm. 'I'm looking forward to seeing your work on display. I've a feeling I'll enjoy

246

it.'

'Come and see it now. Would you like to?' Jenny placed her mug on the tray and stood up.

'Now?' Lesley moved with the alacrity of someone half her size.

Her interest surprised Jenny when she ushered Lesley into her workroom.

Lesley moved slowly round until she reached the shelves of finished work. She examined each piece in silence.

'Pick them up if you want,' said Jenny.

'Can I?'

'Feel free. These are intended for flower arrangements, flowers and containers to be sold complete. People seem to like them.'

Lesley held a tall azure vase up to the light. 'I'm not surprised.' She replaced it carefully. 'The colour of the sky on a summer morning. And this one. Look at the way you've got strands of green and yellow river weed intermingled. Jenny, they're beautiful.'

'I've been working so hard. Perhaps too hard.'

'You have an observant eye.'

Jenny moved to the other side of the room where she had stacked smaller items close together.

Lesley followed her. 'These are lovely too. You're an inspired artist.' She turned over the piece in her hand to inspect the base. 'A tree emblem.'

247

'It seemed a good idea to have my own logo.'

'Brilliant. A tree.'

'The Tidings Tree of course.'

'Yes, I see. Did you know that a tree stands for the eternal certainty of God?'

Jenny turned away, suddenly overcome. She wanted Oliver so desperately at this moment she could hardly bear it. She gripped the side of the bench, leaning forward. Then making a supreme effort she stood upright again.

Lesley picked up another piece on the other side of the room, this time a shallow granite-coloured dish intended for an arrangement of bog flowers and reeds. Relieved that Lesley had noticed nothing, Jenny took a deep breath to calm herself.

When Lesley left Jenny picked up the phone and dialled the number of the hall booking secretary. As she waited she thought over what the vicar had said about ripples on a pond. In her mind's eye she saw a pool of water, calm in the greyness of early morning with a slight mist rising. A stone thrown and a perfect circle of ripples forming and edging out to the perimeter.

'Yes?' boomed a voice in her ear.

Startled, Jenny held the phone further away and explained her requirements.

'The old school? Have you any idea what you are asking?'

Jenny clenched her teeth. She wouldn't back

down but hearing Hilda Lunt's brash tones on the other end of the phone was a shock. Plainly no quarter to be given here. 'I understand the building can be hired by anyone. Isn't that so?'

'Not at that time. Mrs Moore won't allow it.'

'Oh?' Jenny could almost hear Hilda's brain working to produce a good enough reason to justify her statement. It would be funny if she herself wasn't desperate for more space.

'We shall be serving teas throughout the weekend for Wayside Art customers.'

'But it's my exhibition that will bring people to Mellstone to drink the tea.'

'Indeed?'

'And I need the space.'

'So do we. For the teas. I'm sorry, Miss Finlay, you can't hire the building and that's an end to it.'

Jenny sighed as she put the phone down. But wait a minute. Something like this could focus her mind wonderfully if she gave it a good chance. She had always loved a challenge and this setback was certainly that. She would make her contribution to Wayside Arts the success of the decade so that Mellstone folk would sit up and take notice. Karen Moore's orders indeed! She laughed. *Thank you, the pair of you.*

This was the incentive she needed. Sheer determination, and she had plenty of that if she put her mind to it. Tess would back her up,

Nigel too.

Jenny knew that her eyes glowed now. Without knowing it Karen Moore and Hilda Henchwoman had girded her up to produce yet more work that would stun the world whether she had enough space to display it or not.

*   *   *

Cathy could have done without the phone call from Hilda just as she was setting out to visit the Moores at Lynch Cottage. Wouldn't you just know it? A silent phone all afternoon and now when she was later than she had intended, this blast from Hilda Lunt jabbering on about teas for the Wayside Arts Weekend.

'I can't help you,' she said with a firmness that wouldn't have come easily to her a week or two ago. Did that mean she had really grown up at last, no longer fearing other peoples' reactions? About time too. 'That's my busy weekend and I'll be fully occupied. No Hilda, I can't. Sorry.'

'Karen Moore suggested you,' Hilda said with all the assurance of someone who considered the matter settled.

'I'm sorry, Hilda.'

'She won't like it. Not one little bit.'

'I'm just off to see her myself. I'm sure she'll understand.' Cathy put the phone down, marvelling that she was longer the timid girl

Karen had bullied all those years ago. Somehow her concern about Oliver had made everything else fall into perspective. It had been good to talk to Ralph freely about Oliver's interest in Jenny even though they hadn't talked much about it since. She knew that Ralph, being Ralph, had stuffed it to the back of his mind hoping no doubt that it would go away.

For the first time in years she felt really close to Ralph. Metaphorically of course. They had been eating kippers and brown bread and butter when she tentatively raised the subject for the last time. Ralph, red of face after his shower, wiped his hand across his mouth. 'The sooner the boy gets back to Africa the better. I won't be sorry to see him go.'

Cathy sighed. With or without Jenny? Without, of course. How could she even consider the alternative? She had very nearly mentioned the Bronson's proposed visit and her fear that the husband would turn out to be someone from the past. But she had changed her mind about that. Worrying about Oliver was enough at the moment.

*   *   *

Oliver's lecture tour of the Midlands was a relief for Jenny because it kept him away from Mellstone during the following week. She did her best to close her mind to his imagined

251

presence, not always successfully for he often filled her dreams when she finally slept and thoughts of him intruded when she least expected them . . . his delight in the results of her hard work; the way he looked at her sometimes with love in his eyes.

Wayside Arts, once merely a dream, now meant dogged hard work which helped. Plans for the weekend in three weeks time whirled in Jenny's mind. Her workroom would be open to visitors, of course, with her tools of the trade on show. She would give demonstrations on the wheel and visitors would be encouraged to have a go at throwing a pot themselves. As many examples of her work as possible in various stages would adorn the shelves. Then, on tables on the front lawn, she would display the pots and flower arrangements for sale to their best advantage. Weather permitting, of course. She would also need help.

'Of course, Jenny, delighted,' said Tess when Jenny caught her outside her gate next morning. 'What do you want me to do?'

'Man the stalls out here in the front if you would. Talk to visitors. I'll be out here too until anyone wants to see a demo. That's the idea, anyway.'

'Wonderful, dear. How about our front garden? Could you use that too?'

Jenny glanced across the lane to Ivy Cottage. 'Great. I need all the space I can get. My arrangements take up such a lot of room.

Thanks, Tess.'

'We've got a big white patio table. And signs. You'll need big ones outside. Nigel will organise that. He's good at signs. Hand-outs, too. I'm so excited, dear. It's going to be a wonderful success.'

'You're so good, Tess.' Jenny, heart-sore with longing for Oliver, was grateful for any sign of approval from anyone else.

Tess seemed to stand taller than before in her dainty sandals. 'I hope we get better weather than this though. I hate these grey skies and wind I simply can't stand.'

'Nor me,' said Jenny. She hadn't noticed the windy bleakness of the day. The bushes in the front garden rustled and some fallen rose petals fluttered across the path. But she went back indoors, encouraged. This afternoon she'd visit Nether End on her way home from Hilbury to tell Elisabeth that the plans were going ahead well and Tess would make the perfect helper.

A deep sadness to Jenny was that Saskia was out each time she visited Nether End. She longed to see her and yet she didn't. What could they possibly have to say to each other after only this short time?

CHAPTER EIGHTEEN

All evening the wind howled round the house, stirring the branches of the jasmine against the sitting room windows.

Cathy, with uncharacteristic jumpiness, wandered out into the hall and kitchen and then back again, unable to settle to her knitting. There was something in the air she didn't like, a feeling that things were not quite right. Soon after she'd got in from the WI Committee Meeting Oliver had phoned from Kidderminster. He was all right though he sounded a bit down. No problem there. Physically anyway. At least she knew there was no need to worry about her son being with Jenny.

The wind was fiercer now and had given her a headache. Upstairs, as she prepared for bed, Cathy paused with her head on one side, listening. There was a moaning in the wind, a sudden loud gust and then a fading away that seemed odd. She wished Ralph would come up. She found a couple of candles in white china candlesticks that had belonged to her grandmother. They were always kept handy for emergency use and might well be needed tonight if the electricity went off. Matches? She felt for them in the drawer of her bedside cabinet and placed them near the candles just in case.

To her relief she heard Ralph plodding up the stairs.

I forgot to tell you,' he said when he heaved himself into bed at last. 'You've had a cancellation.'

Cathy got in too and pulled the duvet up to her chin. The temperature had dropped and she felt chilly. 'Cancellation?'

'Wayside Arts Weekend.'

Cathy sat up straight. 'Wayside Arts?'

'That's what I said. What's the matter with you, woman, repeating everything I say? They've got a mother in hospital or something. Some crisis.'

'Who?' said Cathy. 'What's the name?' A frisson of relief ran through her, tinged, to her surprise, with disappointment. How could that be when she had been apprehensive for weeks about that particular weekend? Did she actually want to see Arnold Bronson again?

'Can't remember offhand. I wrote it down on the pad.'

Cathy had studied the bookings for that particular weekend so often she knew them by heart. 'Brown, McIntosh, Halstock . . . Bronson?' Self-conscious about that last name her voice faltered a little.

Ralph yawned. 'Not McIntosh or Halstock. I think . . .'

At this moment, as if at a signal from above, the storm broke. Rain battered the bedroom window so hard Cathy thought it would smash. It beat down on the yard beneath the window and she imagined it shooting up high again with the force of the pounding. Thunder boomed across the sky. Lightning flashed.

'Who then . . .?' Cathy's words died in a gasp of fright at a deafening crack that seemed to last for minutes.

Ralph looked up at the ceiling. 'That was close.'

'Has it struck something?'

'Could be.' He pushed back the bedclothes. 'It'll have done some damage somewhere.'

'Where are you going?'

Another flash illuminated the room and thunder rolled, further away this time. I'll check out the back.'

Cathy switched on the table lamp on her side of the bed, her heart thumping. There was no need for artificial light really because the sheets of lightning illuminated the room.

Ralph padded back. 'Everything seems to be all right.' He got back into bed.

The thunder was subsiding now, the lightning less fierce. Cathy got out and felt for her slippers.

'Now what?' murmured Ralph, snuggling down.

'I'm going to check.'

'I told you. Everything's all right as far as I could see.'

'Not that. The bookings.'

256

'It was Mrs Brown. Had a high squeaky voice. I remember now.'

'All the same . . . '

Cathy went downstairs. She had to know for sure or she wouldn't sleep. She switched on the light and picked up the pad by the phone. The electric light went out. Thunder still rumbled but the lightning flashes were further apart. Why hadn't she had the sense to bring a torch down with her or at least a candle? Fumbling, she made her way through the doorway into the kitchen with the pad in her hand and found the torch in the kitchen drawer. She switched it on. Mrs Brown, as Ralph had said, not Bronson at all.

Apprehension about the Wayside Arts Weekend seeped back. In the flickering torchlight Cathy went back upstairs. In the bedroom the table lamp came on. She felt exposed suddenly, caught in some nefarious act. Hastily she switched off torch and lamp and got into bed beside Ralph. A gentle rumbling came from his breathing. He was asleep. How could he be when the wind rattled round the house in this disturbing way?

'Ralph?'

He turned over, mumbling. 'What's the matter now, woman?'

Cathy sighed, and closed her eyes.

Jenny, too, was wide awake listening to the rain buffeting her bedroom window. The thunder excited her and she liked the way the lightning whitened her bedroom more or less continuously. Only one particular crash had her hiding her head beneath the duvet until the noise subsided. Even so the cracking and crashing were amazing.

She waited for a moment and then pushed back the duvet and sat up. The wind blasted the cottage, splintering and thrashing. Had something been hit? She checked at the window and saw that the cottages opposite were still intact with no thatch ripped off or windows caved in. The lightning faded and then came again streaking across the sky in jagged light. The bushes in the Hartlands' garden thrashed and swayed in the sheeting rain. She hoped no one was out on a night like this. Was Oliver missing the storm in Kidderminster, asleep and dreaming? It was hard to imagine that anywhere else was calm with the fierceness of nature surrounding her here.

Sighing, Jenny returned to bed.

By morning the wind had died but rain still fell in a dreary sort of way. Jenny looked out of her kitchen window to check that the brick wall encasing her kiln was still there. Twigs and leaves from the neighbouring trees decorated the grass and a pink rose bloom lay spread-eagled near the steps. One of the fences looked slightly askew. As far as she could see from the front of the house there appeared to be little wind damage. Running water darkened the brick path to her front gate and the grass was sodden with muddy pools of water.

There were a lot of people about for this early hour and in this weather. Surprising. Unless something had happened.

Nigel Hartland, in heavy waterproofs and green thigh boots walked purposely towards her gate. Jenny flew to open her door.

'Have you seen the damage next door?' he called.

Jenny grabbed a jacket and hurried after him to look. She stared in disbelief at the old school building whose roof looked as if a bomb had hit it. Nigel strode through the gathering crowd to the double gate, rope in hand, and tied each section together. From his pocket he extracted a plastic envelope with paper inside which he attached to the gate.

A notice? Jenny craned forward to look.

'*Dangerous. Keep Out,*' someone read out loud.

Rafters hung loose. A tile slid to the ground and smashed. Shocked, Jenny turned away. She nodded to Nigel. 'Is Tess all right?'

'Tess?' he said as if he didn't know what she was talking about.

'Your wife.'

'A bit shocked, that's all.'

'Give her my love. I've got to get back. I'll be off to Hilbury shortly if she wants anything.'

He nodded. 'Watch out for storm damage

then. Trees may be down across the road. Good luck.'

Jenny made herself a strong cup of coffee before setting out. She needed it to get the smell of mud and debris out of her nostrils. Incredible that the damage had happened to the old school building next door and she'd had no idea. How could she not have known? She wondered what would happen now. Hilda Lunt wasn't going to be able to requisition it for her Wayside Arts Teas that was for sure. Unless, of course, the redoubtable Hilda was able to repair the building single-handed in the meantime.

A tree had fallen across the road on the other side of Mepton Parva but the road had been partially cleared before Jenny got there. One or two fences on the outskirts of Hilbury would never be the same again but there was no damage anywhere to rival that of the old school building in Mellstone.

John Ellis, surprised that Saskia refused to accompany him, drove into Mellstone to check for himself that all was well at Marigold Cottage. He left Elisabeth seated comfortably in the sitting room, a pile of magazines at her side and Mrs Horlock to fuss over her.

He parked his car and paused to gaze up at the thatched roof of Marigold Cottage. Nothing untoward there. It was a few minutes before he saw the state of the old school building.

Jenny was not at home. He left his car where it was, headed for Varley's farm and splashed through the puddles in the yard to the back door of the house. Cathy, looking flustered, was glad to fill him in about the storm damage to the old school building. Ralph, too, coming into the kitchen was pleased to see him.

'You've seen the state of the building, John? It's done for now. Solved a problem for us though. Coffee? Something stronger? No? Well then. The place was condemned anyway. Now it'll have to come down at no expense to the village.'

John leaned back in his chair, considering. Rain still slithered down the window panes outside. 'Insured, I hope?'

'Don't worry. Nigel Hartland was here earlier checking on that. He's on the committee. He's come up with an idea. A good one, in fact.'

'And the place was owned by the Village Society?'

Ralph nodded. 'We've only just paid off the mortgage. That's why we're strapped for cash.'

'Will they rebuild?'

'Early days yet, though there's plenty of talk going round. It'll take months for it all to be settled and a new hall built. We need a hall now not in a year's time. More sense to get a hefty loan from the bank with the land as collateral and put in a bid for the Old Bakery.

Up the offer if necessary. Why not? A load of rubbish to think otherwise.'

John stroked his chin. 'I see.'

'I don't see any problem. Sure you won't have that drink?'

'I'll be off, Ralph, thanks. Things to do anyway.'

Deep in thought, John drove back to Nether End along the streaming lanes. Lassie, in the back, breathed heavily in sleep. There was much to consider. Instead of going into the house John pulled on a huge waterproof cape that had belonged to his father and the boots he kept in the porch. With a surprised Lassie at his heels, he headed for the lane again and began walking up it to the top of the hill since the footpaths were unusable.

It was plain that Jenny had no hope of her offer on the Old Bakery being accepted now. It was sad, but inevitable. He'd be a fool to think otherwise.

But there were other ways and means if he could settle something to his satisfaction. At the top of the hill John stopped and looked back at the grey and colourless view smothered with low cloud and sheets of rain. Then, head down, he retraced his steps.

*   *   *

Jenny, deep in thought, took longer than usual at Roselyn Guesthouse. The storm had wreaked havoc on the roses. Last week she had considered using some of them from her garden in her arrangements on the manager's suggestion. Now she was glad she had decided against it and had left her order at the Hilbury florists unchanged. Her fingers moved slowly as she selected the deep yellow pompon dahlias she needed for the blue container she had decided to use on the table on the first landing.

The old school building next door to Marigold Cottage would surely have to be demolished soon. It hardly looked as if it would stand upright for much longer and would be dangerous left as it was. And what would happen next? Maybe the Village Society would be able to afford to rebuild if the place was insured. Surely it would be? Or they might sell the land to a builder. Noise and mess for months on end.

She thought of the petition signed by so many people. The Village had wanted the Old Bakery. Would they still want it? Well yes, why not? And with the sale of the land this would be possible.

She had finished the flower arrangement now. Jenny gazed at it, marvelling that her hands had worked independently of her mind. She collected together the detritus from her work and thrust it in a handy plastic bag that she would dispose of later.

A week after the storm everyone knew that the Old Bakery would soon be the property of Mellstone Village Society unless things went drastically wrong. They also knew that Hilda Lunt wouldn't allow anything to stop the purchase now.

Jenny met Tess one morning outside the Post Office.

Tess looked at her sympathetically. 'Hilda thinks she's won the fight for the Old Bakery single-handed, Jenny. She's going about as if she's solely responsible. She gives Karen Moore no credit but we all know she's the power behind her.

'Maybe she's got a hot line to God.'

'Oh Jenny, it's good you can smile at a time like this. I feel for you so. How can you bear it? Hilda's buying stamps now. I thought I'd warn you.'

'Don't worry Tess, I'll cope.'

Hilda's small eyes glistened as Jenny handed over the packet she needed to be weighed. She could feel Hilda breathing heavily behind her and turned to face her.

'So there we are, Miss Finlay. The vendor of the Old Bakery is holding the sale for us while they sort out the insurance money. Everything comes to he who waits.'

'Or she,' murmured Jenny.

'It's the best thing for Mellstone. We're all

264

agreed on that. Isn't that so, Oliver?'

Jenny spun round to see Oliver standing behind her with several large manila envelopes in his hand. Her knees turned to water as seeing him where she had least expected him to be.

He grinned. 'Don't I always agree with you, Miss Lunt?'

Hilda tapped him on the shoulder with the paper in her hand. 'Don't give me that, young man.' She sounded good humoured, as well she might.

Jenny mumbled something and left, anxious for Oliver to catch her up as she strode up the lane to the Tidings Tree, and yet dreading his company too. Over a week had passed since their last meeting.

She reached her gate. She knew that Oliver would come. Her hands trembled as she undid the latch. It was hard to unearth the front door key from her pocket and insert it in the lock.

She was in the kitchen when the doorbell rang and she flew to open the door. Oliver looked strangely serious now. He reached out for her, and crushed her to him. She thought he would never let her go. When he did she was calmer than she thought possible.

'I needed that,' he said. 'Oh Jenny.'

'I've missed you, Oliver.'

'I know, I know.' He followed her to the kitchen and perched himself on a stool. 'So the Old Bakery won't be yours, Jenny. I've only just heard.'

'Oh that.'

He looked at her searchingly. 'You don't mind?'

Jenny sat down on the other stool. 'I do mind. Very much. But I've got to live with it.'

'That's my girl.' He looked deeply into her eyes for a moment and then took both her hands in his. 'Does it alter the position between us in any way?'

Jenny was silent for a moment. The warmth from his hands was comforting. Her instinct was to throw herself into his arms again but something stronger than herself held her back. 'I wish I knew,' she murmured.

'OK, OK.' He moved his fingers against her hands, stroking them. 'I think of your beautiful hands whenever I'm away from you, Jenny. Your lovely, long fingers, artistic fingers. Your long smooth nails.'

Jenny looked down at them. To her they were workman's hands.

'Let me watch them at work.' He raised her hands to his lips. 'Please?'

She had planned a session at her wheel this morning. She could do with some more pots to exhibit at the basic stage. 'You won't be bored?'

'Bored?' Oliver sprang off his stool. 'Lead the way.'

To her surprise she was able to concentrate as she worked the clay on her wheel, finding the rhythm soothing. Oliver watched her in silence. She wished she knew what he was thinking. She had the strangest feeling he was distancing himself deliberately.

His fingers smoothed the work surface. 'You're really good at this, aren't you Jenny?'

'I've been doing it for quite a while now.'

'Mmn.' He seemed to pull himself together suddenly.

Jenny finished the last pot. She flicked her length of wire beneath it and lifted it off the wheel to place with the others on the shelf. Then she went to the sink in the corner to rid her hands of the slimy mess.

Oliver smiled. 'There's a smudge on your face.'

She glanced at her reflection in the glass doors of the wall cupboard and wiped her face with her sleeve.

'What now, Jenny? Do they go into the kiln?'

'Not yet. They'll stay there until they've dried out and I've got enough to fill the kiln. Then I'll stack it for their first firing. It has to be heated up first of course. But this lot I've just made are different. I want people to see what they look like before being fired.'

Why were they talking like this? Did he no longer care? Jenny felt breathless suddenly, the walls of her workroom pressing in on her. 'Let's go outside.'

The grass was still damp after days of wet

weather. The heavy begonia flowers hung miserably and one or two had sagged off to lie in rich orange and yellow lumps on the soggy earth.

'It smells of autumn,' said Oliver.

'But it's only August. I don't want summer to be over so soon.'

'It's hot and dry out there in Burkino Faso.'

'D'you miss it?'

'Mmn. It looks as if I'll have to go back sooner than I thought. We've got another contract, an unexpected one. There are things I want to sort out first.'

'I see.'

'Do you, Jenny?'

She shied away from him and looked despairingly at the climbing rose dripping jewels of water against the far wall. Above it the bare rafters of the school building were outlined against the grey sky.

'What a mess,' Oliver said, following her gaze.

'I'm glad it's gone.'

'Even though it means you won't get the Old Bakery? The school was never my favourite place. I used to wish it hadn't been shut down when I was a kid. I never liked getting up early to get the school bus to Wernely. A lazy brat. Dad thinks I still am.

'After all your hard work out there, the lectures you give, the articles you write?'

'He won't change now. Too set in his ways.

The farm's the be-all and end-all of everything for Dad.'

'Even above his son's happiness?'

Oliver looked at her strangely. 'Do you still care about that?'

'All the time.' How could he possibly think otherwise? 'Oh Oliver, what are we going to do?'

He moved towards her and his comforting arm was round her. 'I know, I know.' He kissed the top of her head, and released her as the extension bell rang.

'That'll be Tess,' Jenny said. 'It doesn't matter. She'll come back.'

But Oliver was halfway down the steps. They walked to the front of the house, the honeysuckle on the wall shedding drops of moisture on them as they passed.

*   *   *

Saskia wound a strand of hair round her fingers absently. Outside the damp sunlight brightened the Nether End garden. The grass was the colour of emerald. Soon she must leave for dreary work in the church office.

Behind her a chair creaked as her grandmother reached for her reading glasses. 'Won't you have to go off to work soon, dear?'

Saskia turned away from the window, and nodded. 'In a minute.'

'John will be back soon.'

'He's gone into Hilbury? Why didn't you go with him?'

Elisabeth looked troubled. 'I don't really know. He seemed to want to be on his own. Some business to attend to, I suppose.'

'Don't worry, Gran. He'll be back soon.'

Her grandmother's face lit up as she smiled. 'Of course you're right, dear. Now off you go.'

Saskia bent to kiss her and then left. Would Oliver arrive today with another photocopying job now it was the time in the month to assemble the guff for the parish magazine? Or had she frightened him away that time when she had burst out her anger about him and Mum?

Not long to wait now before she had enough money to be off. She didn't care where. Somewhere. Before she left she'd get John to invite Jem here again for another day. Something to look forward to at least.

*   *   *

Disgruntled, Jem stared at his grandmother.

'Why can't I go to Nether End?' he demanded.

The lake's too dangerous and I know you'd be near it, Jem, whatever you say. John should have more sense than to invite you.'

'But Saskia's there. And her gran. I wouldn't be on my own.'

For some reason his grandmother's eyes

270

glittered. 'When I was young we didn't expect our own way, ever. And you're not getting yours now.'

He watched her move out of the room. Then he gathered a pile of books and his notebooks and pens. He stuffed them into his backpack with his spare jersey. When he heard the sitting room door click shut behind her he headed off down the stairs.

As he got down to the tiny hall the front door opened and his grandfather came in. They looked at each other for a moment in silence.

Then Grandad spoke. 'What are you doing, Jem?'

'What?'

'Where are you off to on this damp and dreary day?'

'Me?'

'Yes you, Jem. Don't play the innocent. Where are you going?'

'Nowhere.'

Jem knew his plans had been rumbled. He sprang forward. The tip of his backpack caught on his grandfather's knee, tripping him up. To his horror the old man slumped to the floor and lay still.

Jem opened the door, and ran.

271

CHAPTER NINETEEN

Jenny sat at her kitchen table with her head in her hands. A child had gone missing, the Moores' grandson. At the best he was out there somewhere in the cold and rain, wet through and miserable. At the worst . . . the thought was horrifying. Half an hour had passed since Cathy's phone call saying she had thought of Marigold Cottage because Saskia was friendly with Jem. Jenny had checked her back garden again just in case just as she had when she had first heard from John that the boy had gone missing. She thought of the school building but of course Nigel Hartland had been there like a shot expecting the worst.

Where was the boy? Only half an hour or so but it seemed like an age. Jenny thought of her nine-year-old self dancing on the front lawn of Marigold Cottage in the early morning. Dazzling spangles of light had whirled round her and mingled with the ruby peonies and orange marigolds. She could, in memory, still smell their spicy scent. And all the time she had tried to bury her fear that her mother's exhibition and hoped-for success would bring changes in their lives that had something to do with John Ellis. She had stopped spinning and dashed to the studio in the back garden only to discover the destruction of all Elisabeth's precious work.

She had run away because she thought it was her fault.

Jenny blinked, grabbed her jacket and let herself out of Marigold Cottage to head down the lane. The boy might have turned up by now. She had to know.

At the gate of Lynch Cottage she met Saskia and Oliver. Her daughter's face was pale and her long fair hair, usually so neat, looked bedraggled in the misty rain. Beside her Oliver appeared calm in his grey jacket zipped to the neck.

'He's not here then?' she asked. Have some sense. Of course he wasn't or Saskia wouldn't be looking like this. Was this her mother's fault too in some way not clear at the moment?

'You OK, Jenny?' Oliver said, smiling briefly at her. 'Nether End's been searched. Dad's there now.'

Jenny hesitated, afraid to say more.

Saskia took care not to look at her. 'Mr Moore plans to search the Hollow but he's doing the churchyard and the church first and Lesley's gone with him. I don't know why. Jem won't be there. He hates the church.'

'Robert . . . he's all right then?'

'Worried sick of course. They don't know whether or not to try to get a message to Jem's father in Brittany at this stage.'

'Jem isn't anywhere.' Saskia's voice broke on a sob.

Oliver looked anxious now. 'We don't know that yet.'

'Everything's so wet. He'll be soaked through.'

'I've thought of somewhere down the lane,' Jenny said. 'There's a field sloping down to a bridge over the brook with a wild marshy part in one corner. Brooklands it's called. Have you searched there?'

'That's no good,' said Saskia.

'Why not?'

'They looked there, that's why not.'

'Beneath the brambles there used to be a path. Not many people knew. I found it once. Jem may have too.'

'We'll go again,' said Oliver firmly. He caught hold of Saskia's arm and shot a look back at Jenny. 'Robert Moore's all right. Don't worry about him, OK?'

Jenny watched them go, her daughter and Oliver. She glanced at the shut door of Lynch Cottage, and hesitated. No, not now. Later.

*   *   *

'I'll get myself to Mellstone,' said John. 'I think I'll be needed there. I don't know whether they've contacted the police yet or not. You'll be all right, Elisabeth? I'll be back as soon as I can.'

Heart-sore, Elisabeth got up from her chair. 'I'm coming too.'

'You are? That's good. Karen shouldn't be on her own.'

Now the time had come for the meeting at last with her old rival Elisabeth could feel nothing but deep pity for her. She knew the agony from personal experience. Please God it wouldn't be long before the boy was brought safely home.

Karen Moore, pale and distraught, opened the door to them. 'Robert's searching up the Hollow,' she said so quietly they could hardly hear her. 'He hasn't come back.'

John stepped forward and took her arm. 'The Hollow, you said? I'll get up there right away. No news of Jem?'

Karen shook her head.

'Then let's get you inside. A hot drink would be in order, don't you think? Can you manage that?' He looked over her head at Elisabeth and nodded. Then relinquishing his hold on Karen he squeezed past.

Elisabeth and Karen stood in silence facing each other.

*   *   *

Reversing the car, John drove back through the village and parked outside Meadow Cottages and as near to the start of the track up the hill as he could get. The trees and vegetation lining the banks cast deep shadows on the narrowed path between. Robert was up

275

there somewhere searching for his grandson. He shouldn't be hard to find.

John set off at a smart pace, Lassie at his heels. By the time they reached the top of the track they had both slowed considerably. John leaned on a gate, and looked down the field. Nothing, and no one. Lassie whined a little at the delay but John had little heart to retrace his steps. He would go further down on the other side. Robert would be somewhere near. He called once or twice but got no reply. It was easy to miss somebody with all this thick vegetation in need of thinning.

John rubbed the back of his head. He'd searched like this before and everything had turned out all right when Jenny had been found. The brambles and undergrowth were even thicker than when she had run away after young Joe Barden and his vandal gang had destroyed the paintings. When he had finally located her she raised a terrified face to him. 'I thought you were a ghost.'

'No ghost, Jenny. I'm here to get you back to Marigold Cottage as quickly as possible.'

'No, no!'

'But Jenny, why not?'

She trembled violently. 'The studio'

'But surely you had nothing to do with that?'

'I wished for it. It came true. I didn't know it would be like that. I can't go back.'

Unable to understand her reasoning, he had

276

tried to convince her that whoever wrecked her mother's studio wouldn't hurt her.

She gave a deep shudder. 'He threw stones at the studio when the Tidings Tree was cut down. He'll get me too.'

'No one will get you Jenny, I promise. Everything's going to be all right now that I've found you.' He had wondered what Elisabeth would do after the destruction of all her dreams. But things would be well for Jenny, he hoped. And they had. For Jem too, God willing.

John rubbed his forehead, and looked down at Lassie. 'We've got further to go yet, my girl,' he said.

*   *   *

'Sit down,' said Karen. 'I'll make tea.'

Elisabeth seated herself in one of the deep leather armchairs near the empty fireplace.

Karen switched on the table lamp on the bookcase to relieve the gloom caused by the overhanging yew branches outside. Her hands shook a little as she dealt with the teapot and milk jug.

'It's been a long time,' she said when she had passed a cup and saucer to her guest and placed her own on a table alongside her chair. 'A terrible thing, having to wait. But you know that. How long was it before Jenny was found?'

'A little under two hours.'

'So long?' Karen stared into the fireplace. 'John's very good. He's always been a good friend to me.'

Elisabeth nodded, sipping tea.

'Will you marry him?'

Startled, Elisabeth jerked her hand and tea spluttered into the saucer. She placed cup and saucer on the tray.

'I've done a lot of things in my time,' said Karen. 'Marrying Robert was the best.'

'And you have a son?'

Karen flinched. 'And a grandson.'

Elisabeth leaned forward. 'Jem will be found. Please don't worry. He can't have gone far.'

'My grandson likes looking at things in the countryside. I tried to stop him, but he used to go off and do it all the same.' Her voice sounded thick with remorse. 'I wish I'd let the boy be.'

'Jem will have found himself a suitable hiding place to view some wildlife from,' said Elisabeth gently. 'That's why it's difficult to locate him. But he'll be found, just you see.'

'I wouldn't listen to what the boy wanted to do, what he had to say,' Karen said after a long pause. 'I thought only of myself. That's what I did years ago. I wanted Robert so much, and you . . . I didn't know the right way to go about it. I couldn't bear it you see. Jenny was in the firing line because she was yours.'

'But Robert was never mine.'

'I thought he was. It came to the same thing. From a young child I was programmed to believe anything I wanted could never be mine.' Karen smoothed her hand across her forehead. 'I was even expected to get my first teaching post near home because Mother needed me. The resentment from that was with me for years.'

Elisabeth leaned forward in her seat. 'But surely you realised when you grew up that things would come your way. Not only because you deserved them but because you were you?'

'I could never make myself believe it.' Karen's hand moved across her forehead again, as if smoothing away lines that shouldn't be there. 'When Mother died Robert came to tell me to stay home from school for a few days, that you would come in to school to take over, being qualified too and likely to do an excellent job.'

Elisabeth smiled. 'Not the most tactful thing to tell you.'

She could well imagine the bitterness this had caused. No wonder Karen had insisted on returning to her job at once. No wonder, too, that she had taken her feelings out on Jenny that never-to-be forgotten day when she had leapt forward in bitter frustration, grabbed the child and shaken her so hard that Jenny span across the room and landed up against the partition door to the Infants Room.

The vicar had appeared in the doorway. As he helped the child up and passed her to Cathy for comforting, Karen had known she was finished as the head teacher in Mellstone.

Now she stared into the empty fireplace.

'I'm sorry for the way I treated your Jenny,' she said at last. 'I'm being punished now.'

'But it's not like that. Jem's your grandson and nothing to do with Jenny or what happened in the past.'

'Everything has to do with everything.'

'Everything?'

'Saskia is Jenny's daughter. There's the connection, don't you see? Nothing happens in isolation. Everything is connected. She was kind to the boy, interested in what interested him. John told me. There's the link.'

Elisabeth leaned forward and spoke earnestly. 'You're imagining links like this because of your desperate worry. But someone will find Jem.'

'But Robert . . . '

'Will be home soon with the boy. John will find him and drive him home. We have only to wait.'

Karen sank lower in her chair. 'Yes, to wait, knowing I'm to blame.'

*   *   *

As they ran down the hillocky field to the brook Saskia thought what a wild goose chase

280

this was. 'They've already looked here,' she gasped. 'What's the use? We ought to be looking further afield . . .'

'Jem likes water,' said Oliver, as if that settled the matter.

'Well yes, but . . .'

'Then come on. Stop fussing. There's a job to do, OK?'

She followed, inwardly rebelling. Oliver had turned bossy all of a sudden. There were other places to look and she hated this nasty boggy place.

'Come on, Saskia. We're wasting time.'

He could talk. Ever since he'd turned up at Nether End this morning Oliver had taken charge and organised her when she didn't want to be organised. This was a side of Oliver she didn't like.

She could hear the waterfall now and the brook bubbling away behind the mass of impenetrable brambles.

'Jem!' she shouted above the sound of rushing water, but there was no reply.

Oliver found a way in at one end and forged ahead. Saskia pushed her way along the narrow path after him, calling continuously. Was that a faint cry? She couldn't be sure against the clamouring noise of water.

'Stop, Oliver. Listen!' Her heart quickened, and she was almost afraid to move in case the sound she was hearing wasn't Jem's voice after all.

281

'I'm here. Please, I'm here.'

Even then it was a few moments before they found him. The path was slimy and the overhanging branches tore at their hair and clothes. Then they were on their knees on the wet ground.

Jem shuddered. 'I can't move my foot. It got caught in the tree root. I couldn't get it free.'

'Let's have a look.'

Jem gasped as Oliver touched his swollen ankle. Oliver's voice softened. 'I'll have to get help to get you out of here, Jem. You see that, don't you? We'll have to cut a way through the brambles into the field from here. That's the easiest way. The path's no good.'

He took his jacket off, wrapped it round the boy and pulled out his mobile. 'I won't be long, OK?' He nodded to Saskia. 'Wait here with him. Don't try to move him.'

As if she would. She had some sense even though Oliver obviously considered her an unfeeling fool. She heard the snapping of twigs, a muttered explanation and then except for the brook and the muted waterfall there was silence.

Saskia settled herself on the ground by Jem's side. 'You OK? He won't be long. Your foot's swollen so much that someone will have to cut through the root to set you free so we'll just have to wait.'

'I saw an otter,' he said.

'An otter?'

282

The rain was beginning to penetrate. Saskia thought of the many people searching for Jem, of his grandmother sick with worry. Would it have fallen to Oliver to notify Jem's father if things hadn't turned out right? No wonder he was terse and angry. She would be, too.

Suddenly she thought of Ash. She wanted him here with her now with a desperation that shook her. Oh Ash! Ash with his comforting arms round another girl. Saskia trembled. It was hard not to cry.

'I've only seen one other otter,' said Jem. 'At Nether End. Do you remember?'

'We thought that's where you'd gone today.'

'They'd have known where to look for me then, wouldn't they?'

'So you're hiding. Why?'

'I can't go back, ever.'

'You'll have to as soon as Oliver gets help to get you out of here.'

'No way.'

'But Jem, why not?'

'I can't, that's all.'

'Your grandparents are worried sick. They thought you'd drowned in the lake at Nether End.'

'I wouldn't do that,' said Jem with dignity.

'I know that. So do you. You'd have more sense.'

'You mean Grandma's worried about me? And Grandad?'

'Of course, you dolt.'

'Grandad's all right? He's not dead? He's really all right?'

'Why shouldn't he be?'

'I thought . . . Grandad's really not dead? He just fell over my backpack? So it's not my fault?'

'Nothing's your fault. Only running away.'

'I'll do anything they want,' he said in a burst of gratitude. 'Anything. I mean it.'

The minutes ticked endlessly by as they waited for the sound of voices and for the overgrown brambles to be hacked aside. Down here at ground level the little rustlings in the undergrowth sounded like thunder.

Suddenly Jem threw up his head. 'Listen!'

There was the faint sound of voices, an engine. Someone called that he was about to cut a way through. Then everything happened at once. It took only a few minutes for the tree root to be sawn through and Jem released.

Oliver lifted the boy and carried him out to reunite him with his grandfather whose face was beaming with relief. Out here in the open field the grey light dazzled.

'Grandad?' said Jem. 'Are you mad at me?'

'Indeed I'm not, Jem my boy. I thank God you've been found.'

Robert's expression was so full of joy that Saskia, noticing, turned away. Mr Moore's expression told her that from now on Jem would have his full understanding. She hoped Jem's grandmother felt the same way.

Oliver lifted Jem into the truck, and then stood back as the doors were closed. The vehicle started off back up the rutted field to the lane and home.

Then Oliver turned to Saskia. 'That's that, then.'

'That's that, then,' she said. And meant it.

CHAPTER TWENTY

John wound down his car window. Not coming with us, Oliver? There's room for you as well.' Oliver shook his head. 'I'll walk, OK? Leave the gate. I'll shut it. See you!'

The car started up and set off after his father's Land Rover up the bumpy field. Oliver staggered up to the gate, glad that he was on his own for this short while. Jem's adventure had shaken him more than he realised. Saskia was the calm one, sensible and kind. He was only too aware that he had offended her with his sharp words.

Dog-tired and filthy, Oliver reached the gate into the lane and leaned on it. Saskia hadn't looked at him or made any comment even when Jem's foot had been freed at last from the imprisoning tree root. There had been an underlying feeling in the atmosphere that left him in soreness of spirit. Reaction on his part, most likely, so that he saw things that

285

weren't there. The relief of not having to notify the boy's father if the worst had happened was enormous.

Poor kid, stuck there feeling abandoned and alone. Jem had been courageous and dignified, though obviously in pain. The signs of tears were well hidden. The boy's bravery and his way of dealing with the situation stirred something in Oliver. He had no doubt that Jem would make a success of anything he set out to do and no prizes for guessing what that would be. The boy had the makings of a superb naturalist. He would go for it and achieve heights in his profession hitherto undreamed of. Good luck to him.

Oliver ran his fingers along the rough top bar of the gate and looked at them thoughtfully. Suddenly he saw his own life in perspective. Like Jem he had wanted to follow his own dream. Like Jem there had been people close to him who didn't agree with his plan of action. He had gone for it because it was something he knew he had to do.

His lecture tours had been moderately successful and money had come in. Mid Wales next week and that was that apart from a day in Exeter. Soon he would have to think seriously of the future.

Burkino Faso was beginning to take a hold on his imagination once more instead of being a misty thought in the back of his mind as it had these last hectic weeks. Decision time. Oh

286

God, what should he do? He took a deep breath and thought of Jenny waiting back there in Marigold Cottage.

He was in too much of a stressed state at the moment to go to her to tell her that all was well and that Jem was found. He'd get Mum to do that. But what was he thinking? Saskia was on her way home now with the others. She would see to it.

He was too stressed anyway to contemplate anything other than to get himself home let alone make plans for the future. A shower, food, rest and maybe he'd feel better about everything.

*   *   *

Later, refreshed by all three, Oliver found his mother in the study standing at the desk and looking down at an open page of her booking ledger. She turned to him, frowning.

'Everything OK, Mum?'

'Oh Oliver, yes. Jem's been found, thanks to you and Saskia. How can it not be all right?'

'So what's bothering you then?'

'Nothing, really.'

'I know you too well, Mum.'

Cathy smiled. 'And I you, Oliver. You've got itchy feet all of a sudden, haven't you?'

'What if I have? Why are you looking at me like that?'

'So Africa calls?'

'Maybe.'

'Is it Linda?'

He picked up the ledger, and then put it down again. 'No, not Linda.'

'Does this mean . . .?' Cathy broke off, obviously afraid to say more.

Oliver knew the thoughts that were in the back of her mind and was grateful that she felt unable to form the words. He could always rely on her reticence. Dad, now, was another matter, always shooting his mouth off and not always in the most helpful manner.

'I was just thinking that an extra room here might be useful to you over the weekend with all the extra bookings, Mum.' He said.

'Oh no! It's not that at all. I need you here, Oliver, really I do.'

Oliver looked at her closely. 'There's something more here than meets the eye. You'd better tell me.'

Cathy opened the book, flushing a little.

'Let me see.' He took it from her and ran his finger over the names on the page.

'It's just that . . .' Cathy fidgeted a little. 'Well, I think I might know someone, from the past. Someone I was rather keen on once.'

'An old flame?'

'Oh dear. That sounds ridiculous.'

'So which one is he?'

She pointed and then moved her finger from the page as if it was red hot.

Oliver smiled. 'It's bothering you obviously.

288

What does Dad say?'

Cathy was horrified. 'He doesn't know. You won't tell him?'

'Oh come on, Mum. After all these years? How on earth can it matter now? Are you expecting to be grabbed, slung onto a white charger and carried off into the sunset? I don't think his wife would approve of that. She might make a stab at Dad.'

Cathy laughed rather shakily. 'Don't be silly dear. I don't even know if it's the man I knew. I'm being stupid. It was Mrs Bronson, Betty, who booked the room for the weekend. It might not even be him. Arnold his name was . . . is. But all the same the mind is a funny thing.'

'Heart, you mean.'

She looked at him, her face paler than usual.

'I know, I know. It's not funny.' Oliver's mouth twitched. 'I'll be here to give you support, OK? Not that you need it, dear Mother. I reckon you could deal with anything life throws at you. But I'll be here, if you need me.'

*   *   *

A car pulled up outside Marigold Cottage. Jenny, at her front window, saw that it was John's Volvo and rushed to the door. By the time he had got out of the vehicle she had run

289

down the path and unlatched the gate. 'Has he been found?'

John smiled and she could see he had good news. Elisabeth, at his side, was smiling too. 'Safe and well. Jem's reunited with his grandparents and none the worse in spirits. A bright lad. Brave too.'

'Where was he?'

'Down in a field by the brook. Saskia and Oliver found him.'

'That's great. And Jem's really all right? But what happened?'

'Too soon to know that yet. We left them to it, the Moores and Jem. Lesley Bond will go back later to see if they need help like being run to the hospital . . . '

'Hospital? Oh, poor child.'

'They may need to X-ray the boy's ankle.'

Jenny peered through the open car door at Saskia seated in the back. Her daughter seemed to look right through her in a chilling sort of way.

'Jem's OK, Mum,' she said. 'He hurt his foot but he's OK.'

Jenny wished she could clutch her in her arms and soothe the anguished look from her mud-streaked face. Instead she stood back and tried not to notice the tangled hair, the torn jacket and the cold unseeing eyes.

'And Robert's all right too, even though he rushed off to search up in Hodman's Hollow,' said John. 'I was able to give him a lift back.

Then news came that Brooklands was the place so I drove him down there. The Varley Land Rover was on the scene by then.'

'Thank goodness!' Jenny looked at Elisabeth in concern, noting her pallor. 'Are you coming in?'

Before her mother could say anything Saskia spoke. 'I'm cold. Can we go home now?'

Jenny flinched. Home? Was that how Saskia thought of Nether End? She made an effort to smile. 'Off you go then.'

Later, alone in the kitchen with her half-eaten meal still on the table, Jenny pondered those words of her daughter's. She felt lonelier this evening than she had for a long time. She wished Oliver would come. The rain had gone now, and the pale evening sky showed wispy streaks of pink. She left everything where it was and went outside and climbed the steps to the lawn. Whenever she was troubled she went to her kiln but this evening she found no solace there or in the sweet fragrance of her garden.

If Saskia had got herself in such a state Oliver must have too. Suddenly she wanted to comfort him, to hold him in her arms and to smooth the lines from his forehead. Thank God he had found the boy. Oliver would get to the bottom of things and offer comfort where it was needed.

Jenny walked across the wet grass to the

patio and stood looking down at the walls encasing her kiln. The bricks looked rosy in the evening light. The kiln might not have soothed her a minute or two ago but it was her most precious possession. She remembered poring over catalogues, choosing the kiln that most suited her requirements and the excitement of placing the order. After that she had hardly been able to stop working out glazes and patterns. A wonderful time, full of hopes and dreams. When the purchase of the Old Bakery was a possibility she made more exciting plans and then had to live with the knowledge that the place wasn't going to be hers. But she still had her kiln. Yes, her most precious possession.

What was Oliver's? The vehicle he used abroad and had told her about so often, dwelling on it with pride? A movable object where hers was static.

Averting her eyes from the shattered remains of the school roof next door, Jenny went back into the cottage.

*   *   *

Elisabeth awoke next morning as the first light filtered through her bedroom curtains. For a few moments she lay watching their movement in the slight breeze. Then, remembering, she sat up and got out of bed to reach for her wrap and slippers. Such surprising news John had told her as they sat over their late night cocoa. Impossible to imagine that the land next to Marigold Cottage might one day belong to Jenny. The damaged building would be demolished. So convenient . . . so right if a new building could rise in its stead to house workrooms and showroom. Not for a while, of course, but that was John's idea for the future.

Elisabeth moved to the window to open the curtains. She leaned out, looking at the soft expectant light on the grass and on the downs beyond. Below her the half-heard, half-felt murmur of the brook was a pleasing background as she thought back over the evening before.

She was in the garden and the scented air was cool on her face. Water still dripped from the climbing rose against the wall and the asters hung their sodden faces in the flowerbed. Suddenly sunshine flooded the garden in a last burst of dazzling warmth and John walked towards her across the damp grass.

'Elisabeth,' he said quietly.

She knew what he would say and yet there was no need for words. Two old friends coming together in the last years of their lives . . . what could be more suitable, so obvious, so right for them both?

John smiled. 'You like it here at Nether End, Elisabeth?'

'How can you ask? You know this is where I

293

want most to be.'

'I've been thinking so much about the past,' he said quietly. 'You couldn't have lived your life in Marigold Cottage in that way if it wasn't of the utmost importance to you. It was my fault that I was unable to understand. But now I do. There's room here at Nether End for anything you wish to do. I would like to look after you.'

Elisabeth tried to speak but could not for the tears in her throat. The moment had re-united the present with the past, closing up the chasm of her life away from Mellstone as if it had never been. She felt young again and saw John for a moment as the handsome young man of that long ago morning when she refused to become his wife.

'John?' she said uncertainly. And then she was in his arms. She felt his heart quicken.

'My dear Elisabeth,' he murmured, stroking her hair.

Now, as Elisabeth stood in her bedroom gazing down at John's garden, she knew she had made the right decision in returning to the place she loved. The mist rose from the banks of the brook and in the sudden clearness she saw the line of downs against the sky. Here was her home, the prospective home she had rejected all those years ago after the vandals had wrecked her studio. The early morning had been such as this and she had gulped down breaths of sweet-scented air before

294

confronting the damage. Then, propping open the studio door, she gathered the broken paintings to pile outside. And suddenly John was there too, holding out his hands for them. She saw a portion of one of her earlier ones on which were branches of the Tidings Tree.

'There was trouble from the beginning because of the tree,' she said. It was John who had criticised most, appalled at her financial position and with good reason. He had been right, too, in thinking she had not been fair to Jenny.

He had looked wise, all-knowing. 'Why not give up, Elisabeth, and become my wife? You know how much I'd like you to give up all this.'

She had looked at him in a silence that seemed to last forever. 'I can't, John. I have to think and breathe painting to be able to survive.'

And that's what she had done, heart-sore because of John's lack of understanding that would always divide them if they married.

But not anymore. The knowledge of that was wonderful.

*　　　*　　　*

Jenny also woke early. The memory of yesterday's events crowded in so fast she was unable to lie still. Saskia and Oliver had found the boy and returned him to his grandfather. Robert Moore had been none the worse for

295

his endeavours to locate Jem. Her concern now was for Elisabeth who had looked tired and pale when John brought her briefly to Marigold Cottage on the way back to Nether End.

Leaping out of bed, Jenny pulled on her jeans and shirt. She was aware that the morning was too new for a phone call to Nether End. Her mother needed her rest, John too after all the worry and stress of the day before.

Downstairs she made coffee and carried it through to her workroom. Wayside Arts was looming and although she had plenty of containers made in readiness she felt the need to prepare more. Later she would get down to it. Pummelling clay would give her hands something to do. She dug out her order list of requirements from the florist and checked for the hundredth time. Everything must be perfect for the following weekend. Tess had been wonderful, Nigel too. Tables had been ordered, hand-outs prepared and plans made for the lawn in the front garden. The Hartlands' offer to display some of her work in the front garden of Ivy Cottage too was great. Nigel had planned operations to the last detail but Jenny still couldn't rest.

The phone rang. It was Elisabeth sounding relaxed and happy and wanting to know how things were going. Jenny told her, and then sighed.

'You need a short break from it all,' said Elisabeth. 'Why not come over this evening? Mrs Horlock's laying on a special meal.'

'Someone's birthday?'

Elisabeth laughed. 'You'll see. John asked me to ask you particularly. Do come, Jenny. We want you here.'

'I'll be there. And thanks.'

Jenny frowned as she returned to the kitchen for a second coffee. Three days to Wayside Arts. When she got back from Stourford this morning she would get some more work started here. If she was successful and people snapped it all up she might get some commissions. This afternoon she'd get together with Tess to discuss last minute preparations. This evening . . . Nether End. Remain here and she'd work herself into a stupid state of panic.

*   *   *

Driving herself back home from Nether End later that day, Jenny smiled. Elisabeth and John's celebrations, though low-key, seemed so right for their quiet happiness. They had eaten the meal outside in the shade on the terrace with the lawn sloping away from them to the start of the green hill. Sheep bleated. A host of tiny flying insects hung in the air above the scented roses.

'Does Saskia know yet?' Jenny asked as they

sipped coffee.

John passed her a silver dish of mint chocolates. 'Not yet. We kept the news to ourselves for just a little while.'

'We wanted you to know first, Jenny,' said Elisabeth. 'I shall ask Saskia to be my attendant. She'd like that, wouldn't she? I can see her in pale blue carrying white flowers. I shall rely on you for the selection and arrangement, Jenny. For me too. Roses? Yes, I'd like roses.'

They had discussed the wedding then, to take place as soon as possible. Elisabeth and John would talk to Lesley about the church service. Mrs Horlock, let into the secret soon after Jenny's arrival, promised help with the catering.

'Here at Nether End, of course,' said John. 'Just a few old friends.'

Jenny laughed, and hugged her mother when it was time to leave. 'I'll give you away to John with pleasure as well as arranging the flowers.'

Now, driving along the evening lane, Jenny wanted to talk to Saskia at once and make her peace with her. On impulse she stopped her car outside the Swan Inn. But was this a good idea? The place looked busy. The car park was bursting at the seams. Her daughter would be occupied in serving the customers, perhaps washing glasses, collecting plates. Hardly the moment for a heart-to-heart.

298

A car drew up behind her. Jenny wound down her window as the driver and passenger got out of their dark green BMW and came towards her. A tall man, heavily built whose greying moustache gave him an air of authority. The woman with him was half his size and dainty in a white jacket and pretty skirt.

'Perhaps you can help us,' the man said. 'We're looking for accommodation for a couple of nights. We're booked into somewhere from Friday, but I understand there are no vacancies there at the moment. Not surprising, I suppose with the Wayside Arts Weekend coming up.'

'You know about that?'

The woman smiled. 'That's partly why we're here. I'm a bit of a water-colourist myself. And we're going to be house hunting too. We're interested in what the region has to offer.'

'She's a good artist, is Betty,' the man said as if there could be no possible doubt.

'Anyway it's an excuse for a weekend away, or longer as it turns out. We thought we'd take pot luck.'

Jenny wrinkled her nose in concentration. 'There's a place on the main road. Have you tried there?'

The woman nodded. 'No good, I'm afraid, and we don't fancy the pub.'

'You could ask there if they could recommend anywhere quiet,' said Jenny. 'They

299

wouldn't mind, I'm sure. Sorry I can't be more helpful.'

She smiled as she drove the short distance to Marigold Cottage. So the Wayside Arts advertising was getting results . . . great. Something to concentrate on to keep her mind from wandering to Oliver. She went indoors, prepared to start work at her wheel at once and to continue if necessary well into the night.

CHAPTER TWENTY ONE

Friday was a busy day, Roselyn in the morning and Penmere in the afternoon. The weather forecast was for rain at intervals. But how many intervals and for how long? Jenny, trying hard to concentrate on her morning's work, tried hard not to think of what a wet day would mean to Wayside Arts being at least a reasonable success. After her disappointment about the Old Bakery, she needed the publicity to keep going. Wayside Arts had made it clear that a failure to please the public at this Open Weekend would be disastrous for any hopes of being included in the scheme in the future.

But why was she dwelling on this now?

The manager approved of her arrangements and offered refreshments. Wayside Arts had been busy distributing their eye-catching posters and one was displayed in a prominent position in the foyer. Jenny glanced at it as she left and the enormity of what she was doing hit her. Suppose no one came? Her display would be so public out there in the front garden, like a glorified jumble sale, ostracised by Hilda Lunt.

But the enthusiasm shining from Tess that evening put Jenny to shame. Here was someone who had no doubts. Nigel, too, busy in his front garden making sure the ground was level enough for the tables he planned to put up, seemed happy about it all. He gave the impression he had personally arranged for Saturday and Sunday to be calm and sunny. The posters on his front gate looked magnificent.

So busy was he that he hardly looked up when Jenny walked across to admire them.

'Isn't this exciting?' said Tess. 'Cathy said her place has been booked for weeks. And look, someone's driving along there now. Yes, they've driven into the yard.'

'That's the car I saw the other evening,' said Jenny, her spirits lifting.

'There you are, dear,' said Tess. Didn't I say you've no need to worry?'

*   *   *

Cathy, fiddling about with last minute

preparations in the largest guest bedroom, heard the car arrive. This was it then. Mr and Mrs Bronson. The other guests had checked in earlier. She took a deep breath. Her new cream suit should have given her confidence but she twitched at the skirt as she went downstairs just in case it was too short. She managed not to look in the mirror on the landing wall. She knew what she would see, a middle-aged woman who needed to shed a few pounds. Her grey hair was extra unruly today in spite of her repeated efforts to make it look more elegant. Arnold wouldn't recognise her as the slim girl he once knew, not in a million years.

She heard voices and hesitated. Ralph? What was he doing home at this hour? Clutching the banister rail, she got herself downstairs as Ralph's tone of delighted surprise reached her.

Standing there was a short brown-haired woman in flowered skirt and white jacket looking as pleased to be here as Ralph was to welcome her. Behind her, the tall, broad-shouldered man looked much older. His face was pock-marked and rugged, his hair thin. He stooped a little. Only the shape of his greying moustache gave the faintest hint of the man he once was.

'Here's my wife,' said Ralph, turning to her at once. 'You remember Cathy? Of course you do. Bellringing and all that? Cathy, this is

Arnold Bronson. You remember?'

'Of course,' she said, holding out her hand as he stepped forward to take it. 'How are you, Arnold?'

'Very well, my dear. Glad to be back in Mellstone after all this time.'

Cathy looked at him in surprise. In her memory the young Arnold had rubbished the place and hadn't had a good word to say about the way the council had hacked down the Tidings Tree when in his opinion they should have let well alone. When she remonstrated about its obvious danger he had shut her up in no uncertain terms.

Arnold stroked his moustache. 'You may not have heard of the new woodlands enterprise I set up? Bronson Backwoods is the name. Good name don't you think? We had an excellent launch of it the other day, I may say. Oh yes. The money's rolling in. I have a great deal to tell you, Cathy.'

Cathy smiled. Arnold looked the very picture of a successful tycoon and as out of place here in the farm kitchen as a bug in a duvet.

'What a charming place you have,' his wife said. She looked round with interest. 'I've always wanted a big kitchen like this. Such a wonderful atmosphere.'

Arnold appeared not to hear. 'So how about it, Cathy? You'll be interested in what I have to tell you about the ceremony. Can we go somewhere more comfortable? We don't want to waste time here in the kitchen.'

'All in good time, Arnold,' said his wife calmly.

Cathy looked at her in admiration. How on earth did she cope with him and remain so pleasant a person?

'It's certainly good to see you again after all this time, Arnold,' said Ralph. 'Luggage? Leave it where it is. Our son's here somewhere. He'll get it up to your room. A drink I think to celebrate meeting up with old friends? Come into the sitting room.'

'I've brought the photos of my opening ceremony to show you, Cathy. You'll find them interesting. A great success. All the bigwigs there, of course. Lead the way.'

Cathy shook her head. 'I shall show Mrs Bronson to your room first and then you must excuse me. I have a few things to do.'

'So you'll have to put up with me instead,' said Ralph. 'All right, Cathy?'

Arnold's wife smiled at her. 'I hope you'll call me Betty. And may I call you Cathy? Arnold's mentioned you so much I feel I know you already.'

'I'm so glad,' Cathy said. Arnold was a stranger, a guest arriving in her home to be looked after just like anyone else. She would do her best to make both him and his nice little wife comfortable.

Oliver, joining them at that moment,

winked at his mother as the others moved away.

'Well done, Mum. I knew you had it in you.'

Heartened, Cathy knew the worst was over. Ralph had been here when she needed him. There was nothing to worry about.

*   *   *

Heavy dew on the grass below her bedroom window twinkled up at Jenny in a satisfactory way when she looked out early next morning. Perfect. Already the pale sky was brightening to pure azure.

She dressed quickly and went downstairs. A key turned in the lock and Saskia was there, looking dishevelled against the light in the doorway.

'Saskia!'

'Don't look so alarmed, Mum.'

'What's happened?'

'Nothing. Don't fuss. I came home, that's all.' Saskia slung her laden rucksack inside and dumped it on the floor. 'Say if you don't want me.'

'Of course I want you.' Jenny knew better than to rush at her daughter and envelop her in a bear hug. Instead she breathed deeply in an effort to calm herself. 'But why are you here so early, love? You didn't walk all the way from Nether End?'

'I came to help you, didn't I? Any coffee?

305

And I'm starving.'

Questioning her further at this stage was obviously useless. By the time Saskia had hauled her luggage upstairs and used the bathroom Jenny had the coffee made and some rolls warming. Butter and honey were on the table and a bowl of fruit.

Saskia took an orange and began to peel it. 'I felt I was in the way at Nether End.' Her long fair hair fell over her face and she flicked it back.

In silence Jenny put the rolls in a basket in the middle of the table and poured coffee.

'All that lovey-dovey stuff. I couldn't stand it. I'm pleased about it of course. But at their age!'

Jenny laughed.

'It's all right for you. You didn't have to live with it.'

'Your own choice,' said Jenny lightly as she sat down. Careful now. Play it cool, no pressure. Be thankful Saskia's here in the kitchen of Marigold Cottage and willing to help in her busy day ahead.

'Oh Mum, I'm sorry.' For a moment Saskia's blue eyes looked vulnerable. 'I was totally out of order. I shouldn't have bawled at you.'

'I know. But there you go.' Jenny wasn't going to say she was sorry too. How could she when she had no regrets about wanting Oliver's company whatever the outcome? Later they would talk. Not now. For a moment

306

there was peace between them and she was grateful.

Saskia smiled. 'Will you let me come home again and be useful?'

'Home . . . Marigold Cottage? 'Of course, Saskia. This is where you belong.' Jenny, her heart full, turned her head away.

Saskia finished her orange and pushed the peel to the side of her plate. 'I thought there'd be a lot to do.'

'Oh there is, love, there is. I'll just grab something to eat and get started.' Jenny helped herself to a roll. 'We're putting tables up out at the front.'

'We?'

'Nigel Hartland. Tess too. They're both good friends, helping me out.'

Saskia took a roll, spread butter and ate it almost in one bite. 'I'll take my coffee through. I'll have a shower. I'll be quick.'

The Hartlands had risen early too and already the tables were in place. Jenny and Saskia carried the flower arrangements in their containers out to place in position. Then Jenny vacuumed the workroom and dusted the shelves where they had stood in readiness so she could spread out the rest of her work to its best advantage.

Only then did she allow herself time to inspect the exhibition in the two front gardens. She stood in the middle of the lane and looked back at her own. Her display was the best she could make it. Then she turned to Ivy Cottage. Nigel had done his best for her in his front garden too, and the result was better than she dared hope.

'Wonderful, Jenny.' said Tess. 'People will come pouring in.'

'But where are your books, Tess? They should be on show.'

'Get them out here,' Nigel ordered. 'False modesty doesn't become you, Tess. I've set this small table aside for your display.'

He winked at Jenny as his wife rushed to obey. 'A lot of our Countryside Group will be along to see your work later, Jenny my dear. I've got them all organised. And here is your first visitor now, I believe.'

Jenny darted back across the road to where Saskia had positioned herself behind one of the tables. She herself would be demonstrating inside the workroom when anyone showed interest but she couldn't resist standing out here in the sunshine for a few minutes to get the first reactions.

A figure was coming along the lane in a black coat buttoned to her neck. In her hands she carried a dustbin liner, bulging with something that seemed to be precious from the way she held it. Jenny stared in dismay. She knew at once, with a tingling of nervousness, that this was Alice Pengold. The old lady marched through the open gate into the garden of Marigold Cottage.

Jenny stepped back in alarm. 'Mrs Pengold?'

Alice nodded. She removed something from the black bag and held out a dainty arrangement of twigs and dried flowers. 'I got this for the young maid.' She glanced about her, sniffed and thrust her offering at Saskia.

Saskia smiled in delight as she took it from her. 'For me? It's a fairy garden. It's beautiful.'

Alice glanced unsmilingly at Jenny and then to Saskia. 'Don't you take no notice of they. You'm who you are and don't forget it.'

Saskia examined the arrangement, her mouth curved at the corners.

'Did you make it yourself, Mrs Pengold?' said Jenny, marvelling. 'Have you always made them? Is this why you picked all those dead things in the hedges when I was a little girl?'

'Other folk get they things for me now my screws is bad. The young lad. He was good to an old woman, finding things. And now he's been found. Like the young maid was found thirty year ago.'

'Me?' said Jenny uncertainly.

'The Tidings Tree,' Alice muttered. 'We was under it and the branch came down.'

Jenny saw the bitter twist to her mouth. 'But it wasn't your fault, Mrs Pengold. Surely you didn't think that?'

Alice twisted her gnarled hands together. 'There's things we don't understand and never will till the day we dies.'

'But it was an accident.'

'There's some as didn't think so.' Alice glanced at Jenny's laden table, sniffed again and turned to go. 'Live as long as me and you'll know it's in the nature of things. Our Tidings Tree's not finished yet, not by a long chalk!'

'Phew,' said Jenny when the old lady had gone. She felt shaken. 'A vision from the past.'

'But what did she mean about not knowing it was an accident?' said Saskia hugging her gift.

'There's things we don't understand and never will till the day we dies,' Jenny quoted quietly. She glanced down the lane in the direction of Lynch Cottage and thought of someone else whose bitterness towards her might well be explained by the meaning behind Alice Pengold's words. Should she do something about it or leave well alone?

'I'll just take this inside,' said Saskia. 'I won't be a minute but I can't risk it out here. It might get whipped away by these people coming now.'

Jenny looked up and recognised the man and woman as the couple she had spoken to outside the Swan. They introduced themselves as Arnold and Betty Bronson who were staying at Varley's farm and said that Cathy would be along presently.

'Someone's just turned up out of the blue to see her son,' said Betty. 'Some poor girl

310

looking exhausted. Cathy's busy getting her a meal.'

Arnold Bronson fingered his moustache, frowning. 'Cathy shouldn't allow herself to be put upon. She was always like that in the old days. She hasn't changed.'

'The poor girl has come a long way, Arnold, and looked half-starved,' said Betty. 'Anyway it's no business of ours. Our hostess was sorry for her turning up like that and her son not being there.'

'No excuse. It's not the way to run a successful business and I shall tell her so.'

'You'll do nothing of the sort, Arnold,' said his wife. 'Behave yourself.' She looked closely at Jenny's arrangements in the lovely containers.

Saskia smiled. 'Don't you think my Mum's clever?'

Betty Bronson smiled. 'Talented indeed.'

Arnold looked at Jenny and smoothed his moustache. 'And you have a workroom to show us, I understand? We haven't much time. We've a lot to see.'

Jenny took them indoors. A girl looking for Oliver? Who could she be? But she had no time to wonder about her now.

The Bronsons seemed satisfied and soon left after promising to return later in the day after their proposed tour of other exhibitions in the Vale.

'So that's that,' said Saskia when Jenny

311

looked outside again. 'They didn't buy anything.'

'Not even one of Tess' books,' Jenny agreed. 'But they'll be back.' She stretched, and took a deep breath of warm scented air. Across the lane Tess sat behind her stall. Nothing more doing at the moment. She could afford to relax.

'Go and make a coffee if you want,' Jenny said to Saskia.

'Enough for us all?'

'Why not?'

Another couple came wandering along the lane carrying Wayside Arts leaflets. Then, as they were leaving, three more people who stayed a little longer and asked intelligent questions about firing the pots and the different glazes Jenny used. They bought a couple of her smaller pots with the tree logo on them.

And so it went on all morning. Jenny wondered where Oliver was. She tried not to dwell on his absence but found it difficult.

After a staggered lunch Saskia wandered over to the Hartlands' garden and then down to the shop on an errand for Nigel who needed more drawing pins.

The trickle of visitors continued, among them a tall bearded young man carrying a rucksack like Saskia's who came striding along the lane. Something about him seemed familiar though Jenny hadn't seen the beard

312

before. He looked as if he meant business as he placed his rucksack outside the fence and came into the garden. She saw that he carried a crumpled leaflet as if it had already seen good use.

'Good afternoon,' she said, smiling. In his brown cords and skimpy T-shirt he looked an unlikely customer for her elegant arrangements. How would he carry them? No room in that bulging rucksack. Even a small pot would find difficulty in surviving intact.

'Hi.' He waved his Wayside Arts leaflet. 'I'm looking for someone.' He smiled at her and his worried expression vanished into one of extreme sweetness. 'I hope my detective work's on line.'

'Saskia?'

'She can have a lift back to Exeter with me if she wants.'

'You'll have to ask her yourself. Here she is now.'

Saskia came slowly across the lane. 'Ash! What are you doing here?'

'Hi there, babe.'

Jenny moved away and busied herself rearranging some of her exhibits that didn't need arranging. Saskia looked none too pleased to see Ash and she wouldn't get involved. They spoke quietly for a few moments and then he left, sloping off down the lane towards the Tidings Tree. Shrugging, Saskia went back across the lane.

*   *   *

Oliver came when Jenny was least expecting him. They had cleared the front garden and stacked the tables round the back. The unsold work was in the workroom ready for her to bring out again tomorrow. Nigel Hartland had worked hard. So had Saskia before grabbing something to eat and going off to the pub where she was on duty. Jenny, relaxing with a glass of red wine in her living room, heard the tap on the door with consternation.

'It's only me,' said Oliver when she opened it.

He stepped inside and held out his arms. Jenny relaxed against him for a moment, glad of his presence.

'How did it go?' he asked as he released her.

She shrugged as he followed her into the living room and seated himself on the window seat. 'Not well, I'm afraid. A few visitors, that's all.'

'And I wasn't one of them.'

'You're here now.'

'I know, I know. I intended to be here supporting you, my love, but something cropped up.'

He looked awkward with his back pressed back against the window. Her relationship with Oliver had been easy and relaxed up to now. She indicated the bottle of wine but he shook

314

his head.

'I think I'm going to have to return to Burkino Faso very soon, Jenny. Possibly for six months this time. It seems they need me urgently.'

'Yes, I think I know.' She had seen the girl in the distance wandering about with Cathy. A youngish woman slim and fair-haired. Heavily tanned too and far nearer to Oliver in age than herself. More suitable. Definitely. Jenny drew a deep trembling breath. 'The girl I saw with your mother?'

'Linda?'

'Is she . . . ?'

He smiled with infinite sweetness. 'There's nothing between Linda and me anymore if that's what you're thinking, Jenny, OK? Wouldn't I have said so if there were?'

She knew he would have done. At least she thought she knew, but how could you be completely sure of anyone?

'We leave the day after tomorrow.'

'So soon?'

'That's the way it has to be.'

'And after that?'

'We'll be back for more money-raising. That's the plan at the moment. And there are other parts of the world too that need my sort of expertise.'

Jenny looked down at her hands in her lap and found they were shaking. There was no real place for her in his life out there in Africa.

She had always known it. She might pretend enthusiasm for his work but to her it would become irksome in time. How long would it be before Oliver grew tired of her, met a younger woman genuinely keen on his love of travelling to remote parts of the world? How could she, loving him and knowing how it would be, wish herself on him?

'I want you to come with me, Jenny. Six months, that's all.'

For a moment, filled with deep sadness, she said nothing. He moved slightly and then leaned back against the window again and waited for her answer.

Was her concern for Oliver's happiness a disguise for concern about the loss of her own way of life if she went with him? What of her desire to prove herself in the work she had chosen . . . to show that she could be successful like Elisabeth? And what of the wish to prove to someone . . . who? . . . that the poor little waif, Jenny Finlay, who had been unjustly blamed for the loss of the Tidings Tree could make good and bring good to the village that had once despised her? Add to that her guilt at the hurt she had done to her own daughter and she had no real choice.

'What do you say, my love? Short notice, I know. Will you come?'

She shook her head. There had to be space between them now. At this moment, in the peace of her cottage room, she was sure of that. 'No Oliver. I can't come with you.'

An expression of such tenderness on his face made her tremble. He got up from the window seat and came to her. Perching on the arm of her chair he put an arm round her. His nearness was disturbing. She didn't know how she could bear it.

'I know, I know, you can't simply drop everything. But I have to go back, Jenny. Don't you see? I can't let them down now there's a crisis and they need me.'

'Well, yes. I do see.' Her throat was dry. She swallowed. 'I promise you, it's only you, Jenny. No one else. You know I'm willing to wait as long as you like.'

She gave a little sigh. It was she who had always held back, wanting to be sure because she couldn't bear another false run. Oliver had always understood that. So why, now, was she feeling so devoid of hope?

'Six months? I'll be back then, OK?'

Jenny smiled, though it was an effort. 'I wish you well in whatever you do, Oliver. And . . . thank you for everything. Please . . . I think it's best if you go now. Please?'

'Shall I come tomorrow to say goodbye?'

She shook her head. There would be no privacy tomorrow she could count on. And to take leave of Oliver in public? She shuddered.

'I know, I know.' He stood up, and she got up too. He held her tightly for a long agonising moment. She felt the roughness of his

317

sweatshirt, his warmth and the beating of his heart. Then he let her go.

The room felt empty. He had gone. She went to the window and knelt on the window seat, pressing her forehead against the cold glass of the window where Oliver had been but a short time before. She wouldn't cry but an infinite misery filled her throat with tears.

Turning at last, Jenny saw that Alice Pengold's offering to Saskia was on the small table near the fireplace. *There's things we don't understand and never will till the day we dies.*

Alice's words echoed in her mind long into the night.

CHAPTER TWENTY TWO

Saskia's secret pleasure at Ashley's arrival continued long into the evening although she wouldn't tell him so. She smiled as she went about her duties at the pub, happy that Ash was content to sit in one corner until she was finished. In front of him was a glass of shandy, his second so far and he was making it last. Every now and again he shot an anxious look across at her that she pretended not to see. When at last her duties were done they walked back along the lane together.

At the Tidings Tree Saskia paused, remembering the words her grandmother had spoken not so long ago. Now the thought of her own little family was a joyful one as long as she had Ash too.

'What are you smiling at, Sas?'

'Was I? Gran made a wish on the trunk of the tree. Or maybe it was a prayer? But I'm not going to tell you what it was.'

'Will I find out one day?'

'Maybe. Maybe not.'

'OK then. I can wait.'

At Marigold Cottage a light was on in the front room.

'Mum's still up,' she said.

'Will she want me to stay?'

'Why not? Come on, Ash, don't hang back.'

They went in and Saskia was shocked on seeing the pallor of her mother's face. 'Mum, are you all right? You look dreadful.'

'Me?' said Jenny, struggling up. 'Tired, that's all.'

'We'll be here to help you tomorrow, won't we Ash?'

'Too right, er . . . '

'Jenny,' said Jenny. 'But . . .'

'It's OK, Mum. Don't worry about it. I'm going back to Exeter on Tuesday. With Ash.'

'I see,' said Jenny. Did that mean that they were back together again? Saskia was giving no hint in the way she yawned and flopped down on the sofa.

'He can have my room. I'll sleep down here,' she said, yawning again. 'I've been telling Ash how we came back to live here and how no one's ever stayed long.'

'Until now,' said Jenny.

Saskia leapt up and threw her arms round her mother in a tight hug. 'Great.' She gave another huge yawn as she released her. 'That's all right then.'

Jenny smiled too. 'Well yes, it's all right. I've been sitting here thinking about things. Bed now, I think.'

'Bed,' agreed Saskia.

*   *   *

Next day the weather held until early evening. Nigel, triumphant, was up early again and the tables were all in place by the time Jenny came out into the sparkling morning.

Visitors started arriving at once. No time today to pause and pop over the lane to chat with Tess. The church bells rang, the sun shone. One or two people, interested in the flower arrangements, watched Jenny demonstrate and then asked if the ones she showed them were for sale which of course they were. Others liked the idea of arrangements in her lovely containers that complemented them so beautifully. By lunchtime many of them had sold. Then business eased off a little and gave them all a breathing space. Saskia provided salad rolls for them all and Ash poured lager and iced

320

lemonade. They ate in the front garden of Marigold Cottage, happy that the morning had gone well.

Saskia finished her roll, and took another. 'When's Gran coming?'

'She'll be here later,' said Jenny. 'John too.'

Tess, perched on a low stool, told them with delight how many copies of *Mellstone Magic* had sold. 'And did you hear, Jenny? People asked us things about the village in the past as if we've been here all our lives. They think we're real Mellstone people. Isn't that wonderful?'

Jenny smiled. 'Wonderful.'

'It's all due to you, Jenny. Taking part in Wayside Arts and doing something for Mellstone. The visitors love it here.'

'Not too much I hope,' said Nigel. 'We don't want the place overrun with incomers.'

'Hark at him,' said Tess admiringly. 'He sounds like a genuine native already.'

Jenny laughed.

'Back to our stations now, everybody,' said Nigel. He got to his feet and stretched.

More visitors came, among them Robert Moore and his grandson. Saskia, delighted, left Ashley in charge and took Jem into the back garden where Jenny was showing off her kiln.

'Indeed we're so grateful to your daughter,' Robert said. 'Not only for her successful search for Jem but showing an interest in him and encouraging the boy when he needed it.'

Jenny smiled. 'He's a good boy.'

'Indeed he is. And Jenny, my dear, his grandmother would very much like to have a little talk with you. I hope you'll bear that in mind? And now we must go. We've taken up enough of your precious time.'

Jenny's flower arrangements in their containers had nearly all gone by the time John and Elisabeth came. She saw John park his car further up the lane as Hilda Lunt approached from the other direction.

Hilda's bulky figure was clad in a loose sort of hessian-like top and a long brown skirt. The trainers on her feet were pristine white. She came into the garden and let the gate snap shut behind her. 'I'm here to see what you've been doing, Miss Finlay.'

'Quite well, I think, Miss Lunt.'

'I'm over the moon about the Old Bakery.'

Over the moon? Jenny smiled. Hilda's personality would do something drastic to the moon's gravitational pull for sure.

Hilda glared at the few remaining arrangements on the table. 'So you've almost got rid of the lot?'

Jenny smiled. 'People seem to like them.'

'Puts Mellstone on the map,' Hilda picked up a small pot and turned it upside down. 'I'll take this.'

'You will?'

'The village doesn't need to worry any more now that monstrosity's coming down.' Hilda waved her arm at the school building next door and nearly sent an arrangement flying.

Jenny rescued it just in time.

'The place has been dangerous for years. I told them so. Why don't you buy the land since it's next door to you, borrow the money from John Ellis like you were going to before? Get your own showroom built there. Makes more sense for you than the Old Bakery.'

'Got it all planned out have you, Hilda?' said John, coming up behind her with Elisabeth.

Jenny looked at John in wonder as he stood smiling at her. Elisabeth didn't seem at all put out either by Hilda's suggestion. Could it be they had discussed the plan already? It seemed so from the calm way they both stood there. Hastily she found a chair for Elisabeth.

Hilda took another look at the tree emblem on the pot in her hand, grunted her approval and left.

*   *   *

To her surprise Jenny wasn't exhausted when everything was over and all the clearing up done. Only now did the rain start, gently at first. The church bells had stopped ringing for the evening service but they still echoed in Jenny's mind. She glanced at her empty front lawn that only yesterday had been part of the setting for her first Wayside Arts Open

Weekend and knew a moment's triumph. The gentle rain freshened the air and left a dust of moisture on the gate.

She went indoors to shower and change into something suitably casual for the simple celebratory meal at Ivy Cottage that Tess insisted on providing for them all.

Wayside Arts had been the success Jenny hoped for. But, thinking of Oliver's imminent departure, she had difficulty in relaxing. Six months, he had said. Would she feel differently in six months time? She glanced at Tess, so sparkling and content. Saskia and Ash, seated close together on Tess' sofa, talked with enthusiasm about their imminent return to Exeter. Something was still missing though, something left undone.

'You've been great, Tess and Nigel,' said Jenny. 'You're good friends and you definitely belong here in Mellstone.'

Tess smiled. 'Hilda Lunt said so too.'

'What Hilda says goes, dear,' said Nigel.

'And don't we all know it,' said Jenny, laughing.

*　　　*　　　*

Robert ushered Jenny into the over-warm room at the back of Lynch Cottage and left them alone. Jenny looked at the woman who had been her teacher long ago and who had aged so much she would never have recognised her.

As she seated herself Jenny was conscious of the dark curtains cutting out the light and the heavy scent of carnations mingled with polish.

The woman seated opposite her in a deep leather armchair leaned forward earnestly.

'So, Jenny, you've come at last.' The words were so quietly spoken that Jenny had to lean forward too in order to hear. 'Robert says you are doing well.'

'Well, yes. Wayside Arts.'

'I'm glad there's this chance now to sort things out between us, Jenny. You have a lovely daughter. She's been good to our grandson. Good for us too. She made us see sense. Jem will choose his own future. I've had to learn to sit back, to do nothing.'

Jenny smiled. 'I think that's hard.'

'And your mother and John . . . at last.' Karen's smile reached her eyes for the first time and the bitter twist to her mouth softened a little. 'John's an old friend of many years. We grew up together. Anything he does is right by me. I can say that now and mean it with all my heart.'

'He's doing something else too.' And Jenny told her what John had said about his proposed purchase of the school land and his plans for the future that would involve her.

Karen nodded. 'John was always far-seeing and what he's doing feels right and fitting. It was unforgivable, losing my temper with you all those years ago. And you running away.'

'I blamed myself, you see, for the wreckage of my mother's studio when it was the Barden boy all the time.'

'I didn't know that at the time. I didn't understand a lot of things, then and now. I never could help Joe Barden but your mother managed to get through to him. It was partly because of that I saw red . . . took it out on you, Jenny. I've regretted my actions so much.'

'Please, it's all forgotten now.' Jenny's feeling of relief surprised her.

'I'd like to know how your plans develop, my dear.'

There was a ring on the door bell and Robert showed the vicar in.

Lesley hesitated in the doorway. 'Am I interrupting anything?'

Karen smiled. 'Jenny and I have been talking of old times, something I needed to do. Come back and see us again soon, Jenny.'

Jenny walked back along the lane to Marigold Cottage. Bees murmured among the brambles in the hedge. It was a golden moment after the rain. A startled robin on the front lawn looked up, decided she was no threat and flew on to the white fence. From the thatched roof steam rose into the still air. The scent from the stocks near the front door rose to greet her.

She smiled, and went indoors.